TRICK PLAY

TONYA SHARP HYCHE

ISBN: 1511532300

ISBN 13: 9781511532303

Library of Congress Control Number: 2015906252

CreateSpace Independent Publishing Platform

North Charleston, South Carolina

Novels by Tonya

Data Bank
Faded Memories
Glass Shadow
Breathless
Intersection of Lies
Swept Away
Trick Play

Just for You Trilogy
Just for You
Fearless
Painted Fear

All titles available on Kindle
tonyasharphycheauthor.com

PROLOGUE

The smell of coffee lured Laura Stone from her study. Her husband was awake. Wearing her flannel pajamas and slippers, Laura eased up behind him and wrapped her arms around him. Daniel Stone jumped at her touch.

"Sorry, hun, didn't mean to scare you."

Daniel spun around and quickly lost his frown. "What time did you get up? I didn't hear you."

Laura lovingly placed her hands on her husband's chest. "Too early; I had a deadline." She leaned forward on the tips of her toes and gave him a quick kiss on the lips. "I desperately need coffee."

"I was surprised you hadn't made any."

Laura grabbed a cup from the cabinet. "Knew the smell would wake you." She poured her coffee as Daniel watched with a curious expression. "I woke briefly last night when I heard the shower turn on. Another long night?" she asked.

Daniel turned his back on her and walked to the kitchen table with his coffee. "Yeah. My client is lying to me. My whole case is unravelling before my eyes."

Laura opened a bag of bagels that was sitting on the counter. "I believe the part about the client, but I find it doubtful the entire case is shattered."

At the age of thirty-five, Daniel Stone was one of the most sought-after defense attorneys in Norfolk, Virginia, with 80 percent of his cases ending in not guilty, a hung verdict, or dropped charges. His current client, Gary Bloom, was being charged with assault and battery of a young female college student. The girlfriend, Tricia Bee, Gary's alibi, decided to recant her statement about the night in question. She wasn't with him. She had gotten the dates confused. Of course, her memory conveniently came back after she dumped Gary yesterday at lunch.

"It puts a dent in our bumper, that's for sure. Going to be a hell of a day!"

Laura opened the refrigerator and grabbed the cream cheese. Balancing their breakfast along with her coffee, she stepped toward her husband and froze. Daniel followed her stare and looked out the bay windows. "Oh no, not this again."

"What?" Laura stepped toward the table and set the plates down loudly. "I'm not making this up. And let me remind you, we have a murderer running around town. Police think it's a man, probably with a record."

"And you think the River Strangler is Alec Deluca? Our neighbor?"

She crossed her arms and gave her husband of three years a stern look. "I told you he arrived home after two a.m. the night of Cameron Long's disappearance and then—"

He interrupted, "Yeah, yeah, you told me. That doesn't make him a killer, Laura." Daniel placed a hand on Laura's arm.

"He has a record."

Daniel didn't hide his frown. "Sit down, Laura." He watched her sit with a scowl across her face. "How do you know he has a record?"

Laura looked away, and Daniel immediately had his answer. "You went onto my computer and used People Services? Laura, you're letting your imagination run wild."

"Oh please, Daniel, I write travel reviews, not murder mysteries."

"Doesn't sound like it now. Look, Alec Deluca is not a serial killer. Drop it. You're only going to tick off our neighbor and make a fool out of me in the process."

She jerked her arm away. "Is that what you're concerned about? Your reputation is more important than our safety…my safety!"

Daniel stood and grabbed his coffee off the table. "I don't have time for this, Laura. Not today."

Laura quickly jumped to her feet and ran after him. "Wait."

He set the coffee on the island, pocketed his wallet, and grabbed the keys. Finally, he turned to her as he picked up his coffee cup. "You always manage to turn things around to make me the bad guy. I'm tired of it, Laura. I get that enough at work, and I don't like getting the same at home from you."

She tensed as she remembered his last case. With Daniel's help, the city of Norfolk watched as a child molester walked out of the courtroom a free man. The case was thrown out on a technicality—a technicality that Daniel had found concerning the arresting officer. They had fought that night, with Daniel defending the importance of a flawless justice system.

"I'm sorry." She squeezed his arm. "My flight's at eleven. I don't want to leave like this."

He looked away from her and took a deep breath. Finally, he faced her with a sigh. "Fine." He met her intense stare. "I don't want to leave mad either." He placed his coffee cup down and reached for her. She stepped into his strong arms.

Her lips brushed against his cheek. She whispered, "I love you, Daniel. You're right. I'm being ridiculous. I'll…I'll drop it."

Slowly, he pulled away. "Promise me?"

She nodded.

He picked up his coffee cup. "Good. So you'll be home on Friday for our anniversary?"

She smiled. He hadn't forgotten. "Yes. I got an early flight so I'll be home before you."

He picked up his briefcase and walked toward the garage door. Laura swiftly moved around him and began opening doors for him. He gave her a boyish smile as he placed his briefcase on the passenger-side seat. He closed the door and kissed her on the lips. "I love you too, Laura."

She smiled as she watched Daniel walk around his Jeep Grand Cherokee and climb in. She pressed the button on the garage wall, and the metal overhead door churned upward. She waved as he reversed out of the garage and then walked back in their one-story home. Laura topped off her coffee cup and sat at the kitchen table to eat. Daniel's plate was untouched. She had upset him, and he hadn't eaten. Glancing out the window, she saw Alec Deluca's home. All was quiet, and Deluca was nowhere in sight. She slowly shook her head in frustration and looked up at the clear sky, hoping today would be warmer, leading them closer to spring. It had been a brutally cold winter, and a rocky spell had cast a dark shadow on their marriage.

As she sipped her coffee, she became more upset with her actions. *A perfectly good morning to share with my husband. Wasted now.*

I'll never get this day back. A memory flashed through her mind—a morning with them laughing over coffee, only weeks into their marriage. She was wearing his shirt, and he sat in his boxers. Nowadays, he walked into the kitchen already dressed for the day, and she was in the study. Everything on a schedule. She winced at the thought, and another memory flashed before her. She was lying in bed—their bed— with another man. She looked at her untouched bagel. She no longer had an appetite. Disgusted with her infidelity, she pushed the plate away.

Friday. Yes, Friday, our anniversary. I'll fix this. I want to fix this. I still love him, and I want this marriage. She rubbed her face. *I can't tell Daniel about him; he would never forgive me. We'll talk about this distance between us instead, nothing more. We could plan a trip together. Yes, a real vacation.* She thought about the last time they had taken a trip together, just the two of them. "Oh, that can't be right." She spoke aloud as she thought about their last trip to Punta Cana over eighteen months ago. Punta Cana made her think of Belize. She looked at the time on the microwave and rose. Another business trip for another review.

Laura glanced out the window one last time. Alec Deluca's garage door was closed, and all the curtains were pulled shut. She shook off her vivid imagination that was surfacing once again. *Save it for Belize, Laura!* She walked into the master bedroom and looked at the unmade bed. It would have to wait. She had to pack. The shower lever was turned on to warm as Laura brushed out her long reddish-blond hair and twisted it up into a fat clip. Testing the water, she stripped off her pajamas and stepped in, pulling the shower door behind her.

As she washed, she mulled over what was clean and pressed that was hanging in her closet. Just as she grabbed her razor, she heard a noise. Thinking it was Daniel, a smile formed upon her lips. *He came back. Maybe he'll join me, and we can really make up.* She quickly swiped the razor under her arms and did a fast rinse. Stepping back out from under the spray, she opened the door and called out, "Daniel, I'm in the shower. If we—"

Thump, thump.

Laura turned off the water, stepped out, and wrapped herself in her terrycloth robe that was hanging from a wall hook. She stepped forward and then jerked back at the sound of glass breaking. *Daniel? Why didn't he answer?* Fear gripped Laura. *Oh my God! The garage door. Did I close it?* Laura looked at the unopened bathroom door, waiting, begging Daniel to call out to her, but he didn't.

This is not my imagination running wild! She looked around the bathroom, trying to find something to protect herself. Her eyes rested on the hairspray sitting beside the sink. She envisioned spraying it into an intruder's eyes. *No, not good enough!* She saw the open closet door adjacent to the bath and immediately thought of Daniel's baseball bat. She rushed inside, reached behind Daniel's pressed dress pants, and grabbed the bat. Gripping it tightly, an image of Alec Deluca appeared before her. *What if I wasn't wrong, Daniel?* A tear escaped down her cheek as she had flashbacks of the daily news broadcasting Norfolk's serial killer striking again. Laura took a deep breath, trying to calm herself. *I am not a victim! I am not going to be a victim! I'm going to save my marriage and go on a vacation with my husband! I'm not going to die today!*

Laura firmly held the bat high across her shoulder. She would strike first and then ask questions. Slowly, she crept out of the master bath and peeked into her bedroom. Out of the corner of her eye, she noticed a mobile phone on the nightstand. It was Daniel's phone. She hadn't noticed it earlier. *What? Oh God, I'm an idiot!* Relief began to wash over her. *Daniel forgot his phone. He's returned home to get it. Must have heard the shower running while he searched the kitchen. Didn't hear me call out. He knocked my coffee cup off the counter in his haste. Oh yeah, he's right; I have a crazy imagination!* Laura replayed it all in her head, trying to get the sounds right. Easing her grip on the bat, she stepped into the hall and saw an empty living room. She continued. "Daniel, I got your—"

Whack.

Laura fell forward, and the bat and phone bounced across the tile next to her. Blood oozed from her head, and a bright red puddle formed around her, matting her tangled hair. She moaned in a weak voice, and her eyes fluttered as she fought to stay conscious. She failed and drifted away just as unimaginable pain struck her back repeatedly, blow after blow.

CHAPTER 1

October 29, five years later

The cell door rattled at 4:00 p.m., and a tray slid inside. Alec Deluca sat up and caught a glimpse of the guard as he turned back around. The guard had been placed outside his new twelve-by-seven cell four days ago. The dark, slim guard would be replaced later on tonight by a larger man, older and balding. Tomorrow he would be relieved by a blond man who was also on the heavy side. These three men shared eight-hour shifts and would watch over him for the next two days until execution day. Alec slowly rose from his single cot and shuffled his feet over to his food: hamburger, fries, applesauce, and a chocolate-chip cookie. Alec grabbed the cookie first and washed it down with milk. He ate one fry and slid the tray back over to the rails. He walked back to his bed and lay down on the cot, begging for sleep.

Sleep didn't come. Instead, images of Monica Preston, his first love, filled his mind. They were jumping off a rock in a local swimming hole out in the countryside of Roma, Virginia. They were sixteen and in love. Her smile was golden as she laughed and splashed water toward him. She'd worn her yellow two-piece swimsuit that day, and it matched her hair. It was to be their last day together; her family was moving to Maine the next day. They had promised to send letters each week. They had, but once school started, the letters stopped, each preoccupied by his or her newest love interest that was present and readily available.

Alec thought about how differently his life would have turned out if he'd followed Monica to Maine. Impossible, of course, since Alec was a resident of foster care, still stuck in small-town Virginia. But what if after school? He could have moved to Maine and found a job, possibly even gone to college. Rage consumed Alec briefly and then fear. He would never see Monica again or have the opportunity to visit Maine. He was set to die in two days at midnight.

Alec rolled over and looked at the muted TV. The thirteen-inch black-and-white was his only connection to the world past the cinder white walls. For five years, Alec had wasted away a little each day in his six-by-nine cell at Greenville Correctional Center. He had been sentenced to death by lethal injection for the murder of Laura Stone—a murder he swore he never committed. His lawyer didn't believe him, nor the town of Norfolk, and obviously not the jury. Six months ago, the state of Virginia had appointed a new lawyer to the case, Joy Sutton. She would assist with his case and answer any questions leading up to execution day. Yesterday, she had shown up again and stayed a full hour with Alec, speaking very little. He'd given up. Why not? Everyone he ever knew had betrayed him one way or another; why would she be any different?

One of four channels began the five o'clock news. He pressed the mute button, and sound soon filled his small cell.

"Bob, I'm standing on the shoreline of Lake Maury in Warwick, just south of Newport News, where an unidentified young woman was found dead in the early hours this morning by a local fisherman." Alec jumped up from bed and stared at the TV, which showed the newswoman with the lakeshore behind her. He watched intently and listened to her every word. "Police have barricaded the area and are combing carefully for clues. Her identity is not being released at this time, pending family notification. Sheriff Dunabar plans to hold a press announcement later tonight, but for the town of Newport News, this tragedy brings back painful memories from five years ago when the River Strangler killed four women in the neighboring city of Norfolk, Virginia. As you may already know, Alec Deluca, who was convicted of murdering Laura Stone, one of the four women killed in a span of sixteen days, is believed to be the River Strangler. Deluca currently is serving time at Greenville Correctional Center. He is scheduled to die by lethal injection at midnight on Halloween. Alec Deluca will be Virginia's one hundred and eleventh convicted criminal to receive the death penalty since it was reestablished in 1975. I'm Linda Peet; back to you, Bob."

"Thank you, Linda. Channel Twelve News will bring live feed from Sheriff Dunabar's press announcement later this evening. I'm Bob Free; stay tuned for more breaking news of this tragedy along Lake Maury."

Alec stood and approached the TV. He couldn't believe what he was hearing. *A woman found dead along a river. Coincidental? No.* "Guard! Guard!"

Officer Knots slowly turned. "What is it, Deluca?"

"I want to see my lawyer! It's important; there's been a murder."

The guard stared at the black-and-white screen. "What are you talking about, Deluca?"

"There's been another murder." Deluca started jumping up and down, laughing.

"Knock it off, Deluca, or I'll take the TV."

Alec ran toward the guard and grabbed the bars tightly. The guard placed a hand on his black baton. "Back away, Deluca. I'm not telling you again."

Deluca's eyes were wild as he released the cold metal and raked both hands through his dark hair. "I...I wanna talk to my lawyer. I gotta tell her."

"Tomorrow, Deluca. She comes again tomorrow, nine thirty sharp. The same as the last four days."

"But I gotta see her now! I gotta see her now!" Deluca ranted, and again he ran toward the guard and shook the bars violently. "They gonna kill me. They're gonna kill an innocent man!"

Officer Knots just shook his head and removed his baton. "Tomorrow. Now go sit your ugly ass back down on that cot before I break your fingers."

Alec stopped rattling the bars but didn't back away.

Officer Knots saw true, raw fear in Deluca's eyes. He placed his baton back on his hip and said in a softened tone, "Tomorrow, Alec. Now do us both a favor: don't cause no problems till then, all right?"

Again, Alec was consumed with defeat. Slowly, his fingers unwrapped from around the bars, and his hands fell to his sides. He turned away, walked to the TV, and turned it off. Then he lay back down as instructed.

CHAPTER 2

Halloween, 11:00 p.m.

Hordes of reporters surrounded the state penitentiary where Alec Deluca was scheduled to die at midnight. Joy Sutton honked her way to the front gate, shouting, "Move people!" She honked again, and then armed men stepped in front of the crowd and pushed them back as the gate opened. "Bottom-feeder rodents," she mumbled, pulling forward.

She stopped at another set of gates and rolled her window down. She produced her badge for the gatekeeper, following protocol, but they recognized each other from her many sessions over the last several months. He greeted her kindly. "Ma'am, you doing OK tonight?"

Joy gave the man a weak smile. "As well as expected. Never seen this before."

The guard hesitated before handing the badge back. "Oh, I didn't know. I just…"

"Assumed? Yeah, everyone does. But no, this is definitely my first execution."

"Well then, I guess I should wish you good luck tonight. You'll need it." He gave her a warm smile and then added, "I'll be here when you leave."

Joy nodded and rolled her window back up as she moved forward and found an open slot in visitor's parking. Her black-leather briefcase, the one her father had given her upon graduation, sat on the seat beside her. Inside contained the final letter from the state. She grabbed the briefcase and checked her surroundings. No vultures were lying in wait. She opened the door to her little red Chrysler 200 convertible and walked briskly in her black heels into the building. Immediately, she was met by the warden, Barry Conrad. "Warden," she said in greeting with a handshake.

"Ms. Sutton, this way. He's ready for you." Joy felt a chill run through her bones as they walked down a narrow hallway. At the end was a room familiar to her—the same room where she had met Deluca repeatedly. She could already see him, dressed in orange with his feet chained together. The chains were bolted to the floor. As they neared the final steps, the warden reminded her, "Ms. Sutton, we're on a tight schedule. You'll only have five minutes."

Five minutes? She only needed one. "I understand, thank you. I'll let the guard know when I'm finished."

The warden stopped at the entrance and gave the guard a nod. The gate made a loud clanging noise as it opened, and Joy walked in.

As before, the room felt cold and smelled like stale air. Joy immediately placed her briefcase on the table and took a seat across from her client. She studied him briefly. *Was he lying to me or was he finally telling the truth?* She pushed the thoughts away; it was a moot point now anyway. She had made a decision; there was no going back now. She broke eye contact and took a deep breath. Rehearsing her speech once more in her head as she had done on the long ride from Richmond, she carefully removed the file from her briefcase. She opened it and slid a paper across the table. "I'm sorry, Mr. Deluca.

There will be no last-minute intervening phone call from the governor. We lost."

"Denied" in bold letters jumped from the paper and struck Alec hard. Alec's eyes left the white paper and found hers. "I don't understand. Didn't you tell them about that dead woman on the river?"

Joy, who had mentally tried to prepare herself for this moment, replied, "I told them." Her voice quivered as she spoke. Realizing her mistake, she self-consciously raked a hand over her dark hair, which was pulled into a tight bun at the base of her neck. Then firmly she continued. "I did what I could. I'm sorry."

Confusion filled Alec's face as he slumped down farther in his chair. "But…then why?" he asked in agony.

Joy continued with her lies, ignoring her conscience while trying to appease him. "There's no sound evidence from this woman's death that warrants reopening the investigation of the crime you were convicted of."

Alec's eyes turned sad. He shook his head, and then his chin dropped in despair. He murmured, "I didn't kill those women." He looked back up, and their eyes locked. "And that man from the trial, he shouldn't have been there at her house. You told 'em about that too?"

Joy said nothing. Suddenly, the room began to feel too small. She quickly packed the papers back in her folder and stood. The man in front of her was set to die within the hour. There was nothing more to say. Alec slowly looked away. Tears were flowing freely down his ghostly face. Joy's throat began to tighten as if the oxygen had been sealed off in the room. "Guard, I'm ready!" she unintentionally shouted.

Alec tore into a rage. "No! Don't go!" The table rattled, and the sound echoed loudly as three burly guards came rushing in. Joy froze at his display of anger and betrayal. A hand touched her arm, and she looked up and saw the warden.

"Ma'am, please, come with me."

Joy nodded and took one last look at Alec Deluca, partly afraid and partly ashamed. Finally, she turned away.

***

At eleven forty-five, a blue Honda Accord pulled into Mathews Park, and the driver cut the engine. A female voice from the backseat screamed out, "No! Not here! Are you crazy?"

Liam looked at his rearview mirror and saw Jimmy's girlfriend frowning. He'd already forgotten her name. "Stop being such a girl. Come on, Jenny." Liam's girlfriend turned and looked at her friend in the backseat. She hesitated briefly and then opened her door and stepped out. Liam slammed his door. "Leave them. I want you all to myself."

Jenny looked ahead at the semi lit park. The sidewalk leading down to the sandy beach was empty. She glanced around the parking lot. No other cars were present. She turned back to the captain of the football team, who had given her his letter jacket three weeks ago. She thought about how wrong all of this was, but she bit her tongue and forced a smile. She stepped around the car and grabbed his hand tightly. "OK, just don't run off from me. This place is creepy."

He laughed and pulled her along down the sidewalk. "Now why would I run off? I've got the hottest girl in school by my side."

His words made her heart flutter, and she felt her cheeks warm. She continued freely by his side, swinging their clasped hands.

Their surroundings grew darker the farther they walked. Soon the sidewalk ended, and sand began. Jenny looked around and tried to adjust her eyes to the darkness. The full moon gave very little light with the cloudy sky that threatened rain. The wind blew, and Jenny shivered at the noise from the tree limbs above.

"You cold?" Liam placed his hands on her arms.

"Not while wearing your jacket." Jenny pulled the jacket tighter around her.

Liam let her go and stepped closer to her. His lips found hers, and he kissed her as his hands slowly removed his varsity jacket from her body, revealing a soft cashmere sweater. He tossed the jacket on the sand and pushed her down slowly on top of it. Jenny watched his dark-blue eyes as he lowered himself onto her. He kissed her lips again and then raked his mouth over her neck toward the opening in her V-neck sweater. Jenny opened her eyes wide and looked at the sky. The moon appeared as a cloud rolled away. *What am I doing? This is way too fast.* She softly spoke his name. "Liam, wait."

Liam removed his mouth from her chest and kissed her lips again. She pushed on his chest gently. Liam rolled off and sat up on the sand. Jenny didn't speak. She didn't know what to say. *Was he mad?*

He touched her soft face and then ran his hand through her hair. "What? Nobody ever kiss you like that before?"

Jenny shook her head. "You can say that."

He studied her for a moment and then smiled. "Good." He rose to his feet and pulled her back up. "I feel like a cold swim. Want to join me?"

Jenny watched in shock as he pulled his knit top over his head. Next, he began taking off his tennis shoes. "What? Here? On Halloween at a park where a dead woman was found."

He laughed. "Come on. That was ten years ago. Probably just a rumor anyway."

Jenny shook her head. "Oh no. It's true. My dad was a cop on the case. And it wasn't ten years ago; it was five," she corrected him.

Liam froze at her words. "Your dad's a cop?" Jenny watched as he quickly grabbed his shirt off the beach and pulled it back on. "Geez, Jenny, you think you could have mentioned that earlier." He tossed his letterman jacket toward her.

She dusted the sand off his high-school jacket and pulled it on. "I don't see why that matters." She crossed her arms over her chest and pouted. "Besides, my parents are divorced. My stepdad is who you met. He's a pharmacist."

Liam pulled out his phone and looked at the time. "I'm eighteen, Jenny. You know what your dad can do to me?"

"He wouldn't—"

He interrupted her, saying, "Anyway, I didn't realize it was this late, and it's a school night. Come on, I better get you back home."

Jenny grabbed his hand. "It's not that late."

Liam stopped and looked at her, studying her. "I like you, Jenny. I want to be able to see you again, you know."

Her brow furrowed. "You do? You're not mad?"

He smirked. "What kind of pig do you think I am, Jenny? I'm gonna break up with you because you wouldn't put out? Or worse, your dad's a cop?"

"I..." She looked down and pursed her lips. She felt his hand on her chin, guiding her face upward to look him in the eye. She saw hurt in his expression. "I'm sorry. I just thought you would want someone more..." She looked away down the beach, embarrassed. "More experienced."

"Aw, Jenny. You're only sixteen. I'm glad nobody's kissed you like that before, all right?"

She blushed and looked away again. She felt him tug on her arm, and she turned and followed him back up the sidewalk. As they walked, the moon disappeared again behind a cloud, and thunder boomed distantly.

"Looks like they got the weather right for once." Liam stopped and looked at the sky. "Come on." They began running, but Liam came to an abrupt stop and screamed out in pain, "Damn it!" She watched as he grabbed his bare foot. "I stepped on something." Liam dropped to the sidewalk and wiped at the bottom of his foot. "Just a rock."

He pulled his tennis shoes on as Jenny looked around. The wind was blowing harder at the trees now, and leaves were falling around them. Soon Liam was back on his feet, and they were running again. His car came into sight under the streetlight, and they stopped short when they read the message written largely on the front windshield: "You're gonna die!"

Jenny stuttered, "Wh…what the hell?" She jerked and looked around as Liam eased her closer to the car.

He called out, still holding her hand. "Jimmy?"

Seeing and hearing no one, Jenny watched from behind Liam as he opened the backseat door and announced, "They aren't here."

She moved around him and looked inside. "What? Where are they? Is this some kind of joke?"

Liam walked over to the front windshield and ran a finger across a letter. He rubbed it between his fingers. "It's…I think it's lipstick." He raised it to his noise. "Yeah, funny, raspberry lipstick." He noticed that Jenny had paled. "Hey, Jimmy's just playing a sick joke, that's all.

It's Halloween, remember?" Liam looked around and then closed the backseat door. "I say we should leave them."

"What? No. We can't do that. I can't leave Victoria. I'm staying with her tonight, and besides, that's just—"

"Relax. We're not going to leave them. We're just gonna get in the car and pretend. We'll drive over to the next parking lot, and then we'll sneak over here and watch them freak out."

Jenny backed away. "We can't. It's getting late, remember?"

Liam sighed and looked back toward the beach. "Jimmy! Come on, dude, they're gonna get grounded. We got to go, man!"

Jenny heard giggles and turned toward an area where the trees were thicker. Jimmy and Victoria soon walked out hand in hand. Jenny rolled her eyes, turned back toward the car, and opened the passenger door. "Where's my purse?"

Liam checked the backseat. "I'll pop the trunk. They probably tossed it back there when they left."

"I'm gonna kill her if she used my whole tube of lipstick. It was new!"

Jimmy and Victoria neared. "That was a stupid trick, guys." Liam pulled his keys out of his pocket and pressed a button as Jenny walked around to the trunk.

Victoria pulled out a Kleenex from her purse. "I'll wipe it off."

Jenny placed a hand under the slightly raised trunk. "It's gonna smear like crazy and—" Jenny's scream replaced any other words she might have spoken.

Liam jumped, ran over, and grabbed Jenny, who was stumbling backward. An arm dangled out over the trunk.

From a distance, a man smiled and watched with delight. He glanced at the time on his watch. "Rest in peace, Alec Deluca."

CHAPTER 3

A familiar tune rang out into the dark, quiet bedroom. *Norman Lewis.* Detective Jason Ashmore rolled over and looked at the clock: 12:15 a.m. He groaned. He had just showered off a long night of teenage pranks thirty minutes ago. He sat up, flipped the light switch, and grabbed his phone. "Norman, please tell me we don't have another ketchup-smeared mannequin."

"I wish we did, sir."

Ashmore tensed. There would only be one reason Officer Norman Lewis would call and wake him at this hour. He instantly regretted his words. "Are you sure, not another prank to make us look like asses for the second time tonight?"

"No, sir. I wish. We gotta couple of kids out at Mathews Park. Found a dead woman in the back of their trunk."

"In *their* trunk?"

"Yes, sir. It's all messed up. One of the kids is Detective Lamb's daughter."

"Jenny?"

"Yes, sir. He's already been called. Better get out here. All hell is about to break loose. Lamb's likely to strangle Jenny's boyfriend when he gets here. He's the owner of the vehicle."

"Great! Keep Lamb far away. I'll be there in ten."

"I'll do my best, sir; he outranks me."

Ashmore swore as he ended the call. He quickly threw on jeans and a T-shirt followed by a leather jacket to conceal his sidearm. He had lived alone since his divorce so there was no one to tell that he was leaving. He pocketed his wallet and phone, and he left the house. With the help of a blue light mounted on top of his red truck, he made it to Mathews Park in less than eight minutes. Detective Arthur Lamb's black SUV was nowhere in sight among the four police cruisers that sat before a yellow tape roping off the crime scene. "Good! At least something's going right," Ashmore mumbled as he cut his engine.

Detective Arthur Lamb was his senior by seven years and held a higher rank due to years of service with the homicide detectives at Norfolk Police Department. Lamb was a damn good detective, but he had a quick temper and lost his cool every now and then. Lamb's only daughter, Jenny, lived with her mother, his ex. He'd heard many complaints from his lips about how naïve his ex-wife could be on issues concerning their daughter. Now, his precious sixteen-year-old baby girl whom he had placed upon a pedestal was at a crime scene on Halloween. Yeah, this was sure to test his issues with anger management tonight.

Stepping out of the vehicle, Ashmore nodded at Officer Joe Wilson, who was guarding the entrance. He looked past him and saw several officers standing around a lone vehicle, which was parked with its trunk raised, down below the hill. Norman Lewis and his partner Rick Brown were standing off to the side with four teenagers, all sitting on the paved concrete. Jenny Lamb was easy to spot. "Keep Detective Lamb up here! This is my crime scene, and it's a conflict of interest." Ashmore hurried down the hill, never acknowledging Officer Wilson's grumbling complaint.

With each step Ashmore took, the officers stepped away from the vehicle to reveal what had caused another fuss on Halloween night, waking Norfolk's homicide detective on call. A woman's naked body had been stuffed in the back of the Honda Accord, her arm dangling over the side as if she'd been crying out for help. Her eyes, surrounded by black-and-blue bruises, were wide open. Her long, dark hair covered her shoulders but couldn't hide the dark-blue line that wrapped around her neck. Strangled, just like Hazel Rice, who had been found along Lake Maury shore two days ago. "Damn it! Anybody touch her?"

"No, sir," replied Officer Meriam.

Ashmore looked at the four teenagers sitting at Officers Lewis and Brown's feet. "What the hell happened here?"

Officer Montgomery spoke. "The kids were down here fooling around, doing what kids do. The owner of the car is Liam Wills; he's Jenny Lamb's boyfriend. While they were down walking around on the beach—"

"Walking around on the beach just short of midnight? That's their story?" asked Ashmore.

"Yes, sir. Well, that's what they said. When they got back up to the car, they saw this." He motioned toward the front of the car, and Ashmore walked around and saw the message on the windshield. "Their friends, Jimmy Garner and Victoria Candle, had left this for them to find as a prank. You see, they were part of the group that left the mannequin hanging in the tree earlier."

"Great. Lamb know that yet?"

The youngest officer in the group, Officer Meriam, stepped over. "Yes. I drew the short straw. I called him, sir."

Ashmore stepped forward. "What is this?"

"Lipstick. Jenny left her purse in the car. Her friend, Victoria Candle, used her lipstick to leave the prank. But funny thing is, Victoria says she left the purse on the backseat. It's not there, sir. That's what prompted Liam to pop the trunk. Jenny found the body."

"Where's the purse?"

"Haven't found it. Maybe under the body, but we didn't want to touch her."

"Good call." Ashmore noted, "If it's under her, maybe the asshole left some prints—doubtful but maybe."

"Sir, Jenny's pretty shaken up. Hell, they all are," said Officer Montgomery.

"I bet so. Turns out the prank's on them, but this time it's no mannequin. Damn, no kids deserve to see this!" Ashmore ran a hand through his short, dark hair. "Did they see anybody or a car, anything?"

"No, sir. They said the park was deserted when they got here. Never saw or heard a thing. Sir, she looks to be strangled. Does this mean it's connected to the other woman dumped at Lake Maury near Warwick?"

Headlights flashed over them, and the men looked toward the road. "Good. Medical examiner's here. We'll know soon enough, but God I hope not. Let's get the kids out of—"

Seconds behind the white van was a black SUV. It stopped abruptly, slinging gravel as the engine was slammed into park. Detective Lamb came charging toward the yellow tape, screaming, "Jenny!"

"Great." Ashmore walked down toward the teenagers as he instructed loudly, "Lewis! Send Jenny up. Keep the boyfriend away." Jenny slowly stood up with the help of Officer Lewis. Ashmore began jogging toward her and met her halfway up the hill. "Hey, Jenny, I'm going to walk you up to your dad. Don't be frightened. He's more scared than mad." Together they climbed upward, passed the car, and confronted an outraged father who was teetering on the edge of knowing right from wrong. Officer Joe Wilson was holding him back.

"Are you OK, Jenny, are you hurt?"

Jenny's face was smeared with mascara as she sobbed. She shook her head as she lunged into her father's strong arms. For a split second, Arthur Lamb relaxed as he confirmed with his own eyes that Jenny was alive and unscathed. He pulled away and looked down the hill toward the group of kids. His body tensed. Ashmore stepped closer. "Detective Lamb, we need to take the teenagers downtown. We'll need a statement."

"I wanna talk to that boy who's been dragging my daughter around all night."

Jenny tried to pull away. "Daddy, no! Don't…he…we…we didn't do this."

Lamb looked over his daughter, who was still wearing Liam Will's letterman jacket. Her blond hair was a tangled mess, and she had sand on her jeans. A flash of light was coming toward them. A news van. Ashmore grabbed Lamb's arm and bent close to his ear. "Media just arrived. Not here. Keep it together, Arthur, for all our sakes, or you and your daughter are gonna be splashed all over the news tomorrow."

The news van opened, and Katie Whitten with Channel 2 News stepped out without a hair out of place. She looked at them with a big smile across her face, excited that she was the first to arrive. Ashmore's stomach turned as he wondered if she ever slept. Her pantsuit was pressed, and her makeup was perfect even in this early hour. Ashmore felt Lamb's arm break free from his grasp as he mumbled something inaudible and walked away with Jenny.

At the sight of the news van, Officer Montgomery had run up the hill to assist, leaving the other officers at the bottom of the hill by the body. Ashmore quickly jumped into action, taking charge of the situation. "Officer Montgomery, take Jenny to the station. Arthur, now you go on and follow them." Arthur Lamb let Jenny go and looked back down the hill toward the others. Ashmore spoke pointedly. "You can't be involved, Arthur; you know the rules."

Lamb turned away from Liam Wills, the kid he planned to strangle with his bare hands, and looked back at Ashmore with disgust. He started to say something, but Katie was thrusting a microphone toward them with a cameraman behind her. Lamb walked away from Jenny and moved toward his SUV as Ashmore put out his hands and shook his head. "No comment, Ms. Whitten. Get back; this is a crime scene. You'll get a statement later, like everyone else."

"But…Detective Ashmore, is it connected to the murder of Hazel Rice? Do we have another serial killer? The public has the right to know."

Ashmore hesitated briefly and then spoke the same words as before. "No comment." He quickly turned away.

Officer Wilson took charge. "You heard the detective. I want everyone back twenty feet. Now!"

Ashmore greeted the Norfolk's medical examiner of ten years, who had been busying herself with arranging her kit. "Thanks for coming so fast."

Dr. Marlee Hoyt slammed the door to her government-issued van and looked around. "Are you kidding; how could I miss all this? Good job by the way." She looked at Lamb. "That could've been ugly." Together they watched as Officer Montgomery pulled away in his patrol car with Jenny Lamb in the front seat. Arthur Lamb was right on their bumper.

"Yeah, come on." Together they walked down the hill toward the victim. When they were far enough away from the media, he spoke again. "Female, looks to be strangled."

Dr. Hoyt missed a step and looked at Ashmore. "I see. Oh boy, well, we'll know soon enough." They picked up their speed.

CHAPTER 4

It was nearing one in the morning when Joy Sutton pulled her fireball-red sports car into her gated garage beneath her townhome on the east side of Richmond. The door felt heavy as she pushed it open. She was wiped out, both physically and emotionally. She had been Alec Deluca's last visitor, and she had seen him die by the hands of the state of Virginia. Taking a deep breath, she pushed the image out of her head as she locked the car and headed toward the elevators. She glanced around, expecting to find no one, but wouldn't have been surprised to find a lone man or woman who had gotten past the gate, working for this media or that and looking for a story.

Joy had been assigned Deluca's case back in June; another job the state had assigned, and she would help him appeal to the very end. For nearly six months, Joy Sutton had made the drive from Richmond to Greenville to visit with Alec Deluca and review his case. She had been appointed by her boss, Burt Phelps, to ensure Deluca was given proper and adequate counsel up until the day of his execution: midnight Halloween. "Who the hell schedules an execution at midnight on Halloween?" she mumbled as she walked across the deserted parking garage.

The elevator door quickly opened, and she pressed three. Soon she was unlocking her apartment door and kicking off her black two-inch heels. She dropped her briefcase by the door, tossed the keys on the kitchen counter, and pulled off her jacket. Her phone buzzed, and she immediately turned it off. No more tonight.

Opening a new bottle of red wine, Joy sat at the kitchen table and began to cry. She couldn't get Alec Deluca's face out of her mind. She drank.

Alec Deluca's case had been pretty straightforward. She had reviewed the trial transcript and the state defense attorney's notes. In her eyes, the jury had gotten it right. Alec Deluca had killed Laura Stone and deserved to die on Halloween for his crimes. For five straight months, Alec had said nothing to change her mind or to make her fight harder for him—until yesterday morning. A meeting she wished now had never happened. She poured another glass.

"What have I done?" She sat alone as tears flowed down her cheeks, leaving black streaks. She wiped her face and cried harder when she smeared black mascara on her silk blouse. The same pink blouse she was wearing the night she met Andrew Lane.

A new image filled her mind: Norfolk's district attorney, Andrew Lane. "What were the chances that he'd be the active DA on Deluca's case?" She cussed as she thumped the wine cork off the kitchen table.

Her mind drifted back to the first time they met. They'd shared a dinner, and he had wooed her instantly with a job offer. She'd declined of course, but that's when she began to see her life in a different light. She took another sip.

At the age of thirty-four, she had no husband or children to come home to. Loneliness had taken the place of the thrill of a new case. Since meeting Lane last year, she had begun questioning her career choice. Her initial passion to fight for clients who couldn't afford an attorney had wilted. After all, more clients than not were guilty, and she had put her entire career ahead of her own happiness. All this had taken a toll on her the last few months. As she drank the last of her wine and poured another glass, finishing the bottle, she debated whether she had made a grievous error in judgement.

The look of hope upon Deluca's face as she walked into the room tonight made her conscience twinge again. Denied. *I'm sorry, but the state denied your stay.* Pain and frustration filled his face and then rage. Joy pounded the table. "Damn it, Deluca! Why did you wait so long to tell me? It could've made a difference."

Joy got up and opened another bottle of wine. She refilled her glass, grabbed her phone, and headed toward her master-bedroom suite. She flipped the bedroom light switch, and all was as it should be: a made bed with no one waiting on her. She hiccupped as she set down her glass to plug in her phone. Next, she pressed a button on the wall, and the dark shades began to lower, blocking out the city lights of Richmond. Joy stripped down to her underwear and climbed in bed. Another image of Deluca filled her mind, this one of the needle injected into his arm. She closed her eyes as she took another long sip. When her wine was gone, she lay down and prayed for the drunkenness to take her quickly, erasing all images and thoughts of Alec Deluca and Andrew Lane.

CHAPTER 5

The call came in at 4:35 in the early morning, waking FBI Special Agent Jemma Rhodes from a terrific dream that involved a man, a case of Corona, and a white, sandy beach. Since then, a bag had been packed, trash had been taken out, and a condo overlooking the Potomac River had been locked up tight. Jemma had pushed her Lincoln Navigator hard over the last hundred miles along Interstate 95 as the lights of Washington, DC, faded in the background. Now, she had five more miles to go before reaching Richmond, Virginia. She had been summoned personally by FBI Director Bobby Miller. Her valuable profiling skills were needed. Without any hesitation or the excuse that she had just taken vacation days, Jemma agreed to be present and on time at the Richmond FBI field office at eight hundred hours.

Miller had informed Jemma that there had been two female bodies found, one just south of Newport News and the other next door in Norfolk, within three days of each other. Both strangled and both dumped near rivers. If that wasn't bad enough, this week marked the end of the River Strangler, aka Alec Deluca. The state of Virginia had just finished carrying out his death sentence by lethal injection. Coincidence or were they looking at a copycat? Director Miller was sending her to find out.

The case in Norfolk definitely had her attention, so much so that she had pushed the sweet dream out of her mind and jumped in a cold shower to knock the cobwebs out of her head. Sleep, Jemma had decided years ago, totally was overrated. Sex, on the other hand, was not. A planned extra-long weekend getaway with a rogue, quick-tongued detective she had met about a month ago while on a case in New York City was now canceled thanks to a psychopath in Virginia. Jemma looked at the time on the dash. Seven forty-five. She pressed a button on her steering wheel, no longer putting off what needed to be done an hour ago. "Call Bruce Vines."

A female computerized voice replied, "Calling Bruce Vines on mobile."

Jemma looked in her rearview mirror at her reflection, her emerald eyes appearing darker against her fair-complexioned skin that needed many days of sun before winter set in. "What? Like I have a choice?" she asked herself.

After the third ring, a male voice sounded throughout the SUV. "Well, this is a surprise so early in the morning."

Jemma grimaced. "Sorry, did I wake you?"

"Yeah, but that's OK. Got to get going or I'll miss my noon flight. And missing a weekend with you is something I don't want after the night I had last night!"

Her heart missed a beat at his words. She saw her exit up ahead and her mind quickly took over. "I'm in Virginia. I'm sorry. I got the call early this morning from the director himself." An awkward silence passed as Jemma lifted the lever to signal her exit. "Is your flight refundable?"

"No."

"Mine neither. I'm really sorry, Bruce. I was looking forward to this."

"Yeah, me too, Jemma, me too."

More silence followed as Jemma glanced at her GPS and then turned left at the light. "Look, maybe they'll let us change our flights for another weekend and we could—"

"No, Jemma. I think I'm gonna keep my flight to Miami."

"Oh, well, yeah, I mean, maybe I can wrap this up and catch a later flight out tonight and—"

"I don't think so, Jemma. Look, no hard feelings, OK? This thing we got, it couldn't've lasted anyway. Our jobs aren't suited for each other, you know."

"Maybe not but…" Jemma saw the large FBI building with the dark windows growing larger as she accelerated under a yellow light. "I would have liked to try."

"I know, Jemma, me too. Look, don't say anything else. I don't want this to turn awkward. We're bound to cross paths again with work, so let's just say our good-byes, OK?"

The awkwardness was already there. Finally, Jemma responded, "OK," as she turned into the parking lot and rolled to a stop at the guardhouse.

"Good-bye, Jemma."

Jemma forced a quick smile at the security officer as he approached her car. "Good-bye, Bruce." She pushed a button to end the call and lowered her driver's-side window. "Special Agent Jemma Rhodes." She handed her badge over and was asked to sign in on an electronic notepad. Another moment passed as her badge was examined and she signed in. After a brief exchange, she raised her window and proceeded ahead to visitor's parking as instructed. Cutting the engine, Jemma looked at the time. Like always, she was on time.

The Lincoln Navigator chirped as Jemma dropped her keys in her black briefcase. She checked her surroundings as she was taught—or one could say drilled in her head—by endless training at Quantico and walked with purpose toward the front entrance. She was met again by security. All her items were placed through an X-ray machine, and she collected her weapon and briefcase on the secured side. Jemma pulled her black jacket over her white-silk blouse, hiding her sidearm.

"Agent Jemma Rhodes."

Jemma recognized the familiar voice and turned. "Mark. So nice to see you again." She stuck out her hand, and he ignored it and hugged her. Jemma looked around the empty hallway, saw no one, and relaxed.

He slowly pulled away. "Same to you. How's your father dealing with retirement?"

"About as well as you would expect."

Agent Mark Mitten laughed as he motioned toward the opposite hallway. "Got a room full; just waiting on you."

Jemma fought the urge to look at her watch as she matched his steps toward the conference room at the end of the hall. Mark Mitten was considered old school, just one year away from retirement himself. He and her father, Vance Rhodes, were the best of friends. They had met during their first year with the FBI, and for the next fifteen years, they shared the same office wall in DC, hunted every winter, and went on double dates with their spouses. Mark had been transferred numerous times, but he had been in her life for as long as she could remember. Hell, he had probably changed her diaper. She pushed the thoughts out of her head. When Mark placed a hand on the doorknob, she stopped him. "I know you're my godfather and all, and I love you, but please introduce me as Agent Rhodes."

He chuckled. "Jemma, you proved yourself years ago within this agency. I couldn't possibly say anything that could discredit you now."

She blushed, rose up on her tiptoes, and gave him a peck on his cheek. "I've missed you."

"Well, don't be such a stranger. Come see us sometimes."

She instantly thought of her adorable godmother. "How is Betty?"

"Good, just waiting on me to retire. You should see all the plans she's made. Got next year already planned out and booked."

Jemma gave him a warm smile. "That's good. She deserves this, and so do you." Jemma turned away from him and looked at the closed door. "We should go in now."

The door was opened, and Jemma saw four men seated around a table with files scattered across the shiny, dark, long surface. A heated discussion was taking place and immediately ceased when she and Mark walked in. "Gentlemen, I'd like to introduce you to Agent Jemma Rhodes. She's an eight-year veteran, holds a doctorate degree in psychology from Harvard University, and is one of the agency's top profilers. She's personally been assigned by Director Miller to assist in this case."

"Gentlemen." Jemma spoke with confidence.

"I'm Agent Simon Nichols. I worked the case that convicted Alec Deluca five years ago." He stuck out his hand, and Jemma shook it.

Jemma studied his six-foot-two frame briefly. Totally fit, early forties—must be a health nut. His firm handshake revealed he was a lefty and married. With his warm, green eyes and blond hair, he was beautiful to look at. "This is Agent Howard Novack. He worked with me on the case."

Jemma turned and found a man in his late fifties, shorter at six foot, softer in the middle.

"Agent…actually, retired Agent Novack just came in today to help shed some light if needed." Agent Nichols continued, "Detectives Arthur Lamb and Jason Ashmore, both homicide from Norfolk, also worked the Deluca case."

Jemma studied both detectives briefly and shook their hands.

"Let's take a seat," Detective Jason Ashmore said and was the first to sit. All followed, and Agent Mark Mitten excused himself from the room, but not before he gave an affectionate squeeze to Jemma's shoulder. A glimmer of recognition crossed Ashmore's face. "Agent Vance Rhodes is your father, correct?"

Jemma looked at Ashmore. "Yes, he's retired now."

"Hell of an agent. I worked with him on a couple of cases. He talked about you a lot. Showed me your picture."

Agent Novack smirked. "I'm not surprised. He's very proud of you, Agent Rhodes."

Jemma felt herself blush again within five minutes. She tried shaking it off. "Thank you," Jemma responded as she lifted her briefcase and placed it on the table. She removed a file that Director Miller had sent her that morning. She'd had just enough time to print it off and read over it only once. Her actions brought the topic back to the case. "Now, if I understand this correctly, Alec Deluca was convicted of murdering Laura Stone. The killings then ceased, and everyone assumed he was the River Strangler." She looked at Agent Nichols with raised eyebrows. "So what is your gut telling you now? We've got another serial killer in Norfolk or was he a sleeper who waited on Deluca to die and rub it in our faces?"

The comment seemed to suck the air right out of the room. The thought of Deluca killing only Laura Stone and a serial killer slipping through their fingers brought reality to a screaming halt.

"I don't know," Agent Nichols responded honestly.

Jemma nodded with understanding. "Detective Ashmore, I read you were the first officer on scene with our first victim, Dawn Newberry, five years ago and was lead investigator before the FBI stepped in, correct?"

"Yes, after the second victim, Daisy Gwen, was discovered with the same markings along her wrists and ankles, our department called the FBI."

Jemma glanced over the names of all four victims who were supposedly killed by Alec Deluca, aka the River Strangler. "So do the two victims found recently have any similarities with Dawn Newberry or Daisy Gwen?"

Ashmore picked up a file on the table and opened it. He spread four gruesome crime scene photographs from five years ago on the table: Dawn Newberry, Daisy Gwen, Cameron Long, and the last, Laura Stone. "All the women had been bound and strangled except for Laura Stone." Next, he opened another file and produced this week's victims: Hazel Rice and Jane Doe, who had yet to be identified from last night. "These women were also bound and strangled but also raped. None of our victims five years ago were raped."

Detective Arthur Lamb slid over the file on Laura Stone. "Stone was beaten and had markings on her neck, but the ME said cause of death was from severe head trauma not strangulation."

Jemma studied the photo of Laura Stone. "What's this about her hair dye?"

"That's the strange part that led us to Deluca and his downfall," Agent Nichols explained. "All the victims had dark-brown hair, the same as Deluca's abusive mother. Laura Stone was a strawberry blonde. After the murder, he dyed her hair, walked across the street to his home, rinsed the dye from his hands in the sink, and then showered."

"And what led you to the neighbor?"

Detective Lamb answered. "Laura Stone's husband. He's the one who found her. He'd forgotten his phone and returned home. Said she'd been spying on the neighbor, Alec Deluca, and he was stupid not to have listened."

"Husband has an alibi?" she asked.

Ashmore opened the file on Daniel Stone. "Witnesses place the husband at work, and he placed a call for dinner reservations for the upcoming Friday night, the night his wife was to return from a business trip."

"And where is Mr. Stone now?"

"Still practicing law. He's one of Norfolk's top defense attorneys," replied Lamb.

"So he knows the law well…interesting. He remarry?"

Ashmore leaned forward in his seat. "Yes, to one of his associates."

Jemma nodded. "Even more interesting. I'm gonna want to pay him a visit. Now, what's the key evidence linking Deluca to the other three women?"

Lamb picked up Deluca's file. "Deluca had a record, assault and battery, done time. He'd been released six months prior to the killings. No alibi on the nights the women went missing, history of abuse, grew up in foster care, a true loner."

"So the killings stop after his arrest. You have the hair dye that connects him to Stone, but what physical evidence did you have that would have linked Deluca with the first three women?"

Agent Nichols passed over a photo of nylon rope found in Deluca's garage. "This was used in the trial. Same type and fibers embedded in the first three victims. He had a few rolls in his garage." Another photo was shown. "Deluca's vehicle had traces of mud. Forensics matched it to the same particles found along Lynnhaven Riverbank, where the body of Daisy Green was discovered." A photo of brown hiking boots was presented next. "Deluca's boots found in his garage had traces of sand from the downtown park where Cameron Long's body was found. Oh, and the trunk of his car held the same rope fibers."

Jemma studied the photos and the list given to the jury as evidence. "All from his garage, nothing from inside his home?"

"Where you going with this? You think Deluca was innocent?" asked Lamb.

"The jury thought so." She saw Lamb's vein pulse across his temple. She eased up. "Well, at least with the first three victims anyway. Look, detective, I'm not here to undermine your work. My job is to write a profile for each victim and then, if needed, compare. What's worse than having a new serial killer among us?" She paused and looked at each man. "To have the same serial killer pop back up after we supposedly had him executed."

For the next several hours, case files were read, studied, and compared. The work and evidence on the River Strangler had been top notch. Not one stone was left unturned, not a witness or family member ignored. It was solid criminal investigation work. Jemma studied each of the four victims. All beautiful, young, vibrant women in their early to late twenties. Dawn Newberry, a twenty-one-year-old student who worked as a waitress by night. Daisy Gwen, twenty-five and young mother. She'd gone on a run after her husband returned from work, hoping to drop her baby weight. She'd never returned. Cameron Long, a single twenty-eight-year-old elementary teacher who never made it to her parked car outside a large shopping center. A sales clerk verified the dropped shopping bag by her Ford Escape as her purchases: glue sticks and Post-it Notes. Last, Laura Stone, also twenty-eight, a travel writer about to embark on a trip to Belize and wife to a not-so-liked Norfolk defense attorney.

All four women portrayed strong, independent young women. Someone a man like Alec Deluca was sure to despise. His file was classic textbook for a sociopath who would harbor resentment toward females. His mother, Maria Deluca, had been sentenced to ten years for child abuse. His father, Mickey Deluca, had left before Alec was born. Maria's mugshot was in the file. Twenty-six, dark-brown hair, same weight and height as the victims. Alec was removed from her care and placed in a series of foster homes at age eight. From there trouble always seemed to follow. The juvy record was sealed, but it had been opened during the trial. At age fourteen, Alec had beaten his second foster mother with an iron skillet.

At age nineteen, Alec was a person of interest when a former foster mother had been beaten and left for dead after an apparent robbery. The police officer who was questioned said Alec had done it, but there had been no proof warranting an arrest. At age twenty-four, Alec assaulted his live-in girlfriend, leaving her in the hospital, which led to filing criminal charges. Alec Deluca went to prison. At age thirty-one, seven years later, he was released. Jemma studied the photos of Beverly Fuse, his girlfriend whom he'd beaten and left unconscious. She had dark-brown hair and the same blue eyes as his mother. She'd needed three surgeries to repair the damage he'd done to her face.

Jemma looked around the room and saw Ashmore writing in a file. They were the only two left in the room. Arthur Lamb had been dismissed since his daughter was found at one of the crime scenes. Agent Novack had returned to retired life after having nothing else to add on the case, and Agent Nichols went to retrieve another file. Jemma's neck felt tight as she dropped her pen on the table, and she rolled her neck and rotated her shoulders, lost in thought.

"Well, what do you see?"

Jemma stilled, opened her eyes, and met Ashmore's intense brown eyes. She sat up, picked back up her pen, and wrote on a clean pad of paper. Several minutes ticked by and Jemma passed the paper to Ashmore. He took it after a slight hesitation.

Victims Dawn Newberry, Daisy Gwen, Cameron Long profiler: values beautiful women, needs to control women to show his superiority, kills with great intimacy (strangulation), wants the victim to see him as her last vision, patient individual, intelligent

Profiler of Alec Deluca: uses physical abuse to demonstrate his superiority over women, repetitive learned-abusive-behavior personality, a drifter who wouldn't seek settlement, estranged relationship with women, lacks self-control, easy to manipulate, lack of respect toward elders, issues of abandonment

Ashmore read the notes twice. He frowned. "Deluca doesn't fit the River Strangler."

She shook her head.

"Damn! I was there; I arrested him. We had him on Laura Stone—all the items found in his garage, the murders stopped...we just assumed." He sighed loudly. "What about our newest victims?"

"I'll need more information—need to see ME reports, compare the two victims. But adding rape?" She shook her head again. "He's either changed his game, escalated over his dormant period...hell, if he ever was dormant." She pulled out her briefcase and started stacking files. "Or..." Her voice trailed off.

"We have a third killer." Ashmore stood and began helping with the files. "You coming to Norfolk with me?"

Jemma looked up. "Absolutely."

CHAPTER 6

The door burst open on the fifth floor of City Hall. Andrew Lane stormed out of his office and stopped at his secretary's desk. "Any word from Sheriff Kennedy?"

Jill Eckelberg stopped typing and looked up at her boss of eight years. "I'm sorry; he hasn't called back. I left three messages."

"What about Joy Sutton?" It had been two days since he'd last spoken to her. He tried to remember her exact words as he watched his secretary shake her head. "You want me to try her cell?"

"Yes, I do." Andrew paced back and forth, waiting.

"I'm sorry; there's no answer."

Andrew reached out his hand. "I'll leave the message." He placed the large desk phone receiver to his head. "Ms. Sutton, Andrew Lane. I'd like to talk about Alec Deluca's case. Please stop by my office at your earliest convenience. Thank you."

He handed the phone back. "Call around and see if anyone has heard from her. If she's out giving interviews to the press, I want to know what she's saying."

Jill frowned at his words. "Yes, sir. Right away. I've got a close friend in the press. I'll call her. See if she's heard anything."

"As long as she's discreet. We don't know what direction this Deluca case's going to take."

"Of course, I'll keep you posted, sir."

Andrew didn't comment as he turned and walked back into his office. Andrew began pacing back and forth. He thought he knew Joy Sutton well enough now to predict her moves. Was he wrong? Six months ago, when his new appointment arrived to discuss the final proceedings leading up to the execution of Alec Deluca, little did he know it would be Joy Sutton, the state's appointed lawyer. His idea of a quick meet and greet session just went flying out the window.

A full year had passed since he'd seen Ms. Sutton at the Richmond, Virginia, state conference. They'd shared a dinner among friends and colleagues. He'd immediately been impressed with her. The next night, he pulled her aside, and they dined alone. He tried to convince her to quit her job working for the state and join his side. She had laughed and immediately turned him down.

By the last night of the weeklong conference, they had grown equally fond of each other. She had promised to consider his proposal, and she would get in touch if she ever visited Norfolk. They had shared one more drink that night and had caught the elevator together. When the door opened on the sixth floor, she had held the door and offered him a nightcap. Andrew breathed hard as he thought about how close he came to screwing up his marriage again. Not only was Joy beautiful, smart, and sexy as hell, but willing. He had declined.

Andrew picked up a picture of his wife and three kids off his desk. He sat clutching the frame, remembering how he had walked away from Joy's advances that night. He placed the photo back down and opened his desk's top drawer. The key to Joy's apartment was still in the same spot he'd left it since she'd given it to him several weeks ago.

If you ever change your mind. He picked it up and tossed the shiny metal in his hands. The key looked new; had she made it just for him? Andrew sighed loudly. *I should've given it back immediately. Stupid. But now, should I use it? Why aren't you returning my calls? We made a deal!*

Andrew stood and began pacing once more. He needed to talk to Joy and fast. If she went public on what they had discussed privately and how he had talked her out of presenting a stay of execution to the state, he would be crucified in the media. He looked back into the face of his smiling wife holding their two-year-old daughter. *No. Too dangerous to step one foot into her apartment.* He tossed the key back in his drawer and closed it.

* * *

It was nearing noon when Joy Sutton finally stirred in her two-bedroom townhome. She peeked one eye open and looked at the time lit in green. She slowly rolled over in her dark bedroom and heard the familiar tick of the fan. Her head ached as she closed her eyes once again and buried her face into her soft pillow. The decision to come home and drown her sorrows with a bottle of wine seemed appropriate at the time, but now she was painfully regretting her decision.

She rolled onto her back and tried to convince herself everything would be fine. Last night was just a really bad night. Nothing a hot shower and some aspirin can't cure. She slowly tossed the covers off her body, and just as she rose, the image of Alec Deluca lying flat on his back with a needle in his arm came flooding back to her. She flopped back down on her bed and closed her eyes. A hot shower wasn't going to come close to washing that image out of her mind.

She'd seen the most gruesome crime photos and known in her heart that most of the people she was assigned to defend were guilty. Still, she had mixed emotions about Deluca's divulgence just one day before he was set to die. Moreover, she still had mixed emotions about the death penalty. Slowly, she opened her eyes, but she could still see

Deluca, the look of a frightened, desperate man as she had given him the final word: denied.

Joy turned over on her side and curled up into a ball. Her head pounded at the memory of standing inside the prison and talking to Deluca on October 30, one day before execution. He was rattled and ranting like a madman. Why just one day before his execution did he proclaim his innocence, shedding new light on his case? Joy had left that day so confused, and instead of calling her boss, Burt Phelps, she had driven straight to Andrew Lane's office. Why? Well, she knew the reason; she'd fallen for Andrew and hard.

For two hours, she had listened to Andrew Lane sell a convincing story. After some pleading and sweet talk, she had finally agreed to remain quiet about Deluca's confession. By the time she left Lane's office, she had convinced herself that the conversation with Deluca in his cell had never happened, and she was left holding an offer letter to come work with Lane's office.

Slowly, Joy rose from bed, fighting the pain and memories. She turned on the lights and pushed back against the headboard. When her eyes adjusted, she flipped a switch on the wall and her nightshades covering her floor-length windows slowly rose, revealing a gray, gloomy day. *Perfect. A perfect day to go with my mood.* She stared out the window at the trees, the wind blowing the remaining leaves off. *Winter. A good time to start over.*

Her thoughts led back to Andrew Lane. He was right. It was time to make some changes in her life. She shook off the lingering feelings of guilt over Alec Deluca. After all, he'd done time before for beating his girlfriend to near death. *No, I'm done with guilty no-good criminals.* She thought about her newfound relationship with the good-looking district attorney, and a smile formed on her lips. I think it's time to say yes to Mr. Andrew Lane's job offer. Warmth spread throughout her body as she thought of the chemistry they had shared over the last several meetings before Deluca's revelation. *I should call him and finally tell him yes. Oh, we are going to make a great team, Andrew! An excellent team!*

She reached for her mobile phone, which was plugged into the wall. Last night she had turned off her ringer at 1:00 a.m., refusing further calls from the media that had turned the grounds outside of Greenville Correctional Center into a circus. Immediately, eight missed calls and thirty-two texts appeared on her screen. She touched the phone icon and saw Andrew Lane's number appear several times along with her boss's name and other numbers she didn't recognize. Next, she touched the text icon and scrolled through the messages, all bearing the same tone: *Turn on the TV. Where are you? Was Alec Deluca innocent?*

"What the hell?"

Joy quickly found the remote and turned on the large TV that was mounted on the wall across from her king-size bed. She flipped through a few channels until finally she found a local news channel. A man wearing a black suit was standing behind a podium. The headline read, "Breaking news: FBI Simon Nichols confirms the death of an unidentified woman found in Norfolk, Va., late last night, bringing the number to two victims over three days."

Simon: "At this time, we ask for your patience as we continue to review the crime scenes and allow time for the medical examiner to complete her report before we determine if they're indeed related."

Reporter: "Could these deaths be related to the River Strangler? Did the state of Virginia execute an innocent man last night, Alec Deluca?"

Simon frowned. "At this time, the state and FBI still stand behind the execution of Alec Deluca for the murder of Laura Stone."

Reporter: "What about the other victims: Dawn Newberry, Daisy Gwen, and Cameron Long?"

Simon: "The FBI is working closely with the Norfolk Police Department at this time. More information will follow as soon as it's available. For now, I encourage the community of Norfolk to remain vigilant, and if anyone has any information about the heinous crimes against these two females, please call the Norfolk Police Department. Thank you. There'll be no further comments."

Joy's mouth opened wide as she sat in shock. Another victim had been found last night. When? After the execution? Alec Deluca's words flowed through her head. *I didn't kill those women; he's back. He's back!* Nausea consumed Joy as she slid a finger across her phone and pressed Andrew Lane's name.

"Joy? Where in God's name have you been?"

"Sleeping. I went to bed drunk."

A brief silence passed. "Have you turned on the news?"

"Yeah, just caught the tail end of an FBI press conference. Do you know what this means?"

"Yes, and we need to talk."

Joy was already climbing out of bed and walking toward her master bath. No need to tell her what she needed to do. The lever in the shower was turned to hot. "It's best I come to you." Joy pulled a bottle of aspirin out of the cabinet and took three pills while Andrew remained quiet on the line. "I can be there in about an hour, two tops."

"No, not here."

Joy listened to his directions and ended the call. She pulled off her underwear, tested the water, and stepped in. Immediately, the hot water soothed the pounding in her head. She stood for a long moment, trying to clear her head. *Oh good God, what have I done?*

***

Agent Jemma Rhodes and Detective Jason Ashmore had not stayed behind to hear Agent Simon Nichols's press conference, which had been set up on the first floor of the FBI building in Richmond, Virginia. Ashmore had accepted a ride with Jemma since his early-morning ride, Detective Arthur Lamb, had left hours ago. By the time it took to drive from Richmond to Norfolk, a room had already been set up on the third floor of the Norfolk Police Department and the press conference had finished, leaving the citizens of Norfolk in an uproar. They were immediately greeted by Sheriff Kennedy and four officers assigned to help with the case: Norman Lewis, Rick Brown, Greg Meriam, and Nick Montgomery.

"The press is eating us alive." Sheriff Kennedy spoke with disgust. "And why the hell did Agent Nichols only mention Laura Stone as Deluca's victim? Now everybody thinks we screwed up, and the real River Strangler is at it again." Kennedy's face was flushed, and he rested his hands on his full hips, staring straight at Agent Rhodes for answers.

"Agent Nichols was stating facts only." Jemma eased toward the table in the center of the room and put down her briefcase. "And I suppose the press is going to continue to eat us alive until we find the people responsible for the deaths of Hazel Rice and our Jane Doe." She pulled out a chair and motioned to the men. "Let's take a seat, and I'll share what I learned this morning after reviewing all the facts from your River Strangler files."

Sheriff Kennedy watched her closely as she pulled out a large manila folder and notes from earlier. Finally, he took a seat across from her, and everyone in the room followed suit. Jemma nodded to Ashmore, and he walked over to the blank whiteboard. He had warned her on the car ride over that Kennedy would be mad as hell and have little patience. They had strategized a plan to best deal with the situation that would allow them to start work immediately instead of spending the first hour screaming insults and accusations.

"I was sent to Richmond this morning by FBI Director Miller to take a closer look at the River Strangler files and create a profile. With the help of Agent Nichols and Detective Ashmore, I've created that profile." Jemma watched as Ashmore began writing the profile for the deaths of Dawn Newberry, Daisy Gwen, and Cameron Long on the whiteboard. She explained that not only was the killer smart but patient. Next Ashmore wrote the name of Alec Deluca on another board and listed his personality traits that contributed to his profile. Jemma explained, "As you can see, Deluca has a well-established pattern of physical abuse. Laura Stone had been beaten beyond recognition. Completely out of sync with the River Strangler's trademark."

Sheriff Kennedy asked, "What about all the evidence found at Deluca's house? How can that be explained?"

Jemma picked up a paper. "Just as the defense stated in the trial, Deluca had taken numerous odd jobs over the last year since his release from prison. The ropes are consistent with construction work, and the boots would pick up soil from his various lawn-care jobs. One of the sites happened to be down by Mathews Park where Dawn Newberry's body was found. If we look closely, gentlemen, we can find enough probable doubt that Deluca didn't kill Newberry, Gwen, or Long." She set her notes down. "Just like the jury did."

A loud noise sounded as Sheriff Kennedy stood, his chair scraping against the tile floor. "I can't believe this is happening!" Everyone watched as he began to pace. "The killings stopped with Deluca's arrest and now—"

"They started again with Deluca's execution," Ashmore commented as he began to write the names of Hazel Rice and Jane Doe on a third board.

Kennedy turned to Jemma. "What kind of sick, twisted individual are we dealing with?"

Jemma looked back at the first board. "Someone highly intelligent and, like I said, patient." Jemma stood and walked toward the third board with Hazel Rice and Jane Doe listed at the top. Taking the marker, she wrote "wrist and ankles bound and tied, strangled." She paused, looked at the group, and added "rape."

"This key information does not leave this room. Understood?" They all nodded, and she continued. "Our person of interest has changed his game over the last five years. He now feels the need to degrade the women before death by showing not only his power but his male superiority as well." Jemma looked at Ashmore and nodded for him to speak while she added the extra bio information to his profile on the whiteboard.

Ashmore stepped forward. "Or another scenario, our killer left town."

Officer Greg Meriam asked, "Left town?"

Ashmore nodded. "And this is a separate killer all together."

"Jeesus!" said Kennedy.

Jemma nodded. "We need to look for other victims that match the River murders across the United States. Maybe he stayed active and looked for a new killing ground after Deluca was arrested. Or as I said, he's still here, never left, and added rape after his dormant spell."

"But do you really think a person can stop killing for five years?" asked Officer Norman Lewis.

"Very unlikely, but someone with discipline and self-control, it's possible, yes."

Officer Rick Brown joined in. "Or like you said, left town and now with all the hype in the media over the last several weeks with Deluca, we got a copycat who enjoys sexually abusing women."

Kennedy walked over to the boards and studied them with his arms crossed over his chest. "With the trial coverage, it would've been all in the paper how the women were bound and then strangled so he just added something new to make it his own." Kennedy turned back to Jemma. "Obviously, we got to work together. Whatever the FBI needs, you got my department's full corporation. Now tell me what we need to be looking for where we can stop this sicko before he kills again."

"Thank you. I'm so happy to hear you say that. We'll definitely accomplish more working together, that's for sure." Jemma closed her briefcase. "First, I'd like Detective Ashmore to accompany me to the medical examiner's office. I need to see Hazel Rice and Jane Doe, and then I'll need to visit the crime scenes." Jemma stood. "I'd like your officers to get a name to our Jane Doe ASAP so we can back track her movements over the last few days. Also, take a look at women who've been strangled and tied up across the United States in the last five years and compare it to our first victims on board one." Jemma looked at her watch; it was nearing two. "Let's plan to meet back around five and reassess."

Kennedy nodded. "Five it is. Lewis and Brown, start looking at other cases similar in the United States, and Meriam and Montgomery, get that girl's ID."

Ashmore walked over to Jemma. "Still open to the idea of a third killer?"

"No, not really. Just leaving nothing to chance."

"Why?"

"Because unlike what people see in the movies, serial killers are very rare."

Ashmore nodded, and together they walked out, leaving the sheriff behind with his team.

CHAPTER 7

Andrew tried his luck with Sheriff Kennedy again, and he was rewarded when Kennedy answered immediately in a tired, haggard voice. Andrew asked, "David, you ignoring my calls?"

Sheriff Kennedy, who had worked with Andrew Lane closely for seven years, immediately responded, "You're on the list to call. My phone hasn't stopped ringing since five a.m."

Sheriff Kennedy had been the one to arrest Alec Deluca, and Lane's office had presented the case to the jury that convicted Deluca and recommended the death penalty. Now, everything they accomplished five years ago was being scrutinized and questioned in the media for the whole state and country to review.

"Mine too. What's the latest?"

"The FBI director himself sent a profiler down from Quantico this morning. Special Agent Jemma Rhodes. She just left my office."

"The director? Geez, this is bad! She any good?"

"She sounded smart; got some big degree in psychology from Harvard. Anyway, she thinks Alec Deluca wasn't responsible for the River murders."

"What?" exclaimed Lane. "But the killings stopped. He had to have been the Strangler."

"Hey, I was there too, remember. Now all the files on the first three victims are being reviewed."

Andrew rubbed a hand over his face. His top prosecutor, Wilt Kingston, had handled the case against Alec Deluca beautifully. He couldn't have done a better job himself. Andrew again thought about his meeting with Joy Sutton two days ago when she had walked into his office, dropping her bombshell and hurling accusations. She had asked point-blank if Deluca was indeed innocent of the River killings. Andrew closed his eyes tight and pinched his nose, trying to concentrate. "What about Laura Stone? I saw the FBI press release. Nichols's still standing by Deluca as her killer."

Kennedy sighed. "Yes, for now. Agent Rhodes said Deluca's profile fit the beating of Laura Stone but not the other women." Andrew breathed a sigh of relief. "She talked about how their killer was smart and patient, with self-control—all things Deluca was not."

Andrew bit his lip, contemplating how much information to share with the sheriff. They'd known each other a long time; maybe he could help. No, he couldn't risk it. The decision had been made, and he had helped convince Joy Sutton not to push for Deluca's stay of execution and to remain silent. Andrew looked at his watch. He needed to meet Joy. They had to talk and fast. Would Joy stay loyal, or would she try to cover her own ass by going behind his back and talking to the media?

Breaking Andrew's thoughts, Kennedy asked, "What's Deluca's lawyer saying? What's her name again?"

"Joy Sutton." Then Andrew lied. "I called and she didn't answer."

Kennedy chuckled. "Probably giving an interview now about how incompetent our department is."

Andrew's gut tightened. "Maybe, maybe not. I left her a message, asking her to stop by. I'll keep you posted if she shows."

"Do that. Look, I got another call coming in. We'll talk later, Andrew."

"Thanks. Let's keep each other informed, OK?" Andrew ended his call and glanced at his watch again. It was time to meet Joy Sutton and face the music.

***

Only three blocks away from the Norfolk Police Department was the city morgue. The chief medical examiner, Marlee Hoyt, was sitting in her office and typing up reports when Ashmore and Rhodes arrived. Dr. Hoyt rose immediately, and introductions were quickly made. After working all through the night, she was tired and eager to get this meeting over so she could go home for some much-needed sleep.

"Sorry to keep you waiting, Dr. Hoyt." Ashmore spoke as they followed Hoyt down a long white corridor to a set of double doors.

Hoyt gave him a small smirk. "It's all right. I'm sure you didn't get much sleep last night either." Hoyt opened the doors, and instantly Aerosmith was heard jamming out of a large boom box.

Ashmore couldn't hide his smile. He leaned over and whispered in Jemma's ear, "She never got out of the eighties."

Hoyt, with her big hair and bright lipstick, turned around and said, "I heard that!" She winked at Ashmore, made a beeline over to the boom box, which had stacks of CDs by its side, and turned the music off.

Ashmore teased her, saying, "You should put an iPod on your Christmas list this year."

"Now why would I do that?"

"Less space. You could shuffle your music and never have to change another CD."

"Now you sound like my teenage son. I like my purple boom box just fine, thank you." Then she motioned them over to a steel table where the body of Jane Doe rested under a white sheet. She gave each of them a scented nose plug and a mask.

Jemma looked around. "Where's the body of Hazel Rice?"

"Released two o'clock yesterday afternoon."

This was news to Ashmore. "What? Why?"

Hoyt scowled. "At the time, we didn't have another victim. Her family is laying her to rest tomorrow." Hoyt saw Jemma's worried expression. "Don't worry." She waved her hand in the air. "I'm one of the best. I'm very efficient." She turned on a screen beside her. An image of a woman's neck appeared with "Hazel Rice DOB 12/17/88" at the bottom. Hoyt lowered the sheet to Jane Doe's chest, revealing the ligature mark on her neck. Hoyt made comparisons between the two victims. "I found silk fibers embedded in her neck. Same as Hazel Rice. See the wide and narrow lines?"

"A silk scarf." Jemma had seen strangulation marks like this before.

"Yes, I think our guy used the same scarf. I'm testing a tissue sample now for any traces of DNA from Hazel Rice."

Jemma took a step closer and listened as Hoyt read from her notes. The sheet was lowered again, revealing Jane Doe's arms and wrists. Hoyt pressed a button on the screen, and another image of Rice appeared, this one a close-up picture of her wrist.

"Synthetic fibers were found in the tissue here. The same as the ones on Hazel Rice's wrists and ankles."

"Damn it!" Ashmore could no longer hide his anger.

"He wants us to know. He wants to take full responsibility for both victims." Jemma looked at Ashmore. "Just days apart—he's gonna strike again and soon."

Lastly, the sheet was completely removed. Hoyt explained in a sad voice how the victim was tied up and repeatedly raped moments before her airway was constricted as the rapist pulled the silk scarf tighter, taking her life. "The bruising, tearing…it's consistent with Hazel Rice."

"Marlee, you've got to give us something! Semen, skin under their nails? Jesus, something!" Ashmore pulled the sheet back over the body of Jane Doe, leaving her blank face visible.

Hoyt pressed a button on the monitor, and the screen went blank. "Nothing under their nails, no semen or hair either. Most likely, he's shaved and wears a condom. But I did get the toxicology report back on Hazel Rice. She had chloroform in her system."

Jemma slowly closed her eyes. "They wouldn't have been able to fight." Jemma opened her eyes and stared at Jane Doe. She was so young and beautiful, a life that ended way too quickly. "I assume you put a rush on her toxicology report as well."

Hoyt nodded. "Hope to get it back tomorrow."

Jemma glanced away briefly, taking in the whitewashed walls of the lab. All so cold and sterile. A shiver ran down her back. She quickly shook it off. "OK. We need to shift gears here. You examined the bodies of our River Strangler, correct?"

"I did. Not a happy chapter of my life. Come on back to my office. I already pulled the files for comparisons."

Dr. Marlee Hoyt's office was more inviting than the lab. The walls were painted a warm yellow, and pictures of horses filled the walls among her many framed degrees and certificates of awards. They all took seats. "With the exception of Laura Stone, all three females had been tied up before strangulation, none beaten as Laura Stone. And then there is the obvious: none were raped like our newest victims."

"No." Hoyt opened up the file on Dawn Newberry. A picture appeared, one Jemma had already seen earlier that morning. The ligature mark on her neck was razor thin, nothing like the markings on Hazel Rice and Jane Doe. "Metal particles were found along her neck tissue. So some type of metal wire was used for strangulation. For her wrist and ankles," another photo was pulled out of the file, "tests showed a nylon rope was used. A stronger rope compared to the polyester rope used on Jane Doe and Hazel Rice."

"He drugged them. Any rope would have worked; he wasn't expecting them to fight back," Ashmore said.

The file was closed, and Daisy Gwen and Cameron Long's files were opened. "All consistent with Dawn Newberry. Our River Strangler used the same metal wire and the same nylon-type rope on all his victims."

Jemma looked at all the photos and the conclusive data. "And Laura Stone?"

Hoyt frowned as she put all the photos back in their respective files and reached for Laura Stone's file. "Just weird. She was beaten beyond recognition and strangled with gloved hands, but the true cause of death was head trauma." Hoyt passed over a photo of a bloody and beaten Laura Stone with a bad dye job that had been done too quickly.

"It was the same traces of dye found in Deluca's sink," Ashmore commented.

"The dye is the only thing that convicted Deluca." Jemma looked at Ashmore. "It's so odd. Why? To match his mother, or did someone frame him to look like the serial killer?" Jemma took one glance and passed the photo back. "Thank you for your time, Dr. Hoyt. You've been very informative." Jemma rose from her seat. "We'll let you get home for now."

"Certainly. I'm just a phone call away if someone wants to ID our Jane Doe."

Jemma nodded, and she and Ashmore left. Once inside the truck, Jemma stated, "Evidence points to three different killers, but I think someone's playing with us." She watched Ashmore settle in behind the wheel and start the engine.

"How so?"

"I don't know yet. Just a gut feeling." A brief silence followed, and then Jemma added, "Take me to where Jane Doe was found."

"OK. It's just a few blocks away, our city park."

CHAPTER 8

Darkness was everywhere. Joy Sutton blinked her eyes and felt movement beneath her. "What…what happened?" she mumbled in a state of delirium, her head aching. She reached out her right hand, but it was bound to her left. Determined, she reached forward with both hands and hit something hard. She looked around as her eyes adjusted. Light was filtering in through small cracks. Her body rolled to the left, and she hit something sharp. "Ouch! What the hell?" Red light illuminated the holes, and Joy was shocked to realize that she was in the trunk of a car. As if a bad horror flick were playing before her eyes, she finally came to terms with her dire predicament. She had been taken.

Joy closed her eyes and tried to concentrate, but the pounding in her head was making it difficult to remember anything. The memories of her last few days were running through her head in short clips, out of sequence: sitting across from Alec Deluca behind locked doors, smiling at Andrew Lane over a glass of chardonnay, watching Agent Nichols give a live press conference, and the last image, pouring the remaining wine from the bottle into her glass. *Am I drunk?* The question raced through her head. Then she remembered leaving her apartment and driving to meet Andrew. Cobwebs filled her head again. *What happened next?* No memory returned.

Sudden movement causing her to roll back to the right jarred her back into reality. Her hands were tied. *And so are my feet?* She screamed for her life, but the car continued on without braking. After five minutes, her vocal cords felt inflamed. Her hands were bruised from pounding on the metal above her. She closed her eyes and began taking long, deep breaths, trying to relax. Screaming and pounding were doing no good; the car continued moving. It was time to use her brain.

Two minutes passed, and Joy opened her eyes to adjust to the darkness. She rolled back over to the left and focused on finding the latch for the trunk. *Don't all cars now have a safety latch just for this situation?* She reached around and felt a small metal clip. She pressed and twisted, but nothing moved to release her. Then, just when she was about to give up, she touched a thin strip of fabric. She pulled it, and it easily broke. Twisting it in her hands, she realized with sickness that whoever had taken her had already cut the cord, and this was all that remained.

Nausea began to overwhelm her, and she rolled back over to the right just in time to retch. The smell of alcohol filled the contained space. Wiping her face, she flipped back onto her back. *Oh my God, I'm going to die. Someone has taken me and plans to do…* She cut off her train of thought and angrily turned back toward the left. She felt in the corner for the brake light. *Somewhere I read, no, it was a movie—a girl who had been captured broke the taillight and flung her arm out for anyone to see.*

Joy began to pound on the hard plastic as pain radiated up her arms, causing her to scream again. After another attempt, she realized her legs were stronger. Joy twisted at an odd angle, ignoring the wetness from her own vomit, and kicked with all her strength against the other corner. Her bare feet mashed against the metal around the brake light, causing more excruciating pain, but she pushed on. Finally, on the fifth try, the plastic gave way, and the top of her foot was sliced by the metal as it protruded into daylight. She turned her ankle and painfully pulled her foot back through, feeling the blood run down between her toes.

With more light to see by now, Joy wiggled and crawled until her face was pressed up against the opening. The light was bright at first, causing a lightning bolt to dart through her head. She blinked, trying to clear the fog. The outside world came into focus. She was on a two-lane dirt road surrounded by woods. Not a house or car in sight. Her heart sank. There was no need to scream. She had broken free too late.

CHAPTER 9

The parking lot for Mathews Park was blocked by a police barricade. Detective Ashmore parked his red truck beside the two cop cars and the crime-scene van. Officer Mark Wayne nodded to Ashmore as they got out of the truck.

"Officer Wayne, this is FBI Special Agent Rhodes."

"Nice to meet you, ma'am."

Jemma shook his extended hand and looked around. A lone blue Honda Accord was at the bottom of the hill under a large gray tarp that had been set up in the early morning to protect their evidence from the rain. Standing around the car were three techs and one officer, who were talking. She looked back into the young officer's face. "Thanks. Got a lot of visitors today?"

"Yes, ma'am. Most turn around there when they see me."

Jemma turned to where he was pointing. "What about the beach area?"

"We've got an officer on each side of the beach, turning people away."

"Everybody wants to come look," remarked Ashmore.

"Did anyone look out of place?" asked Jemma.

"Not really, mostly kids. Did have a man and his dog show up. He claimed he hadn't heard the news."

"Maybe, maybe not. Snap a photo of license plates as they come in. We'll run them later against our database." Jemma gave Officer Wayne her card. "E-mail me a description of the man and dog."

"Yes, ma'am. They just finished up. Got a tow truck coming to take the car down to the crime lab."

"Good. Maybe the storm last night didn't wash everything away," said Ashmore.

Jemma and Ashmore ducked under the yellow tape and made their way down the paved road to the parking lot below. All three men stopped talking as they approached. Introductions were quickly made as Jemma looked inside the opened trunk of the Honda Accord. "Find anything?"

"The purse that was missing. Kids claimed it was in the backseat. Found it under the victim in the trunk."

"He wanted them to open the trunk and find the body." Jemma looked at the beige purse that was sealed in a plastic bag. "What else?"

"Trash bags, french fries in between the seats, a sweatshirt, muddy cleats, and a few unidentifiable stains on the front and backseat. Looks like a normal teenager's car."

Jemma stepped around the car and looked into the backseat. Then she walked around and looked at the windshield. Rain had smeared the lipstick into an illegible mess before the car had a chance to be covered. She judged the distance from the parked car and main road.

Last, she turned and looked down toward the beach. "The kids claimed to be down by the beach, right?"

Ashmore walked her way. "Yes. I'll show you."

When they were away from the officers, Jemma spoke in a quiet voice. "I don't think our victim was raped here. I think the killer saw an opportunity to play his own tricks on Halloween. Nonetheless, we need to get DNA samples from all four teenagers."

"That's gonna fly over well." Ashmore smirked.

Jemma had a flashback to that morning, when she met Detective Arthur Lamb. "I'm sure."

Jemma counted her steps as they walked down the winding sidewalk that opened up to the sandy beach below. "Roughly fifty-five feet." Jemma stopped on the sand and looked back up the hill. "The kids stated they never heard a car?"

Ashmore shook his head. "No headlights, no car engines. It was windy; the rain came shortly after the body was discovered." Ashmore motioned to the right. "Jimmy Garner and Victoria Candle claimed to be about a hundred yards over there, making out."

"They said that?"

"Well, not exactly. And Jenny Lamb and Liam Wills were about twenty feet to the left. They were both 'talking.'"

"Oh I bet. What else is the poor girl gonna say with her cop daddy sitting on the other side of a wall listening."

Ashmore looked at the sand. "Rain washed away all footprints. We got nothing but their word."

"Take me to where Dawn Newberry was found?"

Ashmore motioned toward the right. "About where Jimmy and Victoria were standing."

Jemma stopped. "Creepy. These kids sure knew how to get a true Halloween buzz going."

"That's only half of it. The kids were part of a larger group that was hanging ketchup-sprayed mannequins around town last night."

"Mannequins? How can kids afford to buy mannequins?"

Ashmore frowned. "They didn't. Took them out of an old warehouse on Fifth Street."

"Stupid, that's breaking and entering and theft."

"Unfortunately not. Jimmy's dad owns the warehouse. Not pressing charges."

"Then the parent is just as stupid."

Ashmore smiled briefly. He stopped near the bank of the Elizabeth River and quickly lost his smile. He turned and studied the trees behind him. "She was dumped right along here."

Jemma walked past Ashmore and saw an officer ahead of them about thirty feet standing where the beach ends in a marshy steep bank. "How was she dumped again?"

"We think by boat. There had been no rain within the timeframe of her death. The only visible footprints were from the couple walking that found her."

Jemma scanned the river. Two boats were in sight.

Ashmore followed her eyes. "We have a rich fishing history. You can find a fishing boat along these waters day or night."

"Deluca didn't own a boat, did he?"

Ashmore shook his head. "No. But we found fishing poles in his garage. We checked all the charter companies, but there was no record of Deluca renting a boat."

"And the other women, were they all dumped by boat?"

"We think Daisy Gwen was. She was our second victim. Fisherman called it in around six a.m. They were heading out to sea."

"And where was this?"

"East of here, Lynnhaven River. Her body was found lying along the shores of Humes Island. It's a sandy island among the tributaries going out to sea. Judging from the condition of the body, she had never been dumped in the water. No fish bites."

"So someone drops her on the island, knowing she would soon be noticed by fishermen passing by."

Ashmore nodded. "Exactly. If he hadn't wanted her discovered, he would have made the effort to drop her off out at sea. No body, no evidence."

Jemma placed her hands on her hips and looked around the park again. "He wanted the police to make the connections between the two women. He wanted to be labeled a serial killer." Jemma began walking back toward the park. "And the third victim?"

Ashmore met her pace. "Cameron Long. She was found at a neighboring downtown park in Portsmouth, just three miles from the Portsmouth Police Department. Both departments had stepped up river patrol boats after finding the second vic, and so we think he used a car."

"But no trunk fibers were found on her body?"

"Nope. Just like the others, it looked like he submerged their bodies in the water and then dragged them back onto the beach."

Jemma stopped at the paved sidewalk. "Washing away any evidence. Well, we were lucky to get the rope fibers on their wrists and ankles." A tow truck was starting to pull away with the blue Honda Accord bouncing on the flatbed as it climbed the hill to the main road. Jemma glanced at her watch. "Take me to the Portsmouth downtown park. I want to see where the third victim was dropped."

***

Andrew Lane pulled up to the address given to him by Joy Sutton when she handed him the shiny new key to her apartment. He looked at the key in the console beside his gearshift. He cut the engine and looked at the number on the door. His eyes looked up to the third floor, suite 307. A man walked out the front door with a young boy in his arms. The door shut behind them as they walked down the sidewalk. A park was just ahead. Andrew grabbed the key and opened the door, pushing all lingering doubts out of his head. He had to search her apartment.

Another car rolled up, and Andrew stopped and sat back in his car, closing the door. He would wait; best if no one saw him. A man and a woman got out of the car, walked up to the entrance, and pressed a button on the silver box. They looked at each other as they waited. The woman pushed the button again, clearly agitated. Another moment passed. Then she opened up her purse and retrieved a key; they entered. The man turned around and looked right at Andrew's Mercedes-Benz E-Class. *Aw, shit, Burt Phelps.* Andrew looked down, hiding his face from Joy's boss. The man turned back around and followed the woman inside. Andrew slowly looked up just in time to see the door close behind him. "Damn it!" mumbled Andrew as he started his car, backed out, and drove away.

CHAPTER 10

Jemma was deep in thought and spoke very little on the ride over to City Park, the site where Cameron Long was found over five years ago. Long's file was open in her lap, and she was reading it again for the fourth time. Ashmore made a turn beside the cemetery. "The park is located by a cemetery?"

"Yep," confirmed Ashmore as they continued toward the park entrance. "It's a nice park, used a lot by families on the weekends."

Jemma looked at the time and day of discovery. One week after Daisy Gwen went missing. "Body was discovered on early Saturday morning by a jogger. Dr. Hoyt puts her time of death around midnight." Jemma looked up as Ashmore drove through the park, pointing out all the different parking lots.

Ashmore parked his truck at the most secluded spot in the park. "Her body was found straight ahead through those trees."

Jemma noticed how no one else was parked here at four in the afternoon. Visitors had chosen the other carparks. "Then he probably dumped her by car sometime around two or three in the morning." Jemma placed the file on the floorboard with the others and stepped out of the truck.

"There's a path that runs along the beach area that's used by runners."

Jemma counted off her steps to the pathway. Ashmore stopped at the railing, and they both looked on as two women pushing strollers approached. Jemma turned and looked in the opposite direction. "Does this path make a loop?"

"No." Ashmore pointed toward the women. "If you start at the front of the park, it is one and a half miles to the end." Ashmore turned and pointed to the left. "The end is just around the corner."

"So people using this park for the walking path wouldn't park here. They would choose the first parking lot, which is more open and bigger."

"Exactly, just as these women have done."

"Let's move. Not in the mood for twenty questions."

Ashmore began walking in the opposite direction of the women along the path. "This way." Near the end of the pathway, a set of stairs opened up toward the beach. "She was found down there." Together, they descended toward the rocky beach. Jemma continued counting in her head as Ashmore came to a stop. "Here."

"Sixty-five steps. She was five-foot-three and one hundred and fifteen pounds. A strong man could have done this easily by car. And if he used the pathway, and considering the rocks, no trail." Jemma looked across the river at the canal homes with boat docks. "Given the proximity to houses, I think using a boat a third time would be too risky."

"Yes, that's what we thought as well."

"No cameras at the park?"

Ashmore frowned. "Only at the pavilions and restroom areas, mainly to deter vandalism and graffiti. The city was strongly considering new equipment for all the parks in the area, but then Alec Deluca was caught. And as you know, the murders stopped."

"And there're no pavilions or restrooms at this end of the park. A local would know this."

"And Deluca was a local who owned fishing poles and ropes. Nylon ropes that matched the same ones used to tie up all three of our first victims." Ashmore shifted his feet with his hands on his hips. "We really thought he did it."

There was no need to state the obvious. Jemma noticed his pained expression. She spoke tenderly. "I know, Jason. And the killings stopped, just like you said."

Ashmore's brown eyes stared intently back at Jemma. "He played us for a fool, didn't he?"

Jemma stepped forward and placed a hand on Ashmore's arm. "But he won't this time."

* * *

Andrew Lane was reading over Alec Deluca's file when a knock on his door sounded. "Yes." His secretary opened the door.

"Sorry to interrupt, but I thought you would want to know as soon as possible what my contact is saying about Joy Sutton."

Andrew closed the file and dropped his pen. "No, no, come in." Jill closed the door behind her.

"Ms. Sutton isn't talking to the media. In fact, she isn't talking to anyone. No one has seen or heard from her since she left the correction center late last night."

"No one?"

She shook her head. "Oh, and there's more. Her boss, Mr. Phelps, called from the state public defender's office. He wants to discuss the Alec Deluca case."

Andrew rolled his eyes. "Well, we knew that was coming. I hope you bought me some time."

"Yes, sir, I told him you were very busy at the moment but would personally get back with him to arrange a time."

"OK good. Did he mention Ms. Sutton?"

"Yes, he asked if she had been by our office today."

Andrew sat back in his chair and crossed his arms.

"Don't you find her absence in light of today's news odd?"

Andrew sat up in his chair. "Yes, yes I do." Andrew got up, walked over to the window, and looked out at the traffic starting to back up on the freeways.

"Sir, do you think we should alert the police?"

Andrew quickly turned. "The police?"

"Well, my imagination might be getting away from me, but do you think she's in danger?"

Andrew shifted his feet. "Why do you think that?"

Jill walked over closer to Andrew. "I know she was here that day. I saw her get in her car when I arrived back from lunch. She hadn't signed in." She frowned. "We've been working long enough that I know when not to ask questions, but…"

Andrew walked away from her and took a seat behind his desk. Another minute passed as Andrew closed his eyes and tilted his head back in his chair. Finally, he looked back at Jill. "Then don't ask." Andrew abruptly stood, walked over to his private bathroom, and removed his navy-blue jacket from the hanger. "Look, I'm tired. It's been a long day. I'm sure Ms. Sutton will show up sooner or later, and when she does, I'm sure she'll do everything in her power to paint us in a very bad light to the media."

Jill's expression relaxed. "I'm sorry. I shouldn't have implied…"

Andrew walked over and touched Jill's arm. "No, don't apologize. If Ms. Sutton doesn't show up, other people will be looking for her and asking questions. I promise."

Jill nodded. "I'll see you then in the morning, sir?"

He turned with his hand on the doorknob. "Of course. Good-bye, Jill."

CHAPTER 11

The ride back to the station wasn't as quiet. Jemma outlined her thoughts with Ashmore. Mostly, Ashmore listened and only answered questions when asked. By the time they got back to the station at five thirty, everyone was seated in a larger conference room set up for the entire department. The boards from earlier had been brought in for all to see, but Jemma had erased the word "rape" under their newest victims. They had all agreed to keep that knowledge to themselves for now.

Agent Nichols had made the drive down from Richmond, and he was seated by Sheriff Kennedy. Also in attendance were the police chiefs of Newport News and Portsmouth. The mood was bleak; Jane Doe had not been identified yet. After Sheriff Kennedy updated everyone on their team's research efforts, Jemma took the floor.

"First, I'd like to say thank you for everyone's hard work. This is going to be a long road. No research is considered useless. Past cases have been broken wide open with just the smallest investigation that seemed meaningless at the time. Now with that said, I'd like to share with you my thoughts."

Jemma walked over to the board with the names of the first three women found along the riverbanks. "I believe Dawn Newberry, Daisy

Gwen, and Cameron Long were killed by one man. That man is still at large, aka the River Strangler." Sighs and mumbles went through the room, but no one interrupted. "The first two more than likely were dropped by boat and the third, Cameron Long, by a vehicle." Jemma walked over to the board with Laura Stone's name and picture. "At this stage of the investigation, Alec Deluca still appears very guilty for the murder of Laura Stone."

Kennedy could no longer remain quiet. "At this stage of the investigation? What are you saying? We found traces of the same hair dye used on Laura Stone in Deluca's sink."

"Yes. And it is a strong indicator of his guilt, especially when you look at his fixation on dark-headed women who resembled his mother. But why? What is the motive? Did Mrs. Stone go snooping around his home more than what she had told her husband? Did she confront Deluca, or did Deluca catch her spying on him and flipped out? Or was Laura Stone's death convenient for the husband who quickly remarries?"

"Now wait a damn minute here," spoke a man in the back row. All eyes were immediately on Officer Brent Quin. "I know Daniel Stone; he's a personal friend. He was very shaken up over his wife's death. He didn't fake that. He didn't do it, and I'd be careful insinuating he did considering he's one of Virginia's top defense attorneys." He huffed, crossed his arms, and added, "You want to get this department sued for slander?"

Jemma was a little taken aback by his interruption and brash comments, but she remained expressionless as she coldly replied, "A person's status in a community or state does not intimidate me, Officer—"

"Quin."

Jemma nodded. "May I finish?"

Quin looked at Sheriff Kennedy for direction. When it was obvious that Quin wasn't going to answer, Kennedy stepped in. "Please finish,

Agent Rhodes. I'd like to hear where you are going with this. But my officer is right. This department needs to be very careful about what is said about Daniel Stone." Kennedy looked back at his team. "Hold your comments to the end. Everyone will have a chance to speak."

"Noted." Jemma continued. "Or what if one of many of Mr. Stone's enemies killed his wife? For example, a relative of the child who was sexually assaulted by one of Mr. Stone's clients whose case was declared a mistrial a week before Laura Stone's death." She looked directly at Quin with raised eyebrows. "Look, either scenario stated, it ended in murder. Unfortunately, there're questions I won't be able to ask Deluca, nor will anyone else, but I think for the sake of Laura Stone, her death needs another look."

Jemma walked over to the third board with pictures of the latest two victims. "These two women were tied up with a polyester rope and strangled with a scarf, not a metal wire, all of which is different than the River Strangler. Also, traces of chloroform were found in their systems, which explains why they never fought back. This should all point to a third killer, but I don't think we have a third killer, and here's why."

Jemma walked over to the first board and pointed to the profile she'd given earlier that day to the appointed team members. She continued. "He's patient and smart; that's why he was never caught. But he's cocky. With the first three murders, he wanted us to make the connection with the victims by using the same rope and strangulation device and dumping the bodies along the river. He wanted to take credit. He wanted to be known as the River Strangler. Then you had the arrest and conviction of Deluca. His patience and intelligence took over; he stopped. But serial killers rarely ever can stop."

"In fact, there's a good chance he left town, started somewhere new. But he's smart enough to hide the bodies. Why come back?" Jemma looked around the room before answering her own question. "Alec Deluca. With all this public attention given to Deluca's death, he's decided to start up again. He can't take someone else taking credit for his work. And this will be his downfall. His obsession is taking over. He will no longer be this patient man, and he will make mistakes. Unfortunately, given the timeframe of three days between Hazel Rice and Jane Doe, we will see another victim very soon."

Groans were heard among the crowd.

"Even though I anticipate him making mistakes, we can't underestimate his intelligence. Hazel Rice wasn't dumped in Norfolk but instead close to Newport News. He's playing with us. Then he waits until Deluca is executed before dropping Jane Doe at the same park where he left his first victim, Dawn Newberry. He did this to mock us. He's enjoying this very much."

The next hour was filled with an intense question-and-answer session. Agent Nichols spoke and explained how they had the full resources of the FBI, and he would remain in Norfolk along with Jemma until the killer was found. Lastly, Kennedy outlined a schedule for extra patrols around the parks and waterways. Finally, the meeting ended at seven o'clock.

Ashmore came over and stood by Jemma as she packed up her briefcase. "Do you ever eat?"

Jemma glanced at her watch. "Oh, yeah, now that you mention it, I'm starved. Thanks." She gave a warm smile. "Is this really the same day I left my home in DC?"

"I'm afraid so. You never ate any of the pizza in the conference room."

Jemma zipped up her briefcase. "You keeping tabs on me?" She smiled. "Lost my appetite."

"Yeah. Where you staying tonight?"

"Agent Nichols booked us rooms at Rivermont Hotel, just a few blocks away."

Ashmore nodded. "They got a restaurant too."

Jemma picked up her briefcase. "And room service, I hope. Thanks for today, and I'll see you tomorrow, detective."

Ashmore stepped to the side and allowed her to pass. Then Jemma turned around. "Call me anytime if we get a break."

"Count on it."

Jemma walked over to Agent Nichols, and they said their good-nights to Sheriff Kennedy and then left together.

Ashmore was the last to leave after rolling the three whiteboards into the conference room that they had earlier set up on the third floor. The pictures of Hazel Rice and Jane Doe haunted him on the ten-minute drive home. Was Agent Rhodes right? Was their killer the same as the man who killed their first three victims? What if she was wrong, and they had a third killer? Ashmore pulled into his driveway and briefly waited for his garage door to open. He pulled through and cut the engine. Everything was quiet. Rita instantly filled his thoughts along with his daughter. They had pulled into this same garage numerous times with Tracie asleep in her car seat, head to the side, eyes closed with mouth opened. He pushed the image out of his mind and resisted the urge to turn and look in the backseat of the cab. Finally, he stepped out of the truck, closing the overhead garage door.

The hum of the refrigerator was the only sound the house made as he opened the door. Not even a dog to greet him. *Maybe it is time to change that,* he thought as he remembered the city was having a large pet adoption this weekend. Nah, the pup would starve to death in the next few weeks with this current case.

Jason pulled a beer from the refrigerator and took a seat at the kitchen table. He phoned his ex, Rita.

She answered on the fifth ring, just as her answering machine picked up. "Hello, oh, wait, there we go. Hi, Jason."

"Hey, you busy?"

"Not really, just warming up leftovers." A moment of silence followed. "I had a feeling you would call. I heard the news."

Jason thought back to the day that Dawn Newberry's body was found. He and his wife were hosting family and friends for Tracie's one-year-old birthday party. He had left just as the cake was cut. For the following four months during the River Strangler investigation and trial, he had rarely seen his wife or Tracie. "Yeah, I can't say much, but it's not good, Rita, not good at all. FBI is back in town. These next few weeks are going to be crazy."

"It scares me, Jason. I hope you catch whoever is doing this soon. It's like a recurring nightmare for everyone in this town."

"I know."

"Well, the city is lucky to have you. You're good, Jason, don't ever forget just how good you really are. If anyone can stop this, it's you."

Jason's eyes were moist as he took another swig from his beer. After everything they'd been through, Rita was still his biggest cheerleader. "I appreciate that, Rita. More than you know." Another moment of silence passed by, and then he heard the chime of a microwave. "I guess that's your food. I'll let you go. I…I just wanted to hear your voice, that's all."

"Anytime, Jason. Call anytime, you know that. Good-bye."

"Good-night, Rita." Jason's eyes drifted toward the framed photo above his mantle: the three of them sitting on a sand dune with a beautiful sunset behind them. Tracie's olive skin matched his while Rita's ivory skin had a touch of pink. The picture had captured a perfect memory on a special day. Jason tore his eyes away and looked at his beer. He twisted it in his hands and then began to peel at the label. Time seemed to roll past in the form of short clips with Rita and Tracie as the stars, with their smiling eyes and contagious laughter. Finally, Jason drained the remainder of his beer and went to bed. He'd been up almost thirty-eight hours, and making the effort to heat something up to eat seemed too difficult of a task. Ten minutes later, Jason was asleep alone in his queen-size bed with no more thoughts of Rita, Tracie, or the River Strangler.

CHAPTER 12

A noise woke Jemma from a deep sleep. A few seconds passed as she tried to determine the source. Her cell phone. She looked around her dark hotel room and reached out for the light switch. Noticing the time, she climbed out of bed and walked over to the dresser where she had plugged in her phone. As tired as Jemma was last night, she felt it best to force herself to get up when the alarm sounded. However, it wasn't her alarm going off. She was getting a call.

Jemma picked up her phone. Unknown caller. "Hello."

Silence.

Jemma glanced at her screen. The seconds were ticking. The call hadn't been dropped. Jemma repeated, "Hello."

"Agent Rhodes, did I wake you?"

"Who is this?"

"Just a concerned friend. Is the Rivermont comfortable and treating you well?"

Instinct took over, and Jemma grabbed her gun off the nightstand and walked around the room, checking the bathroom. Suddenly, she realized anyone watching the hotel would notice a light come on at 3:00 a.m. Immediately, Jemma turned off the light.

Laughter rung out on the other end. "FBI has sent a smart one. Well, we'll see now won't we? Good-bye, Agent Rhodes, sleep tight."

Jemma stubbed her toe on a chair as she ran toward the window. Carefully, she pulled the curtain back and scanned the street below. She saw no one. Looking down, her phone revealed the call had ended. "Son of a bitch. Where are you?" Jemma stayed at the window, analyzing every shadow. Nothing. A car passed on the street below—a dark car. Then she saw movement in the parking lot below. A man on foot was weaving in and out of cars, crouching low. She watched as he slipped behind a concrete wall and disappeared. "Damn it!"

Jemma scrolled through numbers on her phone and pressed the "call" button for the Norfolk Police Department.

"Norfolk Police Department, this is Officer Wayne speaking."

"It's Agent Jemma Rhodes. I need patrol around the Rivermont Hotel ASAP. Our psychopath just called me. I saw him slip out of the parking lot on foot, going north on Riverway."

"Yes, ma'am." A moment passed and Officer Wayne spoke. "Got a patrol less than three miles away."

"Good, I'm heading down to get the security tape."

Jemma pressed a button on the hotel phone. "Rivermont Hotel, how may I help you?"

"Agent Jemma Rhodes, room five oh eight. I need a copy of your parking lot security tapes ASAP."

"Um, yes, ma'am, um, hold on, let me get my manager."

"No need, I'm coming down." Then Jemma picked up her cell phone and pressed Agent Nichols's number.

"Agent Nichols," he said in a groggy voice.

"It's Jemma. He called me. He was outside the hotel."

"What? Here?"

"Yes, already got patrol coming. I called downstairs to get the security tape of the parking lot. I caught a glimpse of him; he was moving in between the cars in the parking lot."

"Give me two minutes, Jemma. I'll meet you in the hallway."

Jemma pulled on a pair of jeans from her bag and threw on a jacket over her tank top and sidearm. Taking her badge and cell phone, she walked toward her room door and looked out the peephole. When she saw Agent Nichols's door open, she slowly opened her door. Together they carefully checked the hallway and nearest staircase.

"Let's split up. You take these stairs, and I'll take the other set on the other end."

Jemma nodded and slowly worked her way down the five flights of stairs, seeing no one. Jemma checked the hotel lobby, finding it empty except for two men standing behind the front desk. Jemma held up her badge and lowered her gun. Agent Nichols met her from the opposite side. She announced, "Gentleman, I'm Agent Rhodes, and this is Agent Nichols."

The older man spoke. "Chuck Walters, hotel manager."

"We got a patrol coming. We're locking down the hotel. No one leaves and no one enters until we give word, understand?" Jemma asked.

"Yes. Um, Pete, said you needed our security tapes?"

"Yes. I saw a man in the parking lot five minutes ago. I need that tape."

"Of course, I'll go to the security room now and make a copy. Pete, follow their instructions. I'll be right back."

Jemma saw a blue light flashing and turned her attention to the front entrance. A patrol car pulled up under the awning without its siren. They made their way to the front door, and immediately Jemma recognized the officer who had interrupted her at the meeting. "Officer Quin, see anything?"

"No, ma'am. We got two more patrols circling a five-block radius now."

"Cut the light; we'll have more chaos if guests start waking up."

The officer reached in his patrol car and flipped a switch, obeying Jemma.

The next ten minutes felt like thirty for Jemma as she waited patiently for any of the officers on patrol to call in. After another ten minutes, Jemma lost all hope that a man on foot wearing dark clothing would be picked up by Norfolk PD. Jemma and Agent Nichols walked back into the lobby and met with the hotel manager again.

"I'm sorry, ma'am, but the screen is black."

Jemma couldn't hide her disappointment. "Black? You got nothing?"

Walters shook his head. "I'll show you now if you'd like."

"Show us," Agent Nichols said.

Pete was left at the front desk with Officer Quin as both agents followed Walters down a hall to the security room located opposite from the main office. A large screen showing eight windows was sitting on the desk. One of the frames was totally black while the others showed empty hallways, elevators, a fitness center, and indoor pool. "That's our view of the parking lot. Something is wrong with the camera."

Nichols asked him to rewind the tape until the parking lot came back into view. It took thirty-five minutes of playing time. Jemma looked at her phone; thirty-one minutes had passed since receiving the call. She looked at Agent Nichols. "Nothing. He must have come up from the side of the building here." Jemma looked at all eight frames. "No other cameras that would show a different view?"

Walters shook his head. "No."

"And I can assume that no information was given out over the phone about whether or not two FBI agents were staying here, correct?" asked Jemma.

"I already asked Pete. No one called inquiring about you or Agent Nichols."

"So he followed us." Jemma looked at her watch again and did the math in her head. "Can we get a recording of all the frames for the last nine hours?"

"Of course."

"Great." Jemma looked at Nichols. "Let's take a look at the camera outside and see if we can figure out what's wrong with it."

The camera was positioned by a doorway just out of arm's reach. Officer Quin shined his flashlight over the camera. "Looks like black paint." The flashlight scanned the beige stucco wall around the camera, revealing an overspray. "Probably just a can of spray paint."

Agent Nichols stepped back and studied the parking lot. "How did he know your room faced the parking lot and not the river like mine?"

A cold chill ran through Jemma, and she tugged her jacket over her thin tank top. "And how did he get my cell number?"

An awkward silence passed before Quin spoke. "I don't know about y'all, but I don't keep spray paint at my house. We'll contact all the stores in the area and see if a can was sold tonight."

"Good. If he isn't local, I don't see him driving all the way back home to retrieve a can. But he could have. We can't underestimate his intelligence; after all, he managed to get my number and follow us here undetected," said Jemma.

Nichols added, "Go ahead and check all stores within a two-hour radius. Maybe we'll get lucky."

Jemma checked her watch and then tried the side door. Locked. Nichols pulled out his room key. Jemma turned to Quin. "He's long gone. We'll be at the station by seven at the latest, but call us if we get a break."

"Will do." Officer Quin walked back toward his patrol car, and Jemma and Nichols entered the building and walked down the hall that led to the main entrance.

Two officers were standing guard at the front. "I don't think we need them anymore."

Agent Nichols nodded and walked over to relieve the men as Jemma requested another key for her room since she had forgotten hers on the bedside table. "Thanks, we appreciate all your help. I'll be back around six for the tapes."

Pete looked toward the front door as the cops left. "We all good now?"

Jemma gave him a reassuring smile. "Yes, excitement's over."

Nichols joined Jemma, and together they rode the elevator back up to the fifth floor. When everyone had left, Pete looked around and then pulled out his cell phone and made a call.

CHAPTER 13

The sun began to peek through the houses built on stilts as a car bumped along slowly over an unpaved road. Soon the road ended at his home of twenty-two years. The engine was cut, and the car door opened and closed.

Joy Sutton heard the engine of the car, and her eyes popped wide open. The room she was held in was semi lit by the morning light seeping through drapes that hung over a large window across from the bed. Whoever had taken her was back. She struggled against the ropes that were holding her wrists and ankles to an old wrought iron bed. Each movement caused excruciating pain from her bruised and cut foot. Soreness radiated down her arms and shoulders, and she stilled. Tears fell from her eyes; she was helpless.

The sound of a door closing caused Joy's body to jolt in fright. She squeezed her eyes shut as the sound of footsteps grew louder along the hardwood floors. When the sounds stopped, she forced her eyes open and peered at the doorway. She blinked in surprise at who had taken her. *What? Why?* Then, clarity filled her mind. She knew the truth about Alec Deluca and Laura Stone. Alec Deluca was dead and so was Laura Stone. She screamed, but her screams were muffled by the tape that bound her lips shut.

She watched as her clothing and her papers from her briefcase that were scattered on the floor were gathered up. Quickly, they were tossed in a buck stove in the corner of the room. A match was struck, and the papers flamed. Joy's eyes filled with tears at the knowledge that all the evidence of her meetings with Alec Deluca was burning right before her eyes. Lastly, her briefcase, which her father had given her, along with her shoes were tossed inside. The metal door was closed shut, and the lever was turned. She looked away and faced the wall as her body shook uncontrollably, knowing her fate was sealed. She knew the truth about Laura Stone, and that truth would soon die with her.

***

Jason Ashmore and Sheriff Kennedy were seated together at the table in the conference room when Jemma and Nichols arrived at six thirty. "Good morning," Jemma spoke first.

"Is it? I don't think either of you got a good night's sleep," remarked Ashmore as he stood to shake their hands.

Jemma gave a small laugh. "Could have been better, that's for sure."

"You made the morning news," Kennedy said.

"What? How?" Nichols asked.

Ashmore shook his head. "Someone from the hotel must have reported it."

Jemma looked at Nichols. "We saw very few people. You don't think it was him tipping off the media, do you?"

"I don't know, but we need to find out."

"It was Channel Two news. I'll make a call later." Sheriff Kennedy pulled out a sheet of paper. "We keep this handy whenever we get a spree of graffiti artists that pop up over town."

Jemma saw the list of stores in the area that carry spray paint. "Any hits?"

"Still in the works; most stores are still closed. It takes time, but we should have something later today."

"Good. Anything else, maybe a dog walker at three thirty saw a man wearing all black running down the street?"

Ashmore smiled. "No."

Nichols took a seat and opened his briefcase. "Quantico put together a list of unsolved murders over the last five years. I'm going to start with the ones closer to Virginia and work outward across the United States."

Jemma looked at Ashmore. "I thought we would head to Newport News. I want to see where Hazel Rice was found and then observe the funeral at eleven."

"Sure, I just wish someone would come forward with our Jane Doe. Doesn't make sense with all the media hype that someone with her description would go unnoticed."

"Yeah, it surprises me too. Makes me think she wasn't local." Nichols turned on his computer. "Which would make looking at other cases near here important. Maybe our killer did move away and made the trip down here with her body.

Sheriff Kennedy stood and walked over to the map hanging on the wall. "Wish we could spare more patrol along the main highways coming and going into the city. But we can arrange for some early morning roadblocks along some of the smaller roads around the river." Kennedy pointed to two roads on the map. "Highway Four Sixty and Three Thirty-seven. We could check all vehicles between the hours of two to four. That shouldn't put too much burden on traffic at that hour."

"No, it shouldn't, and we could probably expand to Highway Fifty-eight into Portsmouth, but something tells me he won't be using Mathews Park again."

A tap was heard on the door, and they all turned. "Sorry to interrupt, Sheriff, but I thought you would want to know right away."

Kennedy motioned him over. "Not a problem, Officer Ryan." Everyone watched as Ryan entered and handed a sheet of paper over to Sheriff Kennedy.

"Richmond PD just sent a wire that Joy Sutton has been reported missing by Burt Phelps."

"Aw, jeez, just what we need." Kennedy looked at the agents. "Sutton was Alec Deluca's attorney for the last several months, and Phelps is her boss, Virginia's state public defender."

"The report states no one has seen or heard from Sutton since Deluca's execution. Phelps said she hadn't shown at work the next day or called."

"And he didn't say anything yesterday?"

"No, sir. He did check her apartment though."

Kennedy raised his eyebrows.

"He had a key. When he couldn't reach her by phone all day and she hadn't returned his calls, he and his associate let themselves in. Found her red convertible missing along with her keys and purse. Phelps said it was her first execution to witness. He just assumed she needed some space. But this morning when he woke up, well, you know, he felt differently and filed the report. A BOLO has already been issued for her 2014 red Chrysler Two Hundred convertible."

Kennedy shook his head as he scanned the report. "Thank you, Officer Ryan. Keep us posted if she turns up."

Jemma stood up and walked over to the board that listed the profile of the River Strangler.

"You don't think he did it?" asked Sheriff Kennedy.

Jemma turned after a few moments. "It's too much of a coincidence for my liking. If she hasn't shown up by the end of the day, we need to be looking at why he would want Deluca's lawyer."

Ashmore stood and walked over to the board that held Deluca's name. He picked up a marker and added "Joy Sutton missing midnight 10/31."

"God, I hope this isn't related," Kennedy shouted as he tossed his pen on the table. Jemma and Ashmore returned to the table. "We got two dead women, one still a Jane Doe, a district rivalry tonight in town, and now this, a missing lawyer. This is a PR nightmare."

"Football?" asked Jemma.

Ashmore nodded. "Yep, two of Norfolk's teams are undefeated. Tonight's game will decide who moves on to state playoffs."

"Every year, this is the biggest game of the season. Extra patrol is needed around the stadium as well as the pep rally leading up to the game. Men we don't have to spare right now." Kennedy picked his pen back up and started making some notes.

Nichols looked at Jemma. "After last night's visit and everything we've learned over the last twenty-four hours, I think we need to bring in more manpower."

Jemma agreed. Over the next hour, theories were explored, maps were studied, and a call was placed to the Richmond FBI office. They were sending three agents down to Norfolk to assist. All were expected to arrive by two. Kennedy was grateful for the help and left to make a new patrol schedule for the evening and night shifts. With Ashmore taking a call, Jemma and Nichols remained at the table.

"What are you thinking Jemma? Did he take the lawyer?"

She shook her head. "Honestly, Simon, I don't know. His victims have been random. Taking the lawyer makes this a personal connection. It doesn't fit that he would."

"Yeah, that's what I was thinking. So who took her?"

Jemma added, "And what did she know about Alec Deluca that no one else knew?"

"We need to separate the cases?" asked Nichols.

"I think so. When the team arrives, put two of the agents on the missing lawyer. She needs to be found sooner than later."

"Agreed. If she's not found by tomorrow, then we have to reopen the Deluca case against Laura Stone. We've no choice."

Jemma smirked. "The sheriff's gonna flip. He thinks it's a PR nightmare now; wait till the media gets a hold of this."

"Gets a hold of what?"

Jemma turned and saw Ashmore walking in with a folder. "Just talking about the lawyer missing. You ready to head to Newport News?"

Ashmore looked from Jemma to Nichols, studying them briefly. "It's important I stay in the loop."

Jemma stood and packed up her briefcase. "And I plan to." Her emerald eyes found Ashmore. "We're going to put two agents on finding Joy Sutton."

"I couldn't agree more." Ashmore stopped at the table. "And yes, Kennedy will flip." Ashmore gave her a warm smile. "Come on, let's hit the road to Newport News. Gonna be a long day."

***

At 7:40 a.m., Julie waved good-bye to her seven-year-old daughter who was sitting on the front seat of the Norfolk County Public School bus. Her daughter was all smiles, and she was chatting with her best friend as the bus pulled away toward school. Julie turned around and began the quarter mile back to their home. Today, no other moms had joined her. Meredith had parked along the highway and had continued on to the grocery store. Mimi Foster had a doctor's appointment at eight, and she had dropped her daughter off at school on the way.

Julie tucked her hands in her pockets as she walked the narrow, paved road that led to four homes, each sitting on about five to ten acres. Her home was the nearest, just around the wooded curve on the no-outlet street. The wind picked up and swirled the multicolored leaves dotting the ground before her. She looked at the partially bare trees lining their road. Winter would be here soon, bringing her favorite season of the year to an end.

Rounding the corner, the bright morning sun came in full sight, causing her to blink. Her beautiful two-story farmhouse built in the 1940s sat on seven acres. Behind the home was a red barn that housed their two ponies and hay. It had taken the first two years of their marriage to restore the home, room by room. Julie looked down the street once before turning into her driveway. Meredith's house was partially hidden among a wooded lot separating their land. All was quiet, as it should be. All the men in the neighborhood along with Heather Till, the only working female, had all left for work. Julie began humming as she walked along her pebble driveway.

Skipping the front door, Julie walked past her home and straight to the barn. This morning, her adorable daughter Melinda was not so adorable. She had thrown a fit, claiming her pants were too uncomfortable to wear to school. The unpleasant scene had left no time for Melinda to feed her ponies, which caused another meltdown. Somehow, thankfully, Melinda had wiped away the tears and snot by the time they had reached the end of the street to meet the bus. Julie opened the barn door with the sweet memory of Melinda smiling back at her as she seated herself beside her best friend, James.

Both ponies looked her way as she made her presence known. "Sorry, my darlings, for the delay. It's all Melinda's fault, and you have no idea what kind of morning I've had!" LouLou neighed as she rocked her head backward. Julie picked up some hay from across the ponies' stall and tossed it over. Strawberry, the younger pony, stepped back for a brief moment and then moved forward and took the hay. "Good girls. I shall return later—"

Julie heard a noise from behind and spun around. The hay bales were stacked nice and neatly. A frown furrowed her brow as she looked toward the barn door: closed, as it should be. Julie turned back around to the ponies. "OK, well, you girls have a great day, and I'll return after lunch for our walk." Julie reached out and gave each a gentle pat.

"Me-ow!"

Julie's heart leapt into her throat as she spun around again. "Marvin! How did you get out of the house?" Julie walked over, knelt, and picked him up while her mind replayed her morning exit with Melinda. Marvin had been under the couch with only his tail sticking out. Marvin always ran and hid whenever Melinda decided to throw a hissy fit. Julie opened the barn door with Marvin in her arms and headed toward the house. The door on the back porch was closed and still locked from last night, right? Julie stepped up onto the porch and tried the door. Yes, locked. Marvin began to fidget in her hands as Julie continued around the wrap-around porch to the front door. "Ouch, Marvin, what has gotten into you?" She dropped Marvin and watched as he ran and jumped off the porch between the railings.

"Fine. You're having a bad morning too, huh?" Continuing on, Julie noticed the front door was cracked open behind her screen door. She scanned the front yard and street. No one in sight. She turned the silver lever, pulled open the screen door, and pushed the front door open. She dug into her pocket and retrieved her phone. She tapped a name on the screen and a ringing noise was heard just before a familiar voice answered.

"Hey, babe."

Julie knelt down and placed the iron doorstopper up against her front door, letting the cool morning breeze fill the house. "Hey, sorry to bother you at work, but did you come back home while I was in the barn?"

A moment went by and her husband Ken finally answered. "No. Why, something wrong?"

Julie sighed and began walking through the ground floor of their home. "No, I guess not. Marvin got out and I found the front door cracked. It's just been one of those mornings. Melinda decided—"

"Julie, get your keys and get out of the house."

Julie stopped at the sound of his frantic voice. "What?"

"Do as I say, damn it. Get your keys and get out of the house now. I'm on my way."

Her purse was sitting on the kitchen counter beside the house phone. Her keys were inside. She looked behind her, and relief washed over her when she saw no one. She was all alone. Taking a deep breath, she stepped forward and grabbed her purse. Turning back around, she could hear her husband in a hysterical voice reminding her that there had been two women murdered. Julie began to run through the house and urgently pushed the screen door open. She fled down the stairs, leaving the front door wide open. When she got to the middle of the yard, she turned and looked back at her home. No one was chasing her. "Ken, I'm outside in the yard." She spun completely around. "I see no one."

"Get in the car and drive to that gas station just up the road, now!"

"OK, OK, I am." Julie ran around the house and found her Ford hatchback sitting in the driveway. Looking once more behind her, she checked the trunk and the backseat, and then she opened the driver side door and climbed in. She felt the hairs rise on her neck, as if someone was watching her. She hit the lock button before starting the engine. "I'm in the car; I'm leaving now," Julie said as she reversed and then pulled ahead down her driveway.

"Good, I'll be there in ten minutes. Don't hang up; stay on the line."

"OK, I'm hooking up the Bluetooth." Julie placed her phone in the cup holder. At the end of the drive, Julie looked into her rearview mirror. Again, no one was there chasing her. She took a deep breath, looked both ways, and then pulled out onto their street.

CHAPTER 14

Internal rage consumed him. For three days, he had been learning Julie's morning schedule. Why had this morning been so different? Why had she fed the ponies after taking her daughter to the bus? And that damn cat. Why hadn't he seen it earlier? Now with the husband returning home and suspicion raised, he had to walk away from Julie Meek, his mark for his newest victim.

He checked the bedroom a fifth time. All was set to perfection. He closed the bedroom door, walked into the living room, and began to pace the floor of his two-bedroom apartment. It had to be tonight. He had a plan. Finally, he stopped walking in circles and picked up his car keys. "I'll just have to find another," he mumbled to his empty apartment.

***

At 9:00 a.m., Detective Ashmore parked his truck along a two-lane highway that bordered Lake Maury, just south of the city of Newport News. Agent Rhodes pulled out the file on Hazel Rice, the young woman found strangled and raped on Oct 29, just two days before Alec Deluca's execution. Together they weaved in and out of trees for about thirty feet until they reached the lake's edge. Jemma looked up and down the shore of Lake Maury; they were alone.

Jemma held the photo of Hazel Rice's body lying on the sandy bank where a fisherman had found her. She looked back up the small hill to Ashmore's truck. Only one car had passed by in the last five minutes. "Anyone could have pulled off the road as we've done, walked a few steps, and dropped her body unnoticed."

"Rice was found around seven thirty a.m." Ashmore pointed north up the river. "There's a boat launch about a quarter of a mile away; that's where the fisherman had put his boat in around seven o'clock. He was trolling down the lake when he found her. The sun was just starting to rise when he noticed something along the bank, and he flashed his light. He said it about gave him a heart attack when he realized it was a body. Fumbled with his phone and dropped it in the water. Thankfully though, he had it in a plastic bag."

"He must have been hugging the shoreline as he trolled."

"Probably; good fishing here along the banks. Sadly, he'll probably never be able to fish here again."

Jemma looked at the notes from the medical examiner. "Dr. Hoyt states the body wasn't exposed to the elements long after her death." Jemma lowered the file and looked around, shaking her head. "I think he did just as we did: parked along the highway sometime around two or three in the morning and dumped her. No way would he risk launching a boat in the dark. Other fishermen would see his lights."

"Forensic found a set of impressions but nothing concrete. Too many leaves."

"It was him. And he wasn't worried about leaving the prints. Probably even wore boots a couple of sizes bigger than his own feet."

Ashmore sighed. "Huh, I've never thought about someone thinking to do that."

Jemma smiled. "Never came across a perp who has, but I learned a long time ago that there's always a first for everything. And he's a smart one." Jemma's phone began to vibrate just as Ashmore's began to ring. "We just might get a break after all." Jemma pulled out her phone and walked in the opposite direction of Jason, who was also answering his phone.

"Agent Rhodes."

Nichols spoke. "Rhodes, we got a boyfriend coming down to the morgue to view our Jane Doe. Thinks it's his girlfriend, a student at William and Mary."

A wave of heat consumed Jemma. "Poor kid. What're the chances?"

"Better than good. She failed to show up at work. He's been out of the country for a wedding. Just got back last night and found the message on her machine this morning that she'd missed work. It all checks out. He'd wondered why she hadn't messaged him and had no clue what was going on in the media since he was in Europe."

"Wow, OK, keep me posted. Ashmore and I are about to go to Hazel Rice's funeral. I'll touch base afterward."

"Sounds good. And Jemma..."

"Yeah?"

"Be careful."

Jemma turned back around and faced Ashmore, who was walking toward her. "I will, thanks." Ending her call she asked, "About the Jane Doe?"

Ashmore looked surprised. "No, the spray paint. Did we get an ID?"

"More than likely. We won't know for sure until later. What about the spray paint?"

"A can of black spray paint was sold at a Dollar General store on Virginia Beach. Getting the security tape now."

"Virginia Beach?"

"Yeah, I know what you're thinking: probably just a kid out for some graffiti fun."

Jemma narrowed her eyes. "No, I was thinking far enough away but not too far. Could be him."

"So you like to think positive. I like that."

She laughed. "I've never had anyone accuse me of being positive. Well, at least not in this field anyway. Come on." Jemma began walking up the hill, careful not to get her boots dirty. "We don't need to be late for the funeral. I want to blend in."

***

He drove around downtown Norfolk, taking in the sights. Football flags lined the poles in anticipation of tonight's big game. Both schools were represented—a town set on showing no favoritism, only promoting school spirit and comradery among the citizens. A light up ahead turned yellow, and he slowed to a stop, right in front of the Norfolk Police Department. His eyes crinkled behind his dark shades as he smiled at the sight of three news vans parked across the street, all waiting to hear more news about the whereabouts of Joy Sutton. What must the town be thinking? A frown suddenly appeared on his face as he remembered Julie Meek's husband rushing home.

A horn sounded.

The light had turned green. He chastised himself for not paying attention. He noticed two women standing in front of their news vans look his way. He accelerated.

On Highway 460 north, he blended in with traffic. He tapped the steering wheel as he debated where to go. He crossed the river and passed the medical center, and then he was in an oasis of neighborhoods. He chose a random street and signaled. He drove slowly but not too slowly. A house he passed on the right had an open garage with a nice SUV parked inside. He kept driving. He couldn't just pull into a driveway, take a woman, and leave unnoticed. He began to breathe harder, growing impatient as his mind and desire played tug-of-war. Finally, his mind took over, and he passed all the homes and made a turn back toward the same highway.

As he drove, he observed his surroundings. A sign announced a cemetery up ahead. He grinned. Perfect, he thought. He followed the sign, passed under Interstate 64, and turned right into the wooded home of the dead. He drove around the winding roads, seeing very few cars. He drove slowly and took a right down another small, paved road between the rows of headstones. A lone car was parked at the end. He stopped his car, jumped out, and grabbed flowers off the nearest tomb. Back in his vehicle, he drove to the end and parked behind a blue four-door sedan. He looked out and saw a woman kneeling beside a grave. Too old. He reversed.

On the next street, a black 4Runner with names of children etched on the back glass caused him to smile. Someone young. He slowly drove past the vehicle, careful not to stare at the woman who was walking back toward her car about fifty yards away. Once he passed, he glanced in his rearview mirror. She was young. Young and pretty. He turned around and drove back toward her parked vehicle. He stopped ten feet behind her.

Stepping out, he grabbed his stolen flowers off the front seat and began walking straight ahead but alongside her with about twenty feet between them. Suddenly, he stopped and looked around as if he was lost. He raked a hand over his short, dark hair. Then he acted surprised to see her. "Excuse me. I think I've gotten my directions mixed up. Is this not block C?"

Melissa Jarman broke her stride and glanced his way at the sound of his voice. She hesitated then continued walking as she replied, "No. This is block F. I believe it's two streets over."

"Thanks."

She gave him a brief smile. He grinned at the idea that he had this effect on most women. Fit, good looking, and with a nice vehicle. They always relaxed once he made small talk, their guard down. Serial killers—murderers—didn't look like him, right?

"No problem, it's easy to get lost in here. The letters on the markers aren't big at all."

He glanced down the narrow, paved road toward the main road. "Good point."

CHAPTER 15

For Agent Simon Nichols, visiting the morgue was just as unpleasant as the first time when he started his career with the FBI eighteen years ago. His wife, a nurse, reminded him often that the dead don't wake up or grab him from under the sheets. Still, he got the heebie-jeebies every time he got the call to come in. Today was no different. Standing in the front foyer, he waited on Neil O'Hare to show, the boyfriend who'd called about the Jane Doe. Just as Nichols looked at his watch again, the front door opened and a young man in his early twenties entered.

Nichols stepped forward and produced his badge. "Mr. O'Hare?"

The man nodded.

"Special Agent Nichols. We talked on the phone."

Neil appeared distraught and nervous as he shook his hand. "I…I'm probably wrong. I was thinking on the drive down that maybe she took off or—"

Nichols interrupted. "Possibly." He placed a hand on Neil's shoulder. "Let's just take a look, and we'll go from there." Neil's red eyes pierced Nichols's soul as he gestured toward the front desk. "You'll need to sign in and show an ID."

Time slowed as Neil pulled his wallet from the back of his worn jeans. He hadn't even showered since leaving London fourteen hours ago. When Jacklyn had failed to show at the airport and she hadn't answered her phone, Neil had called a friend for a ride home. Once home, he tried Jacklyn's mobile again before getting in his own vehicle and driving fifteen minutes to her apartment on campus. He'd used his key and found the place empty, with dirty dishes in the sink and a stinky, full trashcan. Both were odd and out of character for his girlfriend of six months.

Neil signed his name on the line and looked up at the woman who stood behind the counter. Her expression was sad as she handed him a printed badge with his picture from his driver's license to stick on his shirt. Neil took it without comment and turned just as the door buzzed. A woman in a white lab coat stepped toward them, the door closing behind her.

Agent Nichols recognized her from years ago during the first case. He stepped forward. "I'm Special Agent Nichols, and this is Mr. O'Hare."

The woman gave a slow nod to Nichols. She turned to Neil. "I'm Dr. Marlee Hoyt, the county medical examiner." She paused briefly. "Mr. O'Hare, thank you for coming in. I know how difficult this must be."

A tear escaped Neil's brown eyes and ran down his cheek. "I just want to get this over and know for sure, that's all."

"Of course. We are going to walk through that door, and there is a room just to the right. It won't take long." Hoyt gave a nod to the lady behind the desk, and the same buzz sounded again, unlocking the door. They all stepped forward and followed Dr. Hoyt a few feet before stopping at a room with a clear glass insert in the wall beside the door.

Neil's knees felt weak at the sight of the small ten-by-ten room with a body lying under a white sheet. "Her parents live in Washington state. When I called them, they hadn't heard from her in a few days." He turned to Nichols. "I didn't want to worry them, you know, in case…" His voice cracked. "They don't have the best relationship. They go weeks without talking and…"

Again, Nichols placed a hand on Neil's shoulder. "I understand. You're doing the right thing, Neil, and we're here. You aren't alone."

More tears flowed. "My friend Jacob wanted to come, but I said, nah, it's not her. It just can't be."

From years of experience, Dr. Hoyt knew to continue this quickly. She opened the door, stepped through, and held it open for them to enter behind her. Reality sank back in, and Neil rubbed his face quickly before walking through the door with Nichols behind him. Hoyt walked around to the other side of the table as Nichols stood by Neil and placed a hand on his back for support. Nichols gave a quick nod, and Dr. Hoyt carefully lowered the white sheet.

Neil let out a sharp, piercing cry and began to shake. "Oh, baby, no, no." He reached out and touched her white sunken face, and he jumped at the feel of her cold skin. He stumbled backward as Nichols grabbed his shoulders to steady him.

Dr. Hoyt blinked the moisture away from her eyes and bit her lower lip. No matter how many years she'd been on the job, she was never immune to the pain and suffering of the human soul. "She has a birthmark. Can you tell me where?"

Through a river of tears, Neil tried to speak, but no words formed. Nichols remained by his side, steadying Neil as he tried to pull it together through the pain. Finally, when he realized he couldn't form a word, he pointed toward her leg. Then he covered his face and took a deep breath. Slowly, he lowered his hands and took another step closer. "Her thigh."

Hoyt eased the sheet over and revealed a small birthmark on her left thigh.

Neil shook his head in disbelief that this had happened to the girl with which he had planned to spend the rest of his life. "Oh, Jacklyn, baby." His face crumpled as he studied her lifeless eyes. He whispered, "Who did this to you? Who did this?" Pain turned to rage as Neil shook off Nichols and bolted from the room. Once outside, Neil leaned up against the opposite wall and sank to the floor.

Hoyt covered the face of Jacklyn Riggs. "Find the bastard who did this."

"Oh, I will, rest assured. I won't rest until I do."

"I met Agent Rhodes. She came in with Detective Ashmore. If this is the same guy from five years ago, where's he been hiding?"

"That's what I've been working on—checking every missing-person case and unsolved murder from here to the West Coast."

Dr. Hoyt stepped over to the glass window and peered at Neil O'Hare. "I can call the sheriff and get the ball rolling on her dental records."

"Thanks, doctor. I'll drive him to the station; someone will get his car later."

***

The wind picked up the leaves, swirling them around as thunder boomed in the distance. The Catholic priest dressed in black read from his open Bible. Sobs could be heard among the family and friends of Hazel Rice. Jemma stared at the casket covered with yellow roses and thought Hollywood couldn't have scripted a sadder scene. Light rain began to fall as the priest closed his Bible and led the crowd in reciting the Lord's Prayer. Jemma scanned the many faces, looking for anyone who seemed out of place or alone. Her jacket vibrated as the prayer ended, and she began to back away as the service came to an end.

"Agent Rhodes."

"Nichols. We got a positive ID. Jacklyn Riggs, a twenty-year-old student from William and Mary."

"What's her address?" Jemma spoke with sadness at the thought of another family about to be torn apart by grief.

"On campus. One fifty-five History Row, apartment three B. Campus police are closing it off now."

"Great. Send me everything you have on her. What about Joy Sutton? Anything?"

"No. Still no sign of her car either."

"OK, thanks. Ashmore and I will leave now; we got nothing at the funeral."

"Will do. Keep me posted. I've got two more missing-person cases to go through, but so far nothing on my end either."

"Damn, Nichols, we need a break and fast."

"Yeah, we do."

Jemma ended the call and tucked her phone back in her pocket. The rain was starting to fall harder now. She motioned toward Ashmore, who had walked around the crowd as it quickly dissipated with the onset of the rain. He jogged over, and they left together for his truck.

CHAPTER 16

His hands shook with excitement as he pulled into the private garage of his apartment and remotely closed the garage door behind his SUV. He cut the engine and got out. Once the door was securely closed, he jogged up the four steps to unlock his door. All appeared as it should in his kitchen. Taking a case of soft drinks from the pantry, he propped the door open and returned to the garage. He stopped at the closed trunk.

Stupid Julie, you were supposed to be the chosen one. Not her. He closed his eyes and tried to relax. Slowly, the tension eased from his shoulders. He opened his eyes back up. *Everything is fine*, he told himself. *This woman is here now, and no one is the wiser.* He opened the trunk.

She looked peaceful, with her blond hair flowing over part of her face and her pink lipstick slightly smudged from the damp rag he had held over her face until she had collapsed in his arms. Her arm lay at an awkward angle, broken from the initial fight. He frowned; he had made a slip in judgement. She had screamed at the cemetery and used a self-defense move to protect herself. This woman hadn't completely let down her guard at his good looks and charm. Things he probably would have known if he had had the time to research her first.

Carefully, he carried her into his home and through the small living room to his second bedroom: the room he had set up especially for his victims. He flipped the switch on the wall, and a low blue light filled the room. It held a video camera on stilts in the corner and a twin size bed with a bare mattress. Gently, he laid her down on the bed and removed her gray wool coat. Next, her sweater.

The rope he had used earlier on his other victims still hung on the bedpost. He tied each of her wrists, backed up, and eyed her intently. When he saw her long fingernails, he instinctively touched his left cheek and neck. His skin felt raw where her scratch had left a mark. He cursed as he left her and soon returned with fingernail clippers. He clipped all of her nails and then dipped each finger in alcohol. Gently, he rubbed each one with a clean cloth. When he was finished, he walked over to the camera and pressed a button. Slowly, he removed his clothing and walked toward her. He paused briefly at the side of the bed and took in her beauty. Then he picked up the red scarf hanging across from the footboard and climbed on top of her.

***

The scene was chaotic when Ashmore pulled his truck alongside a curb at the apartment complex one mile from the campus of William and Mary. Several cruisers were blocking the traffic and keeping curious bystanders away. Two news vans had already arrived and set up, waiting for a comment to lead off with on the evening news. "Aw, jeez!" Ashmore slammed his truck into park.

"It just takes one person to say something, and now we got this." Jemma stepped out of the truck and passed a woman dressed in a suit holding a microphone, a cameraman following on her heels.

"Does this have anything to do with the young Jane Doe found on Halloween?"

"No comment." Jemma pushed through a small crowd, mostly students, and made her way to the entrance of the apartment building.

A Williamsburg police officer was stationed by the door. Jemma flashed her badge. "FBI Special Agent Jemma Rhodes."

He stepped aside. "Second floor, apartment three B."

Ashmore followed Jemma up the flight of stairs and they were met by another officer. They passed him and entered an open apartment door. Jemma looked around and found two police officers talking in the middle of the kitchen. They looked her way. "I'm FBI Special Agent Rhodes, and this is Detective Ashmore with the Norfolk Police Department."

The older man stepped forward and shook their hands. "Detective Beck, Williamsburg PD, and Officer Monroe. Place looks untouched."

"Matches the boyfriend's story," Jemma said as she eyed the pasta-stained plate lying in the sink. She turned to Detective Beck. "Still nothing on her MINI Coop?"

"No, ma'am. The only thing we got here is security tape showing her walking out the front door of the apartment on the night of the thirtieth. She went to work, completed her shift at the truck stop, but never returned."

"And the truck stop tapes?" asked Ashmore.

"Shows her walking out the diner the next morning at seven oh five on the thirty-first, Halloween, getting in her MINI Coop, and pulling out in this direction. We got men checking all possible routes she could've taken, but there aren't many. It's only four miles away."

Jemma raked a hand along the Formica countertop. "I saw a few security cameras outside."

"Yeah. The apartment owner said they broke last year, haven't gotten around to replacing them yet."

"He wouldn't have known that." Jemma walked toward the window and peered out at the crowd that had grown in size since she arrived. Her eyes spotted the two broken cameras aimed at the parking lot. "Chances are he was watching her, knew about the cameras when he scoped out the place." Jemma's fingers wrapped around the wand of the blind, and she closed them and then turned. "We need statements from everyone who lives here. Ask if anyone noticed a man in his thirties to forties lurking around."

Detective Beck nodded. "Working on it now."

"Good." Jemma handed him her card. "Send me everything they get, even the smallest of details, everything."

"Yes, ma'am. Don't you worry; we're gonna turn this place upside down trying to find something. These murders can't continue, and now we're about to be bombarded by parents of these university kids. I won't rest until we have statements from all residents."

Ashmore said, "Appreciate it. We need every law enforcer in the state working on this."

All the men looked at Jemma. "He's right. FBI needs all eyes on deck." Jemma looked at Ashmore. "Let's head over to the truck stop. Gentleman, thank you."

The crowd continued to grow. Jemma slowly scanned each face around her, pausing a few seconds on any male over the age of thirty. She felt nothing in her gut. He wasn't here watching. Jemma pushed on through the crowd, making her way over to the truck, avoiding all contact with the media. When Ashmore pulled away from the curb, he asked Jemma, "What are the odds our man dined at the truck stop, and that's how he found her?"

"I would say better than half. If we're lucky, maybe he paid by credit card and then got the notion to come back and take her."

"A warrant won't take too long."

"No. Nichols said the owner was pissing-fire mad. Jacklyn had worked there since she was a freshman. He would've called us sooner, but he's been out of town on vacation. He's driving back today."

Ashmore gripped the steering wheel tighter. "Senseless. All of it. I let him get away, hell, gave him a golden ticket the day we arrested Deluca."

Jemma touched his arm. "Don't...don't do that."

Ashmore looked at her soft, porcelain hand just as she pulled it away. His eyes found the road again. He sighed. "I know; second guessing can be more dangerous than a bullet."

"It can and—" Jemma stopped and pulled out her phone. "This is Rhodes."

Ashmore glanced her way and then accelerated under a yellow light. The diner was just up ahead. He pulled in and found a spot close to the door. He cut his engine and turned to Jemma, trying to decipher her one-sided conversation.

"That was Nichols. He just stepped on a plane to New Hampshire." Jemma smiled. "He got a hit."

"That's great!"

"Yeah, the other three agents are staying here, helping us."

CHAPTER 17

The phone hadn't stopped ringing since Jill Eckelberg stepped foot in the district attorney's office at 7:55 a.m. One reporter after the next kept calling, asking to speak to her boss, Andrew Lane. They all wanted the scoop on Alec Deluca and his possible innocence in light of the new killings. The city was on edge and so was her boss. He'd come and gone all day, never leaving word of his whereabouts. All strange behavior in Jill's mind.

The door to Andrew Lane's office opened. He was back. She looked up and saw him. Their eyes locked briefly, and then he looked away as he removed his coat.

Jill stood and handed over a list of calls. "Phone hasn't stopped ringing."

Andrew took the list and scanned it. "I'm sure. Hold all my calls. I need to finish the Barone file by five."

"Of course. Any word on Ms. Sutton?"

Andrew stopped at the door of his office; he slowly turned. "No, you hear anything?"

Jill shook her head. "Just what the news is reporting." Jill walked out from behind her desk. She crossed her arms and shuffled her feet. "Andrew, what does this mean? Is she some kind of threat to our office?"

Andrew gave her a curious look. "Why do you think that, Jill?" He walked toward her.

Jill stepped back.

Andrew's eyes softened. "Jill?"

She relaxed, walked back behind her desk, and took a seat.

Andrew filled the gap and sat on the corner of her desk. "We've known each other a long time, Jill. What's on your mind?"

Jill gave him a weak smile. "Ms. Sutton. It bothers me that she came by without signing in. She's the opposition, and if I'm questioned down the road, I can't lie."

Andrew gave her a reassuring smile as he reached out and covered her hand, stopping the nervous tap of her fingers. "Joy Sutton wanted to come to work for me. I was planning to hire her once she gave her notice to the state."

She pulled her hand away and sat back in her chair. "That's why she didn't sign in?"

"Yes. It was a private meeting that neither of us wanted on record."

She breathed a sigh of relief. "A job, wow, I had no idea."

"How would you? I was keeping it under wraps. I didn't want her signing in, and I chose a time when you weren't here."

She shook her head in embarrassment. "Thank you for your honesty. I'm…I'm sorry. You know how I can get crazy ideas stuck in my head. It was starting to get the best of me again. And it wasn't helping with reporters continuing to call, and we have dead bodies popping up on riverbanks again."

Andrew laughed. "It's OK, Jill. This office has seen a lot of craziness over the last several years."

"Yes, it has."

Andrew turned serious. "I need this to stay just between us. I don't know where Joy's head is right now." Andrew stood. "I don't even know if she's turned in her notice or if she's changed her mind and working against us in light of the new murders."

Concern crossed Jill's face again. "I don't see how. I mean, what possibly could she know that we don't?"

Andrew forced a smile. "I'm sure nothing. Now, it's my turn for my imagination to run wild." Andrew opened the door to his office. "If the sheriff calls, send it through, but him only. I've got to finish this case. My wife has a sitter lined up for tonight and big plans."

She warmly replied, "Of course."

Andrew closed the door and leaned against it. He shut his eyes as the sound of his heartbeat thudded within him. Slowly, he pushed away from the door and walked toward his desk. The Barone file was still lying in the same spot as yesterday. Pushing all thoughts of Joy Sutton and Jill Eckelberg out of his mind, he opened the file and began to work.

Across the street, Sheriff Kennedy was sitting at his desk and trying to clear his head when Officer Rick Brown poked his head in, tapping lightly at the door. Kennedy looked up with tired eyes and a weary expression. "What you got, Brown?"

"A Mr. Jarman on line two. His wife failed to pick up the kids from school. He can't find her, and she won't pick up her phone."

Kennedy frowned. "He say if this happened before?"

Officer Brown walked in and handed the report to him. "No, sir. Never. With everything going on, he's out of his mind with worry." Kennedy picked up the report as Brown continued, "Sir, they got four kids in grammar school."

Kennedy scanned the report. "Get an APB out on her vehicle." He picked up his phone and pressed a button. "Sheriff Kennedy speaking."

Brown nodded and walked out as the sheriff grabbed a pen and began to take notes while Mr. Jarman retold his story. Kennedy listened intently, trying to decipher truth from fiction. Finally, he was convinced this wasn't another domestic dispute. Something was going on that caused a mother of four to miss carpool. "OK, Mr. Jarman, this is what we need to do. I need you to get someone to watch the kids and come in and make a formal statement so we can proceed with a missing-person case."

Kennedy sat back in his chair as he heard the heartbreak in Mr. Jarman's voice. Somewhere deep down, he knew he was hoping it would just be a slip of time while out shopping or a car accident and her name and emergency contact info was sitting on some nurse's station desk, waiting for someone to make the call. "Sir, I understand. Get your kids settled, and I'll be here waiting for you."

Finally, Kennedy was able to end the call and hang up. He grabbed the report, walked out of his office, and headed straight to the conference room. Six NPD officers and three FBI agents were all working diligently, some on phones, others on computers. Immediately, he was struck with the photos of the dead hanging on the boards. He shook it off and got everyone's attention. "We've got a missing housewife and mother of four. Name's Melissa Jarman. Never missed school pickup before, and she's not answering her phone. Husband is Don Jarman. He's checked the house, called her friends, nothing. He's coming in to file a formal report. For now, I need all my officers in their cars with her photo ID up on their screens and on the lookout for her black Toyota 4Runner." Kennedy looked at his paper. "Two thousand and twelve, license plate six seven F G D eight. Officer Brown already got out the APB. For the next hour, we drive using the city grid we broke down and practiced. If she's in the city, I want her found. Any questions?"

Chairs were shuffled along the tile as all six officers got to their feet and sprang into action. "Sir, Detective Ashmore called. He and Agent Rhodes are on their way here."

"Good. I'll give them the update." As the first officer got to the doorway, he shouted, "Take no shortcuts. I want her found."

Kennedy looked around the room at the three agents the Richmond Field Office had sent: Niki Walker, Slater Taylor, and Val Kicker. "Hear from Agent Nichols yet?"

Agent Niki Walker walked over. "Not yet. Soon I hope."

Kennedy looked over at Kicker and Taylor who had been assigned to Joy Sutton. Taylor made eye contact and shook his head as he continued to talk on the phone. Kennedy pulled out a chair and took a seat. He rubbed his face, and then he removed his cell phone from his pocket and made a call.

"Andrew Lane."

"Kennedy. You got my warrants on the diner where Jacklyn Riggs worked?"

"Judge should be signing them now."

"Good. I need everything done by the book."

"Relax, we are. Just like we did last time with Deluca and every other big case that has come through our office." A brief silence formed. "Hear anything on Deluca's lawyer?"

"No. Nothing. Just add it to the damn list!"

"What now? Something else?"

"Just had a husband call in that his wife failed to pick up their four kids from school."

"Oh, well, that could be a number of things. It doesn't mean he's taken another one."

"God, I hope you're right, Andrew." Kennedy heard someone and turned. "I got to go. Fax the warrants as soon as you get 'em." Kennedy stood and faced Jemma and Ashmore. "I got everyone out making the grid. We just got word a wife and mother is missing."

"Who is it?" asked Ashmore as he walked over.

"Melissa Jarman, husband is Don Jarman. Got four kids, and she failed to show up at school for dismissal."

"When was this?" Jemma asked as she looked at her watch.

"He got the call at three twenty from the school. Left work, picked up the kids, and rushed home to an empty house. No car, nothing missing from their home."

Jemma walked over to a board and wrote the name Melissa Jarman. "What's her age?"

Kennedy looked at the report. "Thirty-three."

"Older," remarked Ashmore as he walked over to a computer that had her DMV license pulled up. "Looks younger, and she's a blonde."

Jemma walked over and looked at her photo. "All our victims have dark hair." She read her height and weight.

"Beautiful woman," remarked Ashmore.

"Yes, she is. And he likes beautiful women." Jemma ran a hand through her loose auburn curls that had fallen from her hairclip hours ago. "When's the last time someone saw her?"

"No one has come forward. We only know she dropped off the kids like normal this morning around seven forty-five, right in front of Revere Elementary School."

Jemma wrote her age on the board and turned just as an officer called out at the doorway, "Sheriff Kennedy, Mr. Jarman's here."

"I want to talk to him." Jemma dropped the marker and walked forward.

Kennedy studied her briefly and then directed his officer. "Officer Dover, take him to conference room five. I'll be down in a moment."

Jemma didn't give him a chance to argue. "Sheriff, with all due respect, I need to be present. Time is of the essence here."

He slowly nodded and waved his hand toward the door. "Don Jarman has no priors. He works an eight-to-five job at National Bank, has a mortgage on his house and cars. All I know."

Ashmore raised his eyebrows at Jemma as they followed the sheriff down a hall to a closed door with "conference room five" hanging on the wall. Kennedy opened the door, and they saw Don Jarman pacing back and forth, his white, starched dress shirt untucked, tie loosened, and jacket thrown over a chair. "Mr. Jarman, I'm Sheriff Kennedy. We spoke on the phone."

Jarman stopped. "Finally! What the hell is being done to find my wife? I called all the hospitals on the way over and no one has seen her. Nothing. It's like she's vanished! Where is she?" His eyes found

Jemma's FBI badge clipped on her jacket, and he stilled. He backed up and started shaking his head. "Whaa…what are you doing here? This…this has nothing to do with those…" His voice trailed off, not wanting to say what he was thinking.

Jemma spoke softly, "Mr. Jarman, take a breath and please take a seat." Slowly, Don Jarman took a step and pulled out a chair. "I'm Special Agent Rhodes, and this is Detective Ashmore. We are all here to help find your wife." Jemma took the middle chair between Ashmore and Kennedy, with Jarman sitting across from them. Jemma opened a notepad and looked at the sheriff for him to start.

"First of all, I want you to know that all my men and resources are out driving the streets of Norfolk looking for your wife. If her car is anywhere in the city, in public places, we'll find it."

Jarman looked up at the ceiling and closed his eyes tightly. Then he wiped his face with his hands before resting his elbows on the table, his hands clasped as if in prayer under his chin. "Thank you. The thought of life without my wife in it is driving me mad. We've got to find her, and she's got to be OK." He looked at Jemma for some kind of reassurance.

"We need to establish a timeline. So far, we know your wife dropped off your kids at school. Then what? What is a typical Friday like for your wife?" asked Jemma.

A hopeless sound emerged from Jarman's lips. "I should know, right? We've been married over eleven years. But I…I can't keep track of everything. She does all that, you know? Be here at six for this game or pick up at seven from this lesson or that. We've got four kids, and they're all involved in something."

Jemma gave a warm smile. "Your wife sounds amazing and super organized. Does she keep a calendar?"

"Oh yes, it's on the fridge. I looked at it but nothing was written down except 'Benjamin singing in the choir tonight at the football game.'" Immediately, sadness filled his face. "She never misses him sing. She thinks he sounds like an angel and swears she can hear his voice out of the twenty-member choir."

Ashmore let out a small laugh as he nodded. "I'm sure she can. All mothers have that special trait."

Jemma looked at Ashmore. *Where had that come from?* "What about the gym, a women's group that meets for coffee, anything you can think of."

"Gym was yesterday. She has a personal trainer." Jarman saw Kennedy make a note. "Don't bother; she's female. Look, my wife has not run off with some man. Hell, neither of us would have time to have an affair. Besides, we laugh, you know—we have good times despite our crazy life."

"So no time for women's groups or volunteer work with the school or church?" asked Jemma.

"Nothing set each week. She does volunteer at the school when asked, but it would have been on the calendar, and the school would have said something to me when I picked up the kids. They all know my wife." He slammed a hand on the table. "I know my wife! Something has happened." He raked a hand over his face again. This time a small tear escaped.

A tap was heard on the door. "Excuse me." Kennedy stood and walked out to talk to an officer. Jemma studied Jarman. His tears were real. She reached across the table and touched his hand. "We started looking the moment you called. We're doing everything we can."

Kennedy came back in the room and closed the door. "Rosewood Cemetery mean anything to you?"

Clear recognition crossed his face. "Melissa's father. Oh wait, what's the day's date?"

Ashmore replied, "November second."

"Yes! Today would have been his birthday. Is she there? Is that where she's been?" A small laugh emerged as relief washed over him. "She must have lost track of time. It's just been three years. They were very close and—"

Kennedy interrupted, "Her car was found unlocked with her purse lying on the front seat floorboard. There's no sign of her. We have officers casing the cemetery now."

"What do you mean no sign of her? She would've just walked over to the grave, stayed awhile, and left some flowers. She has to be—" Jarman jumped up. "Where is she? She's careful. She would have never left her purse in the car if other people or cars were around. She would have locked it up and then…" Anger filled his face. "She wouldn't have just wandered off." He looked at Jemma. "Who the hell has my wife?"

CHAPTER 18

Agent Simon Nichols's uneventful flight landed at Concord Municipal Airport. Immediately, he was met on the tarmac by FBI Agent Will Stepp, who worked and lived a few miles away in Concord, the state capital of New Hampshire. Stepp was a seasoned veteran like himself, but over the course of the last eighteen years, they had never met. At six-five and with a strong handshake, Stepp easily could have passed for a former Hall of Famer. Instead, Stepp had signed up for the Marines his senior year of high school. After an injury early on, he was recruited by the FBI. Nichols watched as Stepp climbed in behind the wheel of his black Lincoln Navigator, seeing no visual injury.

"I wasn't too surprised when I got your call."

"Oh, why's that? This case has been unsolved going on three years now."

Stepp looked his way briefly before pulling onto Interstate 393. "It has, but you found this case because I keep it pushed to the top of the list." He merged into heavy traffic and then continued. "Case has become personal to me. Seeing that young woman strangled and left for dead in an unmarked grave." He shook his head in disgust. "It did something to me. I told my wife I'll never retire until I catch Cherry

Bowser's killer." He looked over at Nichols, and their eyes met. "You ever get a case like that?"

"Yeah, I have. This one is making it number three."

The traffic opened up, and soon they were exiting onto Highway 106, driving north. A few homes dotted the highway along with the trees, which displayed their last stages of color before their leaves dropped off for winter. "You have a wife and kids at home?"

Nichols looked away from the breathtaking scenery. "I do."

"Yeah, me too. Only thing that keeps me sane with this job."

Nichols glanced at his watch. Sandra would be home with their two girls now, making dinner. Friday night was hamburger night. Another dinner he would surely miss. His stomach instantly reminded him that he had skipped lunch—something he had no appetite for after the identification process of Jacklyn Riggs at the morgue. Quickly, he pushed the memory out of his head. "So any thoughts on how this missing twenty-year-old from Ohio got to New Hampshire?"

"Lots of ideas, just nothing panned out. Ohio State Patrol found her car two days after she went missing. Found on the side of a road, keys in ignition, and her driver's license and small cash in the consol. Boyfriend says she was heading to the gym as he was leaving for his nightshift at a local plant. Didn't know anything was wrong until he came home and found their bed unmade."

"And he checked out?"

"Yes. They share one vehicle. Boyfriend gets picked up for work. When he arrived home at seven the next morning, his buddy came in the house with him."

"Convenient alibi."

"That's what I thought at first too, but their story checked out. His buddy came in the house to use his computer. They were booking a trip to Mexico for spring break. They had just got paid."

"So you had nothing until six months later when her body was found."

"That's right. Every lead we got, nothing. Local sex offenders checked out, no new prison releases in the area, all relatives were cleared. Every stone I turned gave me no clue on who abducted that poor girl." Stepp turned onto Route 129, heading east toward Maine. "Just about twenty more miles. Her body was found by hunters."

"I read on private property."

"You read correct. They were hunting on state property. Hunting with dogs, tracking a wounded deer, and they crossed onto private property. That eighteen-year-old kid got one hell of a surprise when he finally found his barking dog digging up her unmarked grave instead of his twelve pointer. Never found his deer."

Nichols looked at the farmland dotting the two-lane highway. The sun was beginning to make its way down, giving way to a beautiful sunset behind the farmhouses and fields to the west. "The land owners know we're coming?"

Stepp smiled. "No. I find that surprises work better in my favor."

"A forty-eight-year-old widow and a mentally challenged nineteen-year-old son?" Nichols asked with raised eyebrows.

"Nothing's ever what it seems." He laughed. "I looked at them hard along with their neighbors. Nothing. It's as if someone drove onto their property and began digging. You'll see when we get there."

Stepp pointed at different farms and gave background information as he drove. He'd done as he claimed. A lot of hard research had gone into this case. Finally, Stepp signaled and they slowed, turning onto a dirt road on his right. He came to a stop when the road made a Y and pointed to his left. "The house is around the corner, hidden by the trees. The road to the right leads to where the body was found. The road borders several hundred acres that get leased to a few hunters every year." Stepp accelerated to the left, and the trees gave way to an old wooden home with cleared, open fields behind it. "Corn, wheat, and pigs. That's how they survive. House built in 1950s by her father. All paid for."

As the Lincoln rolled to a stop, a man stepped out on the large, covered front porch holding a dog that was barking loudly and wiggling beneath the grip of the man's strong arms. "Don't worry about the dog; worry about him. He's messed up." Stepp got out and called out, "Shannon Krammer, I'm Agent Stepp with the FBI. We've met before; remember me?"

The man turned and yelled into the house. "Mom, strangers here! Two of 'em."

Stepp turned to Nichols. "I guess not."

They waited in front of the SUV as an older woman wearing a faded housecoat stepped out onto the porch. She squinted in their direction because the fading sun was behind them. "Shannon, go on back in. They ain't strangers, hun." When he didn't move, she patted him gently on the arm. "Go on back to your dinner. These are policemen here again about that body they found."

Shannon looked confused, but he turned with the dog and went back into the house as instructed. When they were alone, she stepped to the edge of the porch. "Little late for a house call, don't you think?"

"Sorry, Ms. Krammer, but it's important." Stepp flashed his badge. "I'm with the FBI, not the police. I'm Agent Stepp; we met some time ago." He turned to Nichols. "And this is Special Agent Nichols, just flew up from Virginia. He's working on an important case down there."

"Important case? Hmm, well, must be if it got you on my doorstep. Might as well come on in. We'll talk in the living room while Shannon finishes his supper."

"Actually, Ms. Krammer, we'd like to drive out to the grave site first while it's still light for Agent Nichols to view."

"Oh. Well, suit yourself. I'll still be here."

"Thank you, ma'am, we appreciate it."

Nichols took a quick look around and climbed back in with Stepp. As they backed out, he watched Ms. Krammer through his rearview window. She finally walked back inside just as they rounded the curve out of sight. He looked at Stepp.

"I know what you're thinking. Shannon is a big, strong man, quite capable of carrying a woman into the woods and burying her. But he's never left the state of New Hampshire, and he doesn't have a driver's license."

"What about as an accomplice?"

Stepp snickered as he braked and put the car in park. Cutting the engine he said, "People like him don't have friends."

"Siblings?"

"All older. Two sisters and one brother, and they all live very different lives far away from here."

"Interesting." Nichols got out and followed Stepp over to the tree line. A yellow ribbon around a tree marked the spot that led to her grave. The woods were thick, and they walked carefully between brush and briars for about fifteen feet. Stepp stopped and pointed to a small, white cross sticking out of the ground under a large maple tree.

"Cross wasn't my idea. Ms. Krammer said Shannon made it. He was quite traumatized by the circus we created, and his therapist suggested it might help. I don't know whether he knows if the body is still there or not, but I have no intention of explaining to him how the family of Cherry Bowser brought her home to rest in peace by her grandmother in Ohio."

Nichols studied the woods surrounding the marked grave. Whoever dug it knew the area and knew the owners. "He's familiar with this location. Wasn't too worried about his car being discovered." He turned and looked at Stepp. "He took the girl in Ohio and brought her here. But where and for how long before he killed her?"

"We searched the entire property for weeks, looking for more victims. None were found."

"I don't think this is an isolated event. He took more, but we just haven't found them."

Stepp pursed his lips. "There was another young female who went missing just across the border in West Virginia six months later and then two girls the next year in Pennsylvania. Never found them either. You think they're buried too?"

"I don't know. Two more went missing in Maine and Vermont the year after."

Stepp frowned. "Young women go missing all the time. You think it's the same man, and it's all connected?"

Nichols opened the folder he brought from the vehicle. "Don't you? Marcie Barnett, an employed part-time student who lived at home. Morgan Squires, a full-time beautician whom friends described as 'full of life and never met a stranger.'" He closed the file. "I could go on. These women were not runaways or drug addicts; they were employed, well-liked, and with a promising future."

"I know, it's just they were from different states spanning over four years. And only Cherry Bowser has been found."

"Tied up and strangled, just like the women in Virginia."

Stepp placed his hands on his hips. "You really think it's the same man as the one killing your women in Virginia?"

"Think about it. It makes sense. He got his public attention when he was labeled the River Strangler. Then, the wrong man goes to prison. He's smart—so smart that he leaves. But his urge to kill again is too strong. He's already filled the need for fame so he goes into hiding."

"Like taking his women from different states and burying the evidence."

"Yeah, and I think he knows this area, maybe even grew up here. Feels safe enough here to live for a while." The last rays of the sun filtered through the woods, giving way to dusk. "I've seen enough. Let's get back to the house before dark." They took a few steps and stopped at a noise behind them. They turned and scanned the area, both with their hands on their Glocks. They spotted a squirrel running along the ground and up a tree. They relaxed and walked on.

At the house, the front-porch light was on, and they saw Ms. Krammer with Shannon, rocking on the front swing. They climbed the stairs together, and Agent Stepp spoke. "Thanks, Ms. Krammer, for your patience. We won't keep you long."

She lowered a book she was holding in her hand. "We were just reading. Why don't we talk outside? Not too many more nights like this one. Soon it will be too cold to step foot out." She squeezed

Shannon's arm. "Why don't you go brush your teeth and get ready for bed? I'll be in shortly."

The swing made a moaning sound as two hundred pounds was lifted off the wood seat, and Ms. Krammer's small frame swung backward. Nichols stepped aside as Shannon passed by. Shannon said nothing, and he carried a children's picture book with him inside.

"Ms. Krammer—"

"Please, just call me June."

Nichols smiled. "June, is it still just you and Shannon who live on the property?"

"Yes. My girls live in New York and Maine, both married with kids, good husbands who do well and provide nicely for them. They occasionally visit, you know, mostly on the holidays."

"And you have another son?"

A bright smile filled her face. "Yes, my Jonathan. He's in California. He's a lawyer."

Laughter broke out near the window. Nichols looked back and saw Shannon kneeling down, listening behind the screen of the open window. He looked back at June, her smile replaced by a scowl. She shouted, "Shannon, go to your room and brush your teeth, right now!"

"A lawyer. Hahaha, he ain't no lawyer." There was more laughter before Shannon shut the window and left. June got to her feet, walked over to the front door, and watched as he climbed the stairs to his room on the second floor, laughing all the way. She turned red under the porch light, clearly embarrassed. Finally, she moved away from the door when she heard another door shut upstairs. She took her seat again.

"Pay no attention to him. He's e't up with jealousy and envy. He sees his brother leaving for college as abandonment. Well, that's what the psychiatrist says anyway."

"How often does Jonathan visit?" Nichols carefully prodded.

"When he can. Seems like less each year; he made partner in his firm."

Nichols noticed how she'd lost her anger quickly, and she was now consumed with pride. "Do you ever have help with Shannon or maybe able to take vacations to see your daughters or son?"

She shook her head. "I tried. Shannon doesn't do well with anyone, and well, with Martin gone, I'm all alone. He might be different and hard to handle at times, but at least he's here. He fills a void." Shame quickly filled her face. "That came out all wrong. I love Shannon. God gave him to me like that. Martin and I talked about putting him in a home when he was young. We couldn't do it. I'm a stronger person for having Shannon in my life and so are my children—even if they don't see it that way sometimes."

"I'm sure you are, June, I'm sure you are." Nichols walked over and held out his hand. "Thanks for your time, ma'am. We'll leave you now."

June stood and shook his hand. "I hope your case goes well down in Virginia. This world can be a dark place sometimes. Lots of evil lurking out there. I see the news."

"Yes, ma'am," said Stepp. "Thanks again."

They turned and walked down the steps to Stepp's Lincoln. As they pulled away, Nichols caught sight of Shannon standing by his window, watching them. A cold shiver slid down his back as Shannon pulled the curtains closed and disappeared.

CHAPTER 19

Traffic was slow around a three-mile radius of the Norfolk district football stadium where the town gathered for the annual showdown between two rival high schools. Jemma watched as a carload of teenage girls without a care in the world danced to music coming from inside their navy Nissan, which had pulled up beside her. Jemma was envious of their youthful souls not yet exposed to the horrors of the world. The light turned green, and she and Ashmore moved forward ahead of them.

Jemma rubbed her temples as she thought about the long day. Way too many events to keep track of, starting with the killer calling her in the middle of the night. *Why had he done that? Why seek me out? If he's the River Strangler responsible for the murders of five years ago, why call me? He never reached out to any other agents before.* However, he wasn't the one who called Channel 2 News. That was the hotel clerk from the Rivermont. She wondered if he'd lose his job. What was his name? Peter, Pete. She couldn't remember. Then her thoughts led to the funeral of Hazel Rice, surrounded by family and friends filled with sorrow.

"Hey, you OK?"

Jemma dropped her hands from her face and looked at Ashmore. "Yes, just trying to sort through everything. Crazy day." She exhaled loudly. "And to add on top of everything, we've got a mother of four missing, and the FBI agents sent from Richmond have nothing on Deluca's missing lawyer."

Ashmore tapped his steering wheel as traffic slowed again. "It is. A lot to digest. We need Agent Nichols to come back with something… anything to point us in the right direction."

"We do." Jemma looked at her watch. "He's supposed to call when he gets back to the plane."

"Jeez, look at this traffic! Already backing up."

Jemma looked up at the chaos unfolding.

"We're shorthanded for obvious reasons, and we don't have the manpower to protect our walkways heading to the stadium."

Jemma looked around at the large groups of people huddling around the traffic light, waiting to cross. "How many people does this stadium hold?"

Ashmore laughed. "Enough to hold anyone in town who wants to come. It's a community event."

"That's right. Even the Jarmans were attending because of their son's choir concert. Poor family."

"I know of them but not personally. Seems like a good family, always at their kids' events. News of her disappearance is gonna spread like wildfire tonight, if it hasn't already. We need to be prepared."

The traffic came to a stop as the lights of the stadium came in sight. Suddenly, a student darted in between traffic to get to the other side, failing to wait and cross at the light with the mass of people waiting for the light to turn red. Ashmore slammed the truck in park. "Why don't you drive around? I need to get out and stop the traffic before someone gets hurt."

Jemma looked at the crowd, young and old, families and students. "No. Just pull over here with your lights. I'll help."

For the next ten minutes, Jemma stood in the middle of the road with a reflective vest and red wands, helping Ashmore. Ten more minutes passed, and their efforts paid off. Traffic was moving again with thirty minutes left before kickoff. Jemma watched as Ashmore made small talk to many families and high-school kids as they walked by. She clearly saw that his roots ran deep in the community he was born and reared in. Jemma walked his way just as another family approached.

"Jason, how are you?" said a woman holding the hand of a young boy. Her husband was two steps behind her, holding a small toddler.

"I'm good, Cassy." Jason extended his hand and shook her husband's hand. "Randy, good to see you."

"Beautiful night. I've never seen it this crowded."

"Yes, it is. Good for the town right now."

"That's for sure," Cassy said and then leaned down and picked up her son.

"Easy, babe. Don't pick him up. Here, trade with me." Randy switched the kids, and Jason saw Cassy's bump for the first time.

She adjusted her little girl, who was all wrapped up in the high-school's colors. She looked over and noticed Jemma. Ashmore quickly introduced them. Jemma shook their hands as Cassy lost her smile. "I talked to Rita yesterday. She told me what was going on."

Jason glanced around. "Yeah, it's not good." Then Jason looked at Randy. "Stick together until we catch this…" He stopped as he eyed their five-year-old boy. "How are you, Cole? Have a good Halloween?"

"I was a fireman like my daddy."

Jason smiled. "I'm sure you were a great fireman, just like your dad." Jason and Randy exchanged a look, and then Jason continued, "I'll let ya'll get to the game. We're going back out on patrol."

Cassy squeezed Jason's arm. "Hey, don't be a stranger. We miss you."

Jason nodded and watched them walk away, the perfect little family. Finally, he turned to Jemma. "Ready to roll?"

"Sure. But who is that man over there?" Jason followed her eyes. "He's got on a gray sweater, with the blond-headed woman and little girl in the pink jacket."

Finally, Jason's eyes spotted them. "Why do you ask?"

"Because when he saw us, he went out of his way to cross the street and avoid us."

Jason smirked. "I bet. That's Daniel Stone."

Jemma arched her eyebrows. "The Daniel Stone who was Laura Stone's husband?"

"Yep, the very one."

"So is that his new wife?"

"Yes. Liza."

"How old is the little girl?"

"Well, let me think. She's around five now."

Jemma turned and took another glance. They were too far ahead. She turned back around and faced Ashmore. "Explain."

"Adopted. Liza's troubled sister. The Stones have another little girl together. She must have stayed behind with a sitter."

Jason's phone rang, and he pulled it out of his jacket as he hit the unlock switch on his truck remote. "Ashmore."

Jemma continued and climbed into the truck. Ashmore stood outside, finishing his conversation, and then opened the driver-side door. "That was Dr. Hoyt. Drug test came back positive for Jacklyn Riggs. He drugged her with chloroform, just like Hazel Rice."

"No struggle. No DNA. I wonder how he took Jacklyn after she left the truck stop diner."

Ashmore replied, "Still no sign of her car either."

"Any other drugs in her system?"

"No."

Jemma frowned. "We'll probably never know."

Ashmore started the engine. "Where to? Any ideas?"

"Finding Jarman's like finding a needle in the haystack." Jemma looked around at all the parked cars and the lighted stadium up ahead, already playing a school's fight song. "Pick a neighborhood and drive down the streets. See who's home and not at the game," she said with sarcasm.

"How long do you think we have to find her?"

"I don't know…a day, probably less. Hazel Rice and Jacklyn Riggs were found one day after they were taken."

Ashmore recalled the case from memory. "Five years ago, he was more patient. Several days to a week would pass before taking another victim."

Jemma frowned. "With this case, not two days has gone by before we have another victim or woman missing."

Ashmore turned into an older, more-established neighborhood with fuller trees lining the driveways. He drove slowly as they peered at each home, looking for anything out of the ordinary. "At this pace, he's bound to make a mistake."

"I hope so and soon." Jemma felt her phone vibrate. She pulled it out and said, "It's Nichols."

Nichols explained everything he had seen in New Hampshire and filled them in on the several girls missing in the bordering states over the last five years while Deluca was in prison for the murder of Laura Stone. Only one body had been discovered, and it had been by chance. Jemma listened without interrupting and then spoke. "I agree. It could be him. I think you should stay and dig deeper into that farm community. Run another check on the family and neighbors, maybe something was missed from before. Yeah, I'm sure. No, no word on either Sutton or Jarman. Yeah, I'll let you know."

Jemma ended her call. "Nichols ran across an unsolved case involving a woman missing from Ohio who was found strangled in an unmarked grave in New Hampshire. When he dug deeper, he found six more women who were reported missing from surrounding states over the last five years since Deluca's arrest. None of them has been found. So far, all evidence points to abduction by an outsider. No leads on family or friends; they all checked out. He's going to send

Dr. Hoyt the autopsy report and keep snooping around where the body was found."

"He thinks there's a connection to the gravesite?"

"Yes. Medical records indicated the woman had been tied up for some time before her death. I can't imagine killing her near Ohio and then driving with a dead body in the trunk all the way to Concord, New Hampshire, to bury her."

Ashmore nodded. "So he ties her up, drives her to his hideout, kills her, and then buries her nearby."

"Yes, so he can visit the unmarked graves at any time."

Ashmore rolled to a stop at the exit of the neighborhood. He looked at Jemma. "You think he visits the graves?"

Jemma thought for a moment. "I do. Think about the location of the murders here. Two were at a park. He could visit at any time, and no one would suspect a thing. Let's go to Mathews Park. We're wasting time here."

Ashmore pulled out onto the main highway, but instead of turning toward the park, he turned the opposite direction at the light.

"Wait, I thought Mathews Park was to the right?"

"It is. But I'm going to pull into here first and grab us something to eat."

Jemma saw the fast-food deli with a few cars in the parking lot. "OK, well, yeah, this shouldn't take too long."

Ashmore cut the engine and stepped out with a smile on his face. All day long, they had been on the go. He'd grabbed a cold slice of pizza at the station, and Jemma had pulled out some kind of lean protein bar from her briefcase. *Yeah, she has to be starving as well*, he thought.

The counter was empty of lines. The only patrons were already seated and eating their various deli wraps. The young teenager behind the glass counter of meats, vegetables, and condiments was in no hurry as he prepared two sandwiches to their liking. Finally, they paid and walked over to a free table in the corner away from listening ears.

Jemma sat across from Ashmore and unwrapped her sandwich. After taking a few bites, she asked, "Who's Rita?"

Ashmore was taken back and coughed as he lowered his soft drink to the table. "Rita is my ex."

"Oh. I didn't…" Jemma shook her head in embarrassment. "I'm sorry. I didn't mean to pry."

"No. That's OK. Rita and I…" He paused. "Well, let's just say we aren't like most divorced couples. We're still very close, friends even."

Jemma gave him a small smile. "I'd say. No, that's good. Refreshing to hear. I have lots of divorced friends, and well, they all hate each other's guts."

An awkward moment passed and finally ended at the sound of Ashmore's phone ringing. He laid his sandwich down, took a sip of Coke, and answered. "Ashmore." Quickly, he stood and wrapped the uneaten portion of his sandwich with his free hand.

Jemma stood and helped, taking both their sandwiches and her drink, and followed him to the door.

"We're less than ten minutes away." Ashmore stopped once he was outside and looked at Jemma. "They found Melissa Jarman."

"Where?"

"At the football game."

CHAPTER 20

The house was quiet as Andrew Lane sat alone on the sofa in the living room. The TV was muted, and a commercial flashed across the large flat screen. His wife, Bianca, was putting their older children to bed. Their two-year-old, Lexi, had already been asleep in her toddler bed for the last hour. He picked up his glass of wine off the coffee table and took another sip. He glanced around the living room. No toys or games were present. All of it had been picked up by the kids and taken to their game room, a nightly rule Bianca had established years ago. He took another sip and thought about how he was going to appease his wife for canceling her well-laid plans for tonight.

There was no time left to think. Bianca walked into the living room, still wearing her new dress that she had greeted him in when he walked in the door. She said nothing as she picked up the bottle of wine and poured another glass for herself. She turned to Andrew with her full glass dangling between her delicate hands. Her nails were perfectly painted red to match her dress. She said nothing as she took a sip, and then she walked across the room and took a seat on her favorite chair, directly across the room from him.

They played the staring game; the same one Collin, their oldest, liked to play. Andrew looked away first and placed his wine glass down on the coffee table. "I'm sorry, Bianca, but with everything going on, I just didn't feel like going out and celebrating tonight."

She frowned. "I wouldn't exactly call it celebrating. It was just dinner and a movie."

"For God's sake, Bianca, what exactly would you call it? We've got a serial killer on the loose and a botched murder case, and the DA is out on the town partying like nothing's wrong."

"And you think the rest of the town is staying home tonight? They're at the ballgame. Do you know how hard it was to get a sitter tonight?"

Andrew said nothing.

Bianca stood and walked over. She placed her wine on the coffee table and dropped to her knees in front of him. "I would call it spending quality time with your wife. Something that has escaped both of us the last several months." She took his hands in hers. "You promised me that this job would never come first." Her green eyes locked onto his as she continued. "Our marriage, our kids, and then work. You're not living up to your agreement."

Andrew couldn't help but see her disappointment. In his heart, he knew she was right. She'd done nothing wrong. *It's all me. I've done this.* He pulled his hands away and tried to stand, but she pulled him back down.

"Andrew, is there something you need to tell me?"

His mind replayed the last few meeting with Joy Sutton. Their flirtatious relationship that he had equally engaged in, Joy divulging Deluca's claim of innocence, their secret pact, and finally his last meeting with Joy when it had turned for the worse so quickly. He looked back at his wife's pleading eyes and lied. "No, baby. All is fine with us; I promise. It's this Deluca case. They're looking back into it,

and then there's all these young women turning up dead. That's all."
He touched her face, and she closed her eyes and buried her face in his
hand with relief.

Andrew's heart missed a beat as his beautiful wife bought into his
lies. He quickly looked away before his heart could betray his mind.
Keeping it together, he slowly raised her chin in his hands. "Come to
bed with me, Bianca."

Her eyes turned soft. "OK, Mister Lane. I will come to bed with
you."

Andrew helped lift her to her feet and watched as she grabbed the
wine bottle. "Grab another bottle," he instructed, knowing what was
still left to do tonight. Andrew watched as she walked toward the bar
and chose another bottle of wine. He nodded at her selection. "Good
year." Then he picked up both of their glasses and followed her out of
the room, pressing the day's events out of his head.

***

On the fifth floor of the Concord FBI field office, FBI Agent
Will Stepp separated the missing-person cases from the fieldwork
completed around the burial site of Cherry Bowser found on the
Krammer's farm. Nichols had already studied each file on the missing
girls on the flight earlier. A lot of manpower had clearly gone into each
case, resulting in nothing promising and only airing people's unwanted
laundry to the world. Nichols chose to start with the heavy file that was
associated with the location of Cherry Bowser's unmarked grave.

Within the file, he found the report on the Krammer family.
Nichols sat back and read. Martin and June Krammer were married
in 1964 and had four children. Jonathan, the oldest at thirty, was
unmarried and living in Oakland, California. The two daughters,
Veronica, age twenty-eight, and Madison, age twenty-six, were
married and lived with their spouses and children in Maine and
New York, just like June had stated. The reports on them were small

compared to the five-page report on Shannon Krammer, age nineteen. Apparently, he had had a few run-ins with the law: fighting, stealing, lewd conduct, and disorderly conduct in public places, all within a ten-month period following the death of Martin Krammer, his father.

Attached was a medical report, ten times the size of his criminal mischief record. Shannon suffered from bipolar disorder, social anxiety phobia, and dissociative identity disorder. Nichols read about each and then read his doctor's notes given as testimony to a local judge. Charges were filed, but Shannon Krammer served no time. According to his doctor, Shannon had acted out after the loss of his father. The judge, however, did order more therapy sessions, and Shannon Krammer must be supervised at all times when he leaves the Krammer farm. *Huh, could June Krammer possibly supervise her son twenty-four/seven?* Nichols glanced back up at the charges: stealing, lewd and disorderly conduct—not exactly in line with strangling and leaving women for dead. But the fighting?

Nichols found a separate attachment that gave more details on the fight that led to Shannon's arrest. Apparently, Shannon had struck the owner of a store when the owner tried to stop him from leaving with a pack of unpaid chewing gum. Nothing. Nichols placed the Krammer file to the side and picked up a report on the nearest neighbors, Justin and Lucile Grove, who lived a half a mile away. The Groves had two sons, ages thirty-five and thirty-one. Both married and living in the same town, working for their father's dairy farm. Each was married with small children. Agent Stepp had visited with each family member and had made a few handwritten notes in the margins. Kenny Grove, the youngest, was best friends with Jonathan Krammer. They had lost touch when Jonathan left for UCLA after high school. John Grove had an extramarital affair early on in his marriage; wife was still clueless.

Nichols lowered the file, reached across the table, picked up another sandwich that had been delivered earlier, and began to eat again. He scanned more reports on four more families, all within three miles of the Krammer farm. Of the five families, three of them had children similar in age as the Krammers, which meant they would have played and hung out together as children. Nichols was given a report on each with additional handwritten notes in the margin. There was a name highlighted on the second page: Harrison Avery. Below the name was more detail about the neighborhood kids, but no additional information was given on Harrison Avery. Nichols flipped to the next page and saw a handwritten note on the side margin. *Harrison Avery— Shannon's imaginary playmate. Interesting?*

Nichols stood, walked over to the waste can, and discarded his empty sandwich box in the trash. Agent Stepp was on his laptop computer, looking up current information about Jonathan Krammer's place of employment in California. He walked over. "So Shannon Krammer has an imaginary friend?"

Stepp leaned back in his chair and looked at Nichols with a smile. "Yeah, sent me on a wild-goose chase until it was finally explained to me by Krammer's doctor. Harrison Avery doesn't exist. The kid made him up. Just another imaginary playmate he created. The doc said it all started when kids in the neighborhood stopped playing with him because he was so different. He'd been creating friends since he was ten. Harrison Avery just got added to the list when his dad died."

Nichols slowly nodded. "Do they still exist today?"

"No. Krammer's doctor takes great pride in the fact that Harrison Avery and his other friends no longer exist in Shannon's head."

"I bet she does." Nichols looked at the computer screen. "Anything on the brother?"

"Just the fact that the Law Office of Burke and McKinney decided to make Jonathan Krammer partner at such a young age."

"Yeah, but if I'm remembering correctly, he graduated with honors. Must be smart."

"He is that. I met him. He flew out from California when the body was found. Acted just like a lawyer. Didn't want us talking to the family unless he was present."

Nichols leaned closer to the screen and scanned Krammer's bio page. "What kind of law does he practice?"

"Mostly taxes and estate planning."

He leaned back and looked at Stepp. "Huh, well, can't blame him for wanting to protect his family."

"Except where was he when Shannon was arrested?"

Nichols raised his eyebrows and crossed his arms. "When was that? When did Mr. Krammer die again?"

"About four years ago, just a year shy of the body being found."

Nichols did the math in his head. "So Jonathan is twenty-six, graduated, and trying to make a name for himself. Would have already taken time off for his dad's funeral. I'm sure it was tough on him to leave again." Nichols paused and thought. Then he continued, "When the body was found he was twenty-eight. Would have been easier to leave, already been around three years to prove himself. What about the sisters?"

"They rarely visit as well. All have kids and work. The family's only together at Christmas, and that is only two days at the most."

"So bottom line, we got nothing. If they're that busy, then they surely don't have time to kidnap girls and drive them back home to New Hampshire." Nichols picked up another file on the table. "All the kids around that area moved on, except the Grove boys. Grew up to be men and now work for their family farm."

Stepp nodded. "I looked at them the most. Watched them even. I couldn't find anything. Their father was diagnosed with cancer four years ago so he doesn't do much with the company anymore. His sons practically run the place, and it's profitable…very profitable. Kenny and John put in over sixty hours a week."

"So when did he have time for an extramarital affair?"

"Oh, that. She was the secretary."

"Of course. So how did you find that out, and the wife is still clueless?"

Stepp laughed. "Some people are just like an open book. He was more afraid of being accused of murder."

"Would Mr. Grove be healthy enough to carry a twenty-year-old to her grave?"

"No."

Nichols took a seat and sighed. "So all this and we got nothing, no lead, nothing?"

Stepp smiled. "Almost nothing."

***

Ashmore and Jemma arrived at the stadium in less than ten minutes. There were no blue or red lights flashing, and the football game was still underway with a band playing and the crowd following behind with a cheer from the cheerleaders. Ashmore parked in a no-parking zone that was designated for emergency vehicles only. He cut the engine and looked at Jemma. "We'll walk from here. Sheriff was adamant about keeping this under wraps. Word gets out, we'll have a mass panic. People could be trampled to death trying to get out of here."

"He's right. So where are they?"

Ashmore pointed to a small building behind the stadium. Jemma looked and noticed for the first time that an ambulance was backed up to the building on the opposite side from the bleachers. "Looks like a shed to hold lawn equipment."

"It is. Come on."

Jemma opened her door and stepped out. They met up and matched each other's steps, both looking around to make sure they hadn't drawn too much attention. As they neared the shed, they could see an officer standing guard by the back door. He recognized them and looked around before motioning them to enter.

"Brace yourself." He spoke quietly.

Jemma took a step into the semi dark wooden shed and jumped at the sound of the door closing behind her. She took a deep breath and stepped around Ashmore. Kennedy was the first person she saw. He and another officer stepped aside, revealing Melissa Jarman lying at an awkward angle in a wheelbarrow with her eyes wide open. A flash from a camera illuminated the room, followed by another and then another. Jemma looked away briefly and then stepped toward Melissa Jarman. "Who found her?" Jemma asked in a low voice.

Kennedy responded, "The groundskeeper. He was returning some extra cones and immediately became alarmed when he saw the lock broken. At first, he thought it was some kids who snuck in to smoke some weed or make out. Wish that would've been the case."

"Yeah." Sadness filled Jemma as she studied Melissa's face of death. The killer had left her fully exposed with only a red scarf loosely draped around her bruised neck. He had strangled her like the others. Her hand lay upon her bare stomach and showed bruises around her wrist where he had tied her up. Her right arm was at an odd angle. Jemma stepped closer. "Her arm looks broken. She must have put up a fight. Good, maybe we'll find his DNA." She bent down within a few inches of her fingers on her right hand, and then she looked at her left hand to compare. "He cut her nails. They're all jagged. She scraped him." Jemma stood up. "Good job, Melissa. Good job!"

"Bastard! Hurry up with the photos, cover her, and get her out of here. Her family doesn't deserve this."

Jemma turned and saw a red-faced Kennedy. His emotions were getting the best of him now. She didn't blame him. It was his town, his people. Her phone rang, and she dug it out of her pocket, backing away. "Rhodes."

"I see you found my little surprise."

Jemma's face lost all color, and her eyes widened in shock. She mouthed quietly, "It's him!" Jemma quickly walked outside of the shed. "Where are you, you sick son of a bitch?"

Laughter broke out. "You won't find me."

Jemma searched the stands. Everyone had his or her back to her as the crowd cheered and the band picked back up again. She turned around and looked out at the parking lot behind the metal fence that separated the cars from the football stadium. Suddenly, she saw movement. She ran toward the fence just as a dark shadow moved behind a truck. "Oh, I think I will, you bastard!"

Jemma turned back around and saw Ashmore. "He's here! In the parking lot!" She followed the gate back toward Ashmore's parked truck. She was losing time. He was getting away. Finally, she got to the opening by the ticket booth. She ran full speed over the grass and into the adjacent parking lot. She stopped and looked around, trying to listen for the sound of a car, but all she heard was the roar of the crowd as an enthusiastic announcer declared a touchdown. Jemma noticed how there was only one exit to both parking lots. She began running and pulled her weapon, gripping it tightly to her side.

"Boom!"

Jemma stopped and turned. The team's canon had fired. She tightly squeezed her eyes shut and noticed Ashmore waving his hands and running toward her. Jemma turned back around and saw headlights bearing down on her. She dove to the right in between two cars, her gun clattering away. Tires squealed and then the sound of the band playing the school fight song was the only thing she heard.

"Jemma! Jemma!"

Jemma reached for her gun and then slowly rose up. "Over here."

Ashmore ran toward her and wrapped his arms around her. Then he stepped back and touched her forehead. "You got a cut. Are you OK?"

Jemma saw his deep concern, and she quickly looked away toward the parking lot exit. "He got away."

"Agent Rhodes!" Jemma turned and found Kennedy running toward them. "Did you see the car? We got a patrol car three blocks away."

Jemma shook her head. "Too fast, but I think it was an SUV of some sort."

"Yeah, it was a dark SUV, four doors. That's all I got," Ashmore confirmed.

CHAPTER 21

Saturday, November 3

Jemma woke in strange surroundings. A brief moment passed before her mind cleared and she remembered Ashmore's offer of his guest room. She sat up in the oak, four-poster, queen size bed and immediately felt the soreness along the right side of her body. A flashback of the madman trying to run her down filled her mind. She pushed the image out of her head and turned on the bedside lamp. Ashmore's room came into full view. The walls were painted a pale yellow, and the comforter was blue-and-white floral, suggesting the touch of a woman, most likely his ex, Rita. Jemma picked up her phone that was charging beside her and looked at the time. *Eight oh eight!*

Ignoring her aching muscles, she jumped out of bed, quickly went into the bathroom, and turned on the hot water for a shower. Then she opened her luggage, pulled out a new outfit, and closed the bathroom door behind her. Soon she was under the warm spray, trying to clear her head for another emotionally demanding day. After fifteen minutes, her body loosened up, and the soreness faded. She turned off the water and stepped out. She wiped the foggy mirror with a towel and came face to face with tired green eyes that sported circles beneath.

After an extra five minutes added for makeup, Jemma finally stepped out of the bathroom, completely dressed. She made the bed and repacked her luggage. Not knowing if Ashmore was up, she quietly opened the bedroom door and stepped into the hallway. She immediately smelled coffee and smiled.

Ashmore wasn't in the kitchen, but a clean coffee cup with "I heart New York" in large red letters was sitting by the coffeepot. She picked up the black cup and instantly thought of Bruce Vines, wondering how he was enjoying Miami without her. With his good looks, charm, and personality, she had a pretty good idea that he wasn't waking up alone this morning. She pushed the thoughts out of her head, poured the hot coffee into the souvenir cup, and left the kitchen.

She wandered into the living room, analyzing Jason Ashmore's home. Last night she hadn't taken notice of the house; it was late, and Ashmore only had a small lamp on in the foyer. He immediately directed her down a hallway to her room. Now, she sipped her coffee and studied her surroundings. Compared to the guest room, the living room had much more of a masculine feel, with dark, leather couches and rustic tables. The fireplace was stone with a dark, wooden mantle that matched the beams along the ceiling. The framed photo above the mantle caught her attention, and she stepped forward to get a closer look.

Ashmore and an attractive woman sat on a log with fall foliage in the background. Standing in front of them was a little girl with her hands in the air and leaves falling around her to the ground. Jemma immediately smiled. It was a beautiful moment that the photographer had captured perfectly.

"I see you found the coffee."

Caught off guard, Jemma jumped and turned to face Ashmore. "Yeah, thanks, um, I didn't hear you."

"Losing your touch?"

She grinned.

"How did you sleep last night? You sore?"

"A little. Slept like a rock though. Never woke till after eight. Shocking. Don't know the last time I did that."

Ashmore took a sip from his large mug. "Well, your body needed it. I wasn't going to wake you unless something urgent came up. We all need clear minds today to catch this animal."

Jemma nodded. "We do. He made some big mistakes yesterday, contacting me, leaving the scarf at the scene, and then showing his vehicle when trying to run me down. He's cracking." Jemma took a sip from her cup and then looked back toward the family photo. "Beautiful family."

He glanced up at the mantle. "Thanks. That was a good day."

Jemma turned back around. "I assume that's Rita."

He nodded.

"And what is your little girl's name? She's beautiful, has your eyes." Jemma immediately noticed a change appear before her. Was it sadness she saw in his eyes?

"Tracie." Ashmore turned and walked into the kitchen.

Jemma followed behind and decided to drop the family inquires. Divorce was hard and harder when a child was involved. "We should probably get to the station and check in on the latest."

Ashmore refilled his coffee cup and leaned against the counter. "You ever come close to getting married and having the family life?"

Awkwardness filled the room. Jemma thought to herself, *Well, you started this.* "Of course." She took another sip and then moved toward the coffeemaker and refilled her mug. "Just hasn't been the right timing, that's all."

He laughed. "Timing? What's right timing? Everyone said Rita and I were too young to get married."

Jemma didn't want to state the obvious so she just smiled.

"We—" Ashmore paused and picked up his ringing cell phone off the counter. "Ashmore."

Jemma watched how his expression turned serious.

"When…OK. We can be there in fifteen." Ashmore lowered the phone. "An early-morning jogger found Joy Sutton. Bastard strangled her and left her at Mathews Park."

Confusion spread across Jemma's face. "What?" she asked with surprise. "And he had the nerve to go back to Mathews Park? Didn't we have patrol there?"

"With the game and finding Melissa Jarman, we had to pick and choose. Nobody thought he'd be as brash or foolish enough to go back. So just who the hell are we dealing with, Jemma?"

***

Stepp and Nichols were driving down the same highway that led to the Krammer farm. When they were four miles away, they took an unmarked dirt road on the right. Nichols held a map of surveyed land with an orange "X" that marked the spot Stepp had told him about yesterday in the office. The Krammer farm was marked by a yellow line as was a large parcel of state land that bordered the Krammer property. Stepp's black Lincoln Navigator bumped along the dirt road that was heavily marked with private property signs, all provided by the state of New Hampshire. Two miles in, Stepp slowed and then stopped the car in the middle of the road.

Nichols looked out the window at all the dense trees. "How you know this is the place?"

Stepp pointed out his window. "That tree has a funny-shaped limb."

Nichols smiled and shook his head. He stepped out of the car and walked around the front toward Stepp.

"I got it marked on the odometer. We're two point two miles from the main highway. You're no fun, Nichols."

"Oh, I'm fun. I'm just no fun while I'm working and missing my girls' soccer games."

"Fair enough. Let's walk, check it out, and get you back home."

Nichols followed Stepp, who was using his GPS on his phone. For the next twenty minutes, they sidestepped mud puddles and fallen limbs as they made their way through heavy brush and trees. Finally, Stepp came to a stop in front of a manmade shack built of wood. "This is it."

Nichols carefully walked around the structure that was completely sheltered and hidden among the thick forest. "And you said the state surveyor found this?"

"Yes, by accident, last summer. The state plans to cut the timber this spring."

Nichols closely inspected the small frame. Nails had been used to hold various splintered limbs together to form a ten-by-ten hut-shaped structure. The roof had long ago crumbled away, and the remaining branches and wood dusted the floor of the hut. "Any idea how old this is?"

"That's the tricky part. I get different answers, but, yes, it could have been constructed and standing at the same time the girl's body was discovered."

Nichols looked at Stepp. "If that is so, they missed it when they searched the area."

"That would be a fair statement. Yes, but we're looking at just shy of five hundred acres here. Plus, for the last five years, the state has opened this land up for hunters for hunting season. Hunting closed last summer, and that's when the surveyors came out to reassess. Once the timber is cut and replanted, they'll open it back up again."

"Hunters don't build structures like this. They use deer stands."

"Except those weren't allowed by the state," Stepp said.

"And nothing else was found, no trash, nothing?"

Stepp nodded. "Nothing to help our investigation."

Nichols walked around the structure once more and then unrolled the map he was carrying. He studied the distance from where they left the car and the orange X. Then he looked at the property line for the Krammer farm.

Stepp walked over and looked at the map. "What are you thinking?"

"We're only about a ten-minute walk to the Krammer place. What if Shannon Krammer's imaginary friend was real and lived in the woods?"

CHAPTER 22

The morning rays were barely seeping through the wood blinds when Andrew Lane was woken by the sound of his cell phone ringing beside him. He slowly opened his eyes as his vision adjusted to the room. Immediately, his head reminded him of the wine he consumed with his wife and his late-night venture. With it came other intimate images between him and his wife. He looked toward her, expecting to find her still sleeping beside him, but she was gone. Andrew slightly frowned as he turned toward the nightstand to his ringing phone and the time displayed on the clock. *Nine oh five. Who calls this early on a Saturday morning?*

He reached for the phone and saw Sheriff Kennedy's name lit up on the screen. Clarity filled his head, and he rose with a sick feeling in his gut. "Andrew Lane."

"Kennedy. Sorry to call so early, but we got another body at Mathews Park."

Andrew sighed with disgust. "Not again."

"It gets worse."

Andrew slowly stepped out of bed and picked up his trousers. "Is that possible?" He pulled them on, walked toward the bathroom, and flipped the light switch.

"Yeah, I'm afraid so. She's been IDed. It's Joy Sutton."

Andrew looked into the mirror and saw his face: a person he no longer recognized. Quickly he turned away. "I can be there in thirty."

"No need for that. Just wanted you to know ASAP. Why don't you drop by the station this afternoon? That will give us more time to examine the crime scene and give you more time to come up with a statement to give to the press."

"The press," he mumbled.

"That's why I'm calling, to give you the heads up. You need to be on your A game. We need to appear confident, strong, and united."

Andrew walked back into his bedroom and looked at the unmade bed and his wife's new red dress lying on the floor. Two empty wine glasses were on her nightstand beside the empty wine bottle. He had fallen asleep last night in a state of peace and fulfilment. How quickly it all was wiped away by morning light. His temples throbbed as he tried to pull himself together. He took a deep breath and finally replied to Kennedy. "I'll be there at two."

"Good, I'll set up a conference at three."

Andrew ended the call and placed his phone back down on the nightstand. He slowly sat on the bed and buried his head in his hands. *What the hell have I gotten myself into?*

***

As Ashmore's red truck came to a stop, Dr. Marlee Hoyt stepped out of her state-issued van. She looked at Ashmore and Jemma. "We've got to stop meeting like this."

"No kidding," remarked Ashmore.

Jemma gave her a quick nod and waved her hand to get Kennedy's attention. The sheriff left his deputies and climbed the hill to the parking lot. Ashmore held the yellow tape as Jemma and Dr. Hoyt slid under. They all stood surrounded by a sea of flashing lights and officers darting about, patrolling the roped-off border.

"Glad you made it so quickly. News is already spreading fast."

"Then I better get started," Dr. Hoyt said and then walked down the sidewalk that led to the beach below.

Jemma looked around at the scene. "Pretty bold for him to come back here. Please tell me he's made a mistake."

For the first time, Sheriff Kennedy smiled. "He did. He left a set of footprints, trailing away from the body."

Jemma looked surprised. "What?"

"Yeah, I'll show you. Just follow my steps in the sand."

Jemma and Ashmore left the sidewalk and walked in a straight line that had already been marked off. Up ahead they could already see Joy Sutton, naked and lying in an unnatural position. A white tarp had been set up behind her to prevent unwanted peering eyes. Jemma continued, following Kennedy's steps as instructed. When they were five yards away, they stopped. Dr. Hoyt was carefully kneeling beside their victim and making notes. Joy's eyes were open, and a dark-blue line wrapped around her neck.

That same chill ran down her back. Jemma pulled her jacket tighter around her silk blouse. Death appeared to be by strangulation again. "Any idea how long she's been dead?"

Dr. Hoyt stopped writing and stood up. "Between twenty to thirty hours. I can narrow it down later."

Ashmore asked, "Do you know how long she's been at the park?"

She frowned. "Hard to say, but judging from all her bites, she laid here all night."

Jemma crossed her arms. Coldness turned to numbness as the realization sank in. She'd been unable to stop him again. She heard Kennedy talking about the evidence so she pried her eyes off Joy Sutton and looked at the yellow markers Kennedy was discussing. The stick markers with numbers had already been placed in the sand around Joy Sutton. Kennedy pointed. "Number three shows a set of footprints leading away from the body toward the tree line. Number six shows a clear set of size-eleven boot prints toward the parking lot."

Ashmore spoke. "Alec Deluca wore size-eleven boots."

"But he's dead, executed by the state," Kennedy replied.

Jemma said nothing as she processed the information and scanned the immediate area around Joy Sutton. *He could have waded into the water and walked out farther down the beach. Why leave the prints?* she thought to herself.

Kennedy directed their attention back toward the beach and the body. He continued, "Another set of prints along the shoreline. But those are Steven Bell's prints. They're consistent to his story. He was running and came to a dead stop within fifteen yards. Then he walked up toward the body and called nine one one. Luckily for us, he was smart enough to backtrack and preserve the scene of the crime."

Ashmore turned to Jemma. "He's never left prints before. Why now?"

She shook her head. "He's changing the game, and I don't know why. Nothing's making sense."

"Maybe he's at his breaking point, spiraling out of control. Leaving two victims within hours of each other. Is he cracking?" asked Kennedy.

Ashmore added. "And he did call you last night and let us get close enough to see his vehicle."

"Yes, but…" Jemma mumbled as she looked around, thinking to herself. *There are many different ways to leave her body without leaving prints. Why did he do it?* She frowned. "It doesn't fit his MO. He's smart. This doesn't make sense."

Kennedy let out a small laugh. "Does brutally killing women and leaving them for dead ever make sense? I say it's a gift, and we need to run with it and be thankful he's screwing up."

Jemma raked a hand over her forehead, pushing back her hair that had fallen across her face as the wind picked up. "Don't get me wrong, Sheriff, I hope you're right. I hope he's cracking up, and if so, it's just a matter of time then before we find him."

Sheriff Kennedy nodded with a smile. Then he turned and walked back up the hill toward one of his deputies. Ashmore touched Jemma's arm. "He could have heard a vehicle or seen a boat, causing him to panic and dump Ms. Sutton quickly."

"Yes, maybe."

"Come on. Let's get to the station and see what the night crew came up with. They should have a very long list of vehicle registrations that match our SUV by now."

Jemma nodded and took one more last look at Joy Sutton. Sadness filled her heart as she bit back the pain of failure. The failure to find Joy Sutton in time and the failure again to catch her killer.

***

Stepp drove as Nichols studied the timeline associated with Shannon Krammer. At age seven, Shannon loses his brother Jonathan to UCLA, who at the time was his best friend. At age ten, Shannon creates imaginary playmates once the kids in the neighborhood reject him since he is so different. Martin Krammer, his dad, drops dead of a heart attack when he's fifteen, right about the same time Harrison Avery appears in his life as a new imaginary friend. Then, over the next ten months, Shannon is in and out of trouble with the law. Jonathan is nowhere around nor his sisters, just his mother for support. Then only one year later, a body is discovered on their property. Today, Shannon lives alone with his mother and is highly dependent on her as his caregiver. He continues to receive therapy twice a month.

Nichols looks over at Stepp. "If I'm reading this right, Shannon Krammer has had a history of imaginary playmates from age ten to what, sixteen, when the state mandated extensive therapy with Dr. Raven Lisbet, who now claims he's free of imagined friends?"

Stepp chuckled. "That sounds about right."

"But what if among all those friends, Harrison Avery was real. We can't ignore that he shows up right around the time Deluca was sentenced for Laura Stone's death and assumed to be the River Strangler."

"No. But we also can't ignore that Harrison Avery also showed up with the death of his dad."

Nichols frowned. "Yeah, a good time to have a new friend." Nichols dropped the papers to his lap and looked out the window. "Even my gut tells me I'm reaching. There was no evidence that a serial killer built that shack. Hell, it could have been some neighborhood boys' summer fort. And we don't even know how long it's been standing."

Stepp brought his Navigator to a stop by the main road. "All is true, but we did find the body of Cherry Bowser in a place we shouldn't have."

Nichols looked at him and then his watch. "Too early for a house call?"

"You mean the doctor?" asked Stepp.

"No. The Krammers. Doc will just feed us bullshit on confidentiality."

Stepp smiled. "I do like how you think." He accelerated and turned right toward the Krammer ranch. "Never too early for a visit in my book when Cherry Bowser's killer is still at large."

As they drove the few miles toward the Krammer ranch, Nichols looked over the paperwork once more. Stepp slowed when the mailbox came in sight and turned down the dirt road. Nichols shoved the papers back in the manila envelope and dropped it on the floor. The two-story farmhouse came in full view. The Krammers' blue truck was parked in its usual spot.

"Looks like they're home," said Stepp as he pulled to a stop. He turned to Nichols. "What's our approach?"

"The truth. I think we'll get more cooperation from Ms. Krammer if we level with her."

Stepp opened his door. "I hope you're right."

As Nichols got out of the car, June Krammer stepped out on the porch, wearing a yellow housecoat and holding the same barking dog. She was the first to speak. "Well, this is a surprise. I thought you would be long gone by now."

Nichols gave her a warm smile as he approached. "Sorry for not calling ahead of time. We were just down the road on state property. Just took a chance you'd be home."

June commanded her dog, "You be quiet. I can't hear!" June tossed the dog inside and closed the door behind her. "So what can I do for you this time?" As if realizing she wasn't dressed yet, she crossed her arms over her chest.

Nichols climbed up the stairs. "Last summer, a handmade shack was discovered on the state property that borders your land. It's just about a ten-minute walk to the gravesite of Cherry Bowser."

Confusion spread across June's face. "OK, but what does that mean?"

Stepp neared them. "Well, honestly, ma'am, it could mean nothing. But we feel that we would be doing Ms. Cherry Bowser a disservice if we didn't explore every avenue surrounding her death."

June's facial muscles relaxed. "I understand. I would want someone to do the same for me if the situation was reversed. It's just... well, I just wish none of this would have ever happened. Lord knows I got a lot to deal with without it."

"Yes, ma'am. I appreciate all your cooperation," Stepp said sincerely.

"Why don't we take a seat?" June sat in the swing and motioned to the two wooden chairs beside her. "Shannon is inside watching cartoons. On a Saturday morning, he's in another world. Happy and content for hours."

Nichols smiled. "Then we will do our best not to hold you up during your free time."

June nodded with appreciation.

"The truth is, we don't know when that shack was constructed. It's hidden well among thick trees and brush. So it could have been there three years ago when the body was discovered, and we just missed it."

"I see. Funny how you take responsibility for missing something when you weren't up here looking."

He smirked. "We all work for the same agency, ma'am." Nichols turned serious. "I've been reading all the files, and I came across a name: Harrison Avery. Shannon's supposedly imaginary friend."

Sadness filled June's face. "Shannon's had a lot of friends that weren't real. Until he started working with Dr. Lisbet. Now he has none, real or imagined."

"I know this is difficult, but—"

She laughed. "Oh, Mr. FBI Agent, no you don't know difficult until you've spent a day in my shoes."

Nichols nodded. "You're right, I don't." A brief moment of awkward silence followed, and then Nichols pushed it away and continued. "The reason we asked about Harrison Avery in particular is due to the timing. He entered Shannon's life around the same time as the murder of Cherry Bowser."

June shook her head. "Dr. Lisbet said Harrison Avery was created as a direct result of Shannon losing his father, my Martin."

Stepp interjected, "And that may be correct, ma'am, but since we found that shed and there is even a hint of a slight possibility, well, we just can't sweep it under the rug. Not until we know for sure. For the sake of Cherry Bowser, we have to ask."

Nichols looked at Stepp. In his mind, he was laying it on a little thick. Stepp got the message and allowed Nichols to speak next. "We don't want to cause Shannon any duress so we thought it best to just ask you: what exactly do you remember about Harrison Avery?"

June pursed her lips. "It feels like a lifetime ago, and some days it doesn't. When Martin died, I wasn't myself, one reason Shannon got in so much trouble with the law." She looked into Nichols's eyes. "Life isn't fair sometimes, you know. I questioned God many times after Martin passed on just how much pain and suffering a person is expected to cope with and survive and remain faithful to the Almighty."

Nichols didn't make the same mistake twice of trying to understand her pain. He waited patiently without interrupting.

"I think your theory is off base, but what do I know. I'm not a detective."

"Anything you remember about Harrison Avery would be appreciated," Nichols prodded gently.

She began to swing as she searched her memory. Nichols and Stepp gave her all the time she needed. Finally, after what seemed like a full minute, she suddenly stopped swinging and her face turned white. "Ms. Krammer, are you all right?" Nichols stood and laid a hand on her arm.

"Shannon asked me one day to make him a picnic to take in the woods. When I did, he looked at the basket and turned mean. I didn't make anything for Harrison."

Nichols released her arm and took a seat again. "That's good, June. What else do you remember?"

"He insisted on me making another sandwich." June buried her head in her hand.

Nichols looked at Stepp and then back at June. "Take your time."

She dropped her hand and looked at Nichols with glassy eyes, as if she had seen a ghost. "He said Harrison would be hungry since he was building a house."

Nichols immediately pictured the shack in his head. *Was Shannon capable of building it alone?* "Ms. Krammer, I want you to think real hard. Has Shannon ever built something with a hammer and nails?"

Color returned to her face as she rubbed it, and then she dropped her hand to rest it on her chest. Nichols did everything in his power to hold his tongue as he sat on pins and needles, waiting on her reply. Finally, she shook her head and responded, "No, never."

CHAPTER 23

The police station parking lot was full when Andrew Lane pulled in. He circled around and then left to park at his office just a few blocks over. He walked swiftly down the sidewalk, taking in the activity around him. News vans lined the opposite side of the street in anticipation of the afternoon press conference set for an hour from now. He had thought of coming in earlier but felt it was best to stay home with Bianca since their youngest one woke up with a fever this morning. Fortunately, by the time he left, the fever had responded to the children's Motrin. Teething was the suspected culprit.

Andrew climbed the stairs to the police station and opened the door. Immediately, he was met with extra security. He was waved to the front of the line by Officer Byron. He relinquished his keys, wallet, and ID and then walked through an X-ray machine. They talked briefly as he pocketed his items and was directed straight back to Sheriff Kennedy's office. The sheriff was expecting him.

Officer Williams was seated outside of the sheriff's office, talking on the phone. She pointed over her shoulder for him to go on in as she answered questions. Andrew nodded, stepped forward, and opened the door. Kennedy was alone, sitting behind his desk in the room. He looked up at Andrew and dropped a paper he was holding. He looked as if he hadn't slept in days, probably the same thing someone would say about him if Andrew bothered to ask anyone. Of course, he didn't ask, but Bianca had made flippant comments about his red eyes when he left the house, confirming the fact that he looked like shit, just like Kennedy. Andrew took the chair in front of the sheriff.

"I wrote a statement. I think it's not enough…hell, I know it's not enough. Here, take a look. Add to it if you can."

Andrew took the paper and began reading aloud. "I would like to confirm that at eight o'clock this morning, the body of Virginia state lawyer Ms. Joy Sutton of Richmond, Virginia, was found along the shores of Mathews Park by an early-morning runner. Ms. Sutton was last seen at Alec Deluca's execution and was reported missing two days later. Our department and the FBI are working closely…Um, I think you need to start with Melissa Jarman."

Kennedy frowned. "I thought of that. But I already made a brief comment late last night, and they ran it with the story first thing this morning. And again at noon," he said, raising his voice.

Andrew looked back at the statement and finished reading it. When he was done, he gave the paper back to Kennedy. "Start with a follow-up on Melissa Jarman and then confirm Joy Sutton. Treat them the same and link it all to our unknown psychopath terrorizing the city."

"OK. And what do you plan on saying when they ask about Alec Deluca?"

Andrew took a deep breath and sat back in his chair. "I don't know."

Kennedy leaned forward. "You don't know? You've had all morning to think about it."

Andrew stood, walked over to the window, and opened the blinds. The crowd along the front entrance had begun to spill over onto the sidewalks and street, closing off traffic. He closed the blinds and turned to face Kennedy. "We stick with the same story. We strongly feel Alec Deluca was guilty for the murder of Laura Stone."

"But not Dawn Newberry, Daisy Gwen, or Cameron Long? We just openly admit we never caught their killers?" Kennedy stood. "We'd be walking into a shitstorm with the media."

Andrew smirked. "And we aren't already?" Andrew walked toward Kennedy. "We're screwed either way. The best thing we can do at this point is give the facts. When Deluca was arrested, the killings stopped. No, the jury didn't convict Deluca of Newberry, Long, and Gwen, but the killings stopped. And then we just keep reminding them that we are working and patrolling nonstop with the help of the FBI until this madman is caught."

"Andrew, we've got four dead women in one week. Nothing I'm going to say is going to calm their fears and rightfully so. Hell, my own wife's afraid to leave the house and wants to keep our girls out of school next week."

There was a long pause, and both men took their seats again. Andrew took the paper back and reread Kennedy's prepared statement. When he laid it on the desk, he asked, "Is the FBI gonna stand with us at the press conference?"

Kennedy nodded. "Not Nichols but Rhodes. Nichols is in New Hampshire working on a lead."

Andrew's interest was piqued. "New Hampshire? Why didn't you say something before?"

"Because at this point he's got nothing, and the last thing I want to do is look like a moron with egg on his face if he still comes back with nothing."

"OK, what does Agent Rhodes plan to say?"

Kennedy shook his head. "FBI has nothing. There's nothing she can say other than what's right here."

Andrew looked at his watch. "Thirty minutes." Andrew removed his pen from his shirt pocket. "Let's make this the best we can."

***

On the third floor, Agent Rhodes was sitting at a table viewing the list of motor-vehicle registrations that had been pulled from earlier. The list of dark SUVs registered in Norfolk County was high. What made it worse, most people who drove SUVs fit the right age category of their profile. Jemma grabbed a peanut-butter cookie off a platter that had arrived at the same time as sandwiches. *My third or fourth cookie?* She shook her head as she tossed some papers aside and looked at Ashmore sitting across from her. "You find anything, because I'm not."

"No."

She twirled a pencil between her fingers. "Whatever came of the spray paint bought on Virginia Beach?"

"Credit card tracked it to a local art teacher who lives four miles away from where the paint was sold."

Jemma frowned. "Figures. If we could get so lucky. And that dog walker who was asking all those questions at Mathews Park? I never got that e-mail from the officer."

"Sorry about that. But there was nothing to report. He probably just got busy with something else."

Jemma reached for another stack of paper. "There's always something to report."

Ashmore nodded. "I'll make sure you get it."

Jemma's phone vibrated on the table. She laid down the MVR printout and picked it up, seeing Nichols's name. "It's Nichols." Jemma stood and slid the screen to answer his call. "Rhodes." She paced as Nichols replied on the other end. "What? Hold that, I'm going to put you on speaker for Ashmore." Jemma sat back down, and Ashmore came around the table and stood beside her.

"I said I think we have that break we've been looking for."

"Tell us."

"Remember what I told you about the Krammer farm where the body of Cherry Bowser was found?"

"Yes," Jemma responded.

"Well, the son Shannon Krammer has had a history of imaginary playmates, but new information has emerged. I think one of those playmates, Harrison Avery, was real. "

"You think Shannon was an accessory to a crime and didn't know?" asked Jemma.

"I don't think he knew his imaginary friend was evil, but he told stories about spending time with him in the woods."

"Wow, unbelievable. Everyone just thought it was in his head."

Nichols explained, "It was around the time of the death of his father, so, yeah, everyone contributed his imagination to his state of mental health. Look, the mother has agreed to bring Shannon in and let him meet with our psychologist and sketch artist. We're setting it up later this afternoon."

"So you think this Harrison Avery was a drifter and killed Cherry Bowser."

"Maybe."

"What about the other missing women over the last five years? Anything?"

"No. The work done up here was top notch. They just disappeared."

"So all we have to go on is that Cherry Bowser was tied up and strangled."

"Just like the work of our river rat," Nichols replied.

"We need Dr. Hoyt to compare Bowser's medical records to our first three victims'."

"Already got in touch with her. She should get back with me later today."

"Hopefully. She has her hands full with Joy Sutton now. But hey, if they're anywhere close, then this Harrison Avery could be our River Strangler who did in fact leave town and continued taking lives," remarked Jemma.

Nichols sighed. "It's the only thing we have close to a lead so it's definitely worth a shot. Besides, I've got a good feeling about this."

Jemma rested her chin on her hands as she stared at the phone, contemplating his every word. Finally, she replied, "Well, OK then. Let's run with it, and I'll try to connect the timeline from what you sent me earlier."

"Thanks, Jemma. I'll be in touch after the therapy session."

Jemma pressed the "end" button and looked at Ashmore. "What do you think?"

Ashmore shook his head. "I didn't see the timeline he sent you."

Jemma nodded and picked up the printed email for Ashmore to read. It listed the dates and locations of the women missing along with the details of Cherry Bowser's body found on the Krammer farm. Jemma reread it as Ashmore read it for the first time.

"Only one woman found. Man, it does sound like a longshot, but like ya'll said, we've got nothing else to go on."

"And she was strangled with her hands and feet bound together." Jemma laid down the timeline. "We need to hear from Dr. Hoyt."

"We can't ask her to stop working on Ms. Sutton. She probably won't get to the Bowser file till evening."

"No, we can't. We'll just have to wait." Jemma picked up her pencil and began to tap on the timeline.

"You said earlier that serial killers are rare. So you're saying the chances of another serial killer at large taking women from the northeast so soon after the River Strangler is slim?" asked Ashmore.

"Yes. Especially since Nichols has come across six missing women over the last five years. It's like our guy up and left Norfolk and the spotlight but continued killing. Who knows how many were killed that were never reported."

"We need to search our databank for renewed licenses in the last six months," Ashmore said as he made a note on some paper.

"Or he has always lived here and travels with work," Jemma added.

Ashmore frowned. "Yeah, he could have picked up hitchhikers, young teens who ran away. Lots reported every year that go unsolved."

Jemma looked at the e-mail again. "But maybe not. He was gone long enough on the Krammer farm to befriend a mentally challenged kid. Check the records for someone renewing his driver's license from living out of state. Maybe, just maybe it's that simple."

Ashmore stood and walked back around to his computer. He sat and looked at Jemma across the table. "There's that optimistic spirit coming back."

Jemma smiled, but it was short lived. She spotted Sheriff Kennedy and Andrew Lane walking in. "You stay here and keep working. There's no need for you to be at the press conference."

Ashmore turned around and saw Kennedy and Lane. He turned back to Jemma. "You gonna tell them about Nichols in New Hampshire?"

Jemma stood. "Not now. I want to see what he's got first."

Ashmore nodded. "I'll keep working then. Good luck."

She turned back around. "Thanks, we're all gonna need it."

CHAPTER 24

The muted TV flashed different shades of color across the semi dark living room as it advertised a washing detergent. The thirty-year-old brunette actress, an all-American housewife, picked up her equally adorable toddler off the floor and looked into the camera with a big smile. He laughed as he sat alone, drinking a cup of coffee and waiting on the much-anticipated news conference that was promised to take place shortly. Another commercial and then a special report from the local Norfolk news channel flashed on the screen. He picked up his remote and pressed the mute button. Sound filled the room as Bob Free, looking somber, appeared behind a desk with Channel 12's logo displayed largely for the viewing audience.

The screen switched to a new scene with Linda Peet front and center. Her voice took on a serious tone as she explained that she was downtown at the Norfolk police headquarters waiting on a press conference from Sheriff Kennedy and the FBI. Noise erupted behind her, and she quickly stepped away from the camera as it zoomed in on a group of three individuals who walked up behind a podium and took their places. Sheriff Kennedy, who looked as if he had swallowed a lemon, gripped the podium. The man held back his laughter as Kennedy began talking and his face took on a rosy peach color. He needed to hear what they had to say.

"Today, it is with great sadness that I confirm the deaths of two women."

"Two?" He turned up the volume.

"Melissa Jarman, mother of four and a loving wife, resides here in Norfolk with her family. She was reported missing yesterday, and her body was discovered last night in Norfolk. The second woman, Ms. Joy Sutton, a Virginia state public defender who was representing Alec Deluca in his final days, was discovered early this morning at Mathews Park."

Noise erupted from the crowd, and Sheriff Kennedy raised his hand. "My staff and I will answer questions at the end. Please allow me to finish."

The crowd grew quiet except for the flash of cameras.

"I'm saddened by this news, and my department, along with the FBI, is working around the clock, trying to apprehend this killer living among us and terrorizing our community."

He smiled as Kennedy recapped the past. His chest swelled with pride at the mention of the River Strangler and his victims. His eyes left the TV and moved toward his second bedroom, his death chamber. His need to kill again was strengthened.

Kennedy concluded, "At this time, I'd like to introduce FBI Agent Rhodes, who is assisting in this investigation."

He smiled and leaned forward as the camera gave the viewers a close-up of the five-eight, auburn-haired, fit thirty-two-year-old. He looked into her emerald eyes that were accentuated by her fair-complexioned skin. *Agent Rhodes. Nice to see you again. Oh, I see that nasty cut. I really wasn't going to hit you. I must say though, the camera agrees more with you than the sheriff.*

Jemma moved in behind the microphone. "Good afternoon. First of all, I'd like to give my condolences to the families of Hazel Rice, Jacklyn Riggs, Melissa Jarman, and Joy Sutton." The hardness of her face softened to tenderness as she paused after speaking each name. "As Sheriff Kennedy spoke earlier, we are working around the clock and following every possible lead. Please understand that we will provide only information that will help our investigation instead of hampering our efforts."

She paused as she glanced around the room, as if she was studying each face. He wondered if she thought he was there, watching. *Not today, Agent Rhodes.*

"We are actively searching for a dark-colored, new-model SUV that was seen speeding away from downtown from the south side of the football stadium at the block of eighteen hundred River Drive, approximately at eight fifty-five p.m. The suspect is believed to be male, in his late thirties to late forties. If you happened to see this event last night, please call the sheriff's department at the number on the screen. Please do not approach this man or his vehicle; he's considered armed and very dangerous."

Oh just perfect! Looking for the SUV now. Following along right on schedule, Agent Rhodes.

Low whispers filled the room, and Agent Rhodes paused for the information to sink in. "Also, we believe the body of Joy Sutton was dropped off at Mathews Park sometime between sunset yesterday evening and sunrise this morning. Again, if you were in that area and remember seeing anything unusual or a dark SUV, please call the number on the screen."

Deep laugher filled the apartment. *Oh my, what have we here? This is getting more interesting by the minute. They think I killed Joy Sutton?* He leaned back on his couch and placed a hand over his mouth to stifle the sound of his laughter. *I couldn't have thrown a better curve ball myself.*

Agent Rhodes's face turned serious again as she reminded the great citizens of Norfolk to call the number if they had any further information. Next up behind the podium was Andrew Lane. *Oh, Andrew, my, oh my. I would say the years have been very kind to you. Is Bianca still that sweet little Southern peach I met at the ballpark? Or did she turn thick and round after birthing all your babies?* On the screen, Andrew Lane gave his condolences as well. *Yeah, yeah, yeah, get on with it. What do you have to say?*

"At this time, the District Attorney's Office is working actively with this investigation as the case against Alec Deluca is revisited. Until proven otherwise, the state still stands behind the execution of Alec Deluca for the murder of Laura Stone, of which he was convicted. I would like to remind the public that Alec Deluca was not charged for the murders of Dawn Newberry, Daisy Gwen, and Cameron Long."

Of course you want Deluca responsible for the death of Laura Stone. Tsk-tsk, Andrew. We both know the real truth. Now, what did you do to Ms. Sutton, hmm? She find out something she wasn't supposed to? Your little perfect house of cards will soon fall, and it couldn't happen to a better man.

Noise erupted among the crowd. Lane raised his hands and waited as the noise ceased. His face was a ruby red now as he continued. "Once Alec Deluca was arrested, the murders ceased. Alec Deluca was looked at for all the murders but was only convicted of Laura Stone's death based on the evidence presented to the court. I, along with this community, wanted to believe Alec Deluca was the River Strangler. And when there were no more murders, we all turned a new page and began living our lives once again without the constant fear."

Still a smooth talker, aren't you, Andrew? Well, I guess you wouldn't be where you are today if you weren't.

"Again, the District Attorney's Office is in full cooperation with the Sheriff's Department and the FBI. Every file in the Deluca case will be combed over again and again, looking for anything we might have missed five years ago."

The man laughed. *I'm sure you'll be leading the way, Andrew.*

Sheriff Kennedy placed a hand on Andrew, cuing that he was done. *Yeah, better stop now, Andrew, before you make too many promises that you sure aren't going to be able to deliver.*

The OK was given for the news media to ask questions. It was to no one's surprise that Sheriff Kennedy called on Linda Peet, the leading newscaster in Norfolk.

"Agent Rhodes, earlier you said a dark-colored SUV was speeding away from the football stadium. Are you saying that our River Strangler, who obviously isn't Alec Deluca, was in attendance at our high school rivalry game last night?"

Agent Rhodes moved behind the podium. He could tell she wasn't happy with the comment about Alec Deluca. He smiled as she kept her cool under pressure.

"I was at the football stadium when I received a phone call from whom I believe is the man who killed Melissa Jarman. When I spotted him, I gave chase and was almost run over in the process. So yes, I believe the man who killed Melissa Jarman was at the stadium last night, and if anyone saw the dark-colored SUV of interest, please call the Sheriff's Department."

"Where was the body of Melissa Jarman found?" asked Linda Peet.

Agent Rhodes looked at Sheriff Kennedy briefly and then faced Ms. Peet. "I'm sorry, but at this time, that information will not be released. And also, that unfortunately ends this press conference."

Noise erupted again as everyone realized no more questions would be accepted contrary to what was stated earlier by the sheriff. Agent

Rhodes spoke loudly in the microphone, silencing the crowd. "We have a job to do, and we're going to get back to it. You'll receive more information when available if it doesn't hamper our investigation. This concludes our press conference."

The man took a sip of his coffee and realized his afternoon shot of caffeine had turned cold. He placed the cup back down and lifted the remote, turning the TV off. *I think it's time to hit the coffee shop downtown, see what's going on.*

Jemma Rhodes rushed out of the room that had held the press conference with Kennedy on her heels. When they were out of earshot of the media, he grabbed her arm and spun her around. "We agreed to answer more questions."

Jemma narrowed her eyes and pulled her arm back. "We gave them enough." She looked at Andrew Lane. "What was that all about? You went off script!" Jemma looked from Lane to Kennedy. "What we believe doesn't matter. It's what the killer believes we think that matters. Don't pull that bullshit again. The less we put out there, the less our killer will know our direction." She took a step back and took a deep breath. She was letting the killer rattle her. She looked at Kennedy. "Nichols has a lead, and at this time, it's our only lead. Come back to the situation room, and I'll fill you in."

Lane followed them down the hall. Jemma pressed the button on the elevator and turned to Lane. "I'm sorry, Mr. Lane, but this doesn't concern you. Someone will contact you if needed."

Andrew looked hurt as he stepped away, raising his hands in the air as if he got it and it was no big deal. Kennedy stepped forward as the doors opened. Once inside, he turned and remarked, "Call me if you find something."

Andrew Lane nodded as the doors closed.

CHAPTER 25

The room was painted white with a long table in the middle surrounded by eight chairs. One wall had a mirror that allowed people on the other side to listen and watch. This room on the fifth floor of the FBI field office in Concord, New Hampshire, was known as interrogation room number three. Nichols had gone back and forth on which room to use for the interview with Shannon Krammer. If he chose another room that was warmer in color and had comfortable seating, would his potential witness become too relaxed? In the end, Nichols followed his gut. He would rather Shannon feel scared than comfortable.

Nichols and Stepp had greeted June and Shannon Krammer downstairs in the lobby. June had informed them that she had called her son, Jonathan, and he would be calling them later. Nichols was still trying to figure out why June had divulged that information when they stepped on the elevator. Clearly, she was here with Shannon and no lawyer. What was she implying? A threat of some kind?

Shannon hovered in the corner of the elevator. He was looking at his faded white sneakers as he shifted his weight from one foot to the other. He had not yet made eye contact with anyone that lasted longer than a millisecond. June stood near him with a hand on his arm, patting it gently. No one said anything as the group rode the elevator. Nichols stepped out and motioned down the hall. "Second door on the right."

Shannon looked up at Nichols but quickly looked away when Nichols reciprocated. Nichols began to second-guess himself about the room choice.

Stepp opened the door and walked in, holding the door for everyone to enter. Inside the room were two other agents, both strangers to Shannon. He stopped when he saw them, but June, who was right on his heels, slightly pushed him. "Why don't we sit here, Shannon, beside each other?" She pulled a chair out for Shannon, and Stepp closed the door.

"Ms. Krammer and Shannon, I'd like you to meet Agent Phillips and Agent Cashmere. Agent Cashmere is also a licensed psychologist, and Agent Phillips is an artist." Nichols spoke as he pulled out a chair and took a seat across from June and Shannon. Handshakes were exchanged between June and the agents only. June looked at her son to comply but then quickly dismissed the idea and looked back at Nichols.

"Shannon knows why he's here. I told him that we have come to help that poor girl who was buried on our property. Shannon wants to help. He feels very sad about her death." June patted Shannon's arm as she talked.

Shannon peeled his eyes off the table and looked at his mother. "Yes, Momma." He looked back down at the table. June gave a nod to Nichols, indicating that they were ready.

Nichols couldn't help but feel sorry for Shannon Krammer. He was a grown man dressed in a vintage *Sesame Street* T-shirt. He knew June had chosen the T-shirt not for style but because Grover, Cookie Monster, Big Bird, Elmo, and Burt, his friends from Saturday morning TV, would bring him much comfort today. Nichols lifted a pad of paper from the table and signaled to Agent Cashmere to begin.

With a honey-warm voice, Agent Juicy Cashmere made small talk with June and Shannon. After about three minutes, she had Shannon's full attention and eye contact. Nichols hid his smile. He had called Cashmere hours ago and told her to drop everything and get her butt on a plane to Concord. She readily agreed after hearing about Shannon. Juicy Cashmere lived for challenges, and she was one of the top psychologists in the agency. Thankfully, she lived nearby in New York, where this could happen today before June Krammer changed her mind.

"Now, Shannon, I'd like to go back in time. A few years ago when you met your friend, Harrison Avery."

Shannon's eyes showed a hint of confusion, and Nichols grew worried that the other doctor had erased Harrison Avery away with all his other imaginary playmates.

"Think back to the woods. You used to have picnics and watch Harrison build his new fort." A glimmer of recognition twinkled in his blue eyes. "I bet Harrison sure was hungry after working so hard on that fort. Did you ever help him, Shannon?"

Slowly Shannon nodded.

"I thought so. It sure looked good. Strong enough to hold both of you while you picnicked inside."

"Very strong. Harrison used my daddy's hammer and nails."

A sense of pride filled Shannon's face. Cashmere responded, "I bet it was. Your daddy was a hard worker on the farm; his tools were the best."

Nichols noticed June look away, doing her best to say nothing or add to the discussion. Nichols had instructed her earlier on the phone on what was expected along with the procedure to follow.

"I never got to meet Harrison. I live in New York City. The big city with lots of people. If I ever come across Harrison, would you like me to say hello for you?"

Shannon gave a big nod up and down, up and down. Cashmere smiled. "I tell you what. I will tell him, but, Shannon, like I said, there are a lot of people in New York City. Why don't you tell me his hair color?"

"Brown."

She looked over toward Agent Phillips. "Does it have a little gray like his?"

Shannon shook his head no.

Cashmere turned on her charming voice again. "So Harrison looks younger?"

He nodded.

"How about his eyes. Does he wear glasses?"

"No," Shannon replied.

Cashmere continued. "What about his—"

Shannon interrupted, "They were blue like mine."

Nichols noticed how Cashmere twisted her lips to hide her smile. She looked over at Nichols briefly and then back to Shannon. "Wow. Good memory. You must have spent a lot of time with Harrison Avery to remember his eye color."

"We built fort every day, and I would—" Shannon paused and looked at his mother. He suddenly stopped talking.

Cashmere made a little cough. "I'm getting thirsty. How about you, Shannon and Ms. Krammer?"

June made no effort to hide her frown. Cashmere had just given her the cue to leave and come back in five minutes with drinks. June removed her hand from Shannon's arm. "I'll go get some drinks. My legs need walking anyhow. Shannon, can I get you your favorite soft drink?"

His eyes beamed at his mother. June didn't allow Shannon to have soft drinks except on holidays and birthdays. "Yes, Momma, please."

June closed her eyes and nodded. When she opened her eyes back up, she looked at Nichols as she pushed back her chair. Nichols stood also. "I'll go help." Outside the room, Nichols directed her to the room next door. They entered and walked over to the mirrored window to watch and listen.

Cashmere gave them enough time to get into the other room by filling the moments with comments about the weather. "Shannon, when you built that fort, was it snowing yet?"

"No. It was hot. That's why I had to bring Harrison lots of water. I made many trips during the day."

"What a good friend you are, Shannon."

"Sometimes I told Momma I was washing the pigs with the water."

"Oh, well, that was a good story you told her."

June looked at Nichols. "I don't…never mind. That's not important now."

Nichols lifted his hand and placed it on her arm. "We really appreciate this. I know this isn't easy."

"And terrifying! My son interacted with a stranger, and I had no knowledge?" She quieted as Shannon answered another question.

"Harrison wasn't here in the cold. He left in shorts."

"Did he say good-bye?"

Shannon nodded.

"Did he say he would come back?"

"He said he would try."

"I'm sure he would. Now, if I see Harrison on the streets of New York, will he be taller than you?"

"Yes. He was taller than Jonathan."

Cashmere nodded and made a note. She looked back up and met Shannon's eyes. She smiled. "Going back to his brown hair. Did it grow long while he lived in the fort?"

Shannon smiled really big. "That was funny. I brought him scissors. He cut it before he left."

"Did he cut it very short or more like your hair, Shannon?"

"Very short. I had to go back and find a mirror for him to use."

"You have a nice laugh and smile, Shannon. I've been told I have a cute little dimple right here when I smile." Cashmere pointed to her cheek as she smiled. "Did Harrison have one of these?"

Shannon became frustrated when he didn't have the answer. "That's OK, Shannon. What about a tattoo? With it being hot, Harrison probably removed his shirt. Did he have any tattoos?"

Shannon relaxed. He knew the answer. "A baseball. And 'mom' on his arm." Shannon busted out laughing. "No, he didn't. 'Mom' on your arm is stupid. That's what Jonathan told me."

Cashmere looked at the window to signal a break. Nichols picked up the tray of drinks on the table and left with June. They reentered and took their seats after passing out the drinks. Several moments went by as Shannon poured his drink over a cup of ice. He quickly drank the entire cup and refilled it.

"Not so fast, Shannon," June spoke quietly.

Shannon gave her a pouty look and continued drinking until the drink was gone. Cashmere quickly intervened. "Hey, Shannon, you getting hungry?"

He nodded.

"Yeah, me too. I've got some change, and there is a vending machine down the hall. Do you want to go with me and help me pick out something?" Shannon didn't immediately answer so she prodded. "I'll need some help carrying it."

Finally, he stood without answering and walked straight to the door without turning around to face his mother. When they left, Nichols said, "She knows what's she's doing. Trust us; trust her."

June let out a deep sigh that she'd been holding in a long time. "This is excruciating. I keep thinking next I'm gonna hear he helped dig a hole."

Nichols looked at Agent Phillips at the end of the table. "Were you able to get anything?"

He laughed as he flipped it over. "Just blue eyes and short brown hair."

Nichols grinned. "I'm not complaining; we already got more than I'd hoped."

"And she'll get more while in the break room. You'll see."

Nichols hoped he was right. The break room had a wall of moveable body parts. If Shannon was willing, maybe Cashmere could get him to play a game to construct Harrison Avery. Nichols looked at his watch. If they were gone more than five minutes, he'd have his answer. He looked at June. "You OK?"

"Yes, well, I think."

"How tall is Jonathan?" Nichols asked.

"He's right around six feet. And that other thing about the tattoo." She smirked. "Harrison wanted to get a tattoo, and Jonathan had joked around with Shannon that maybe it should read 'mom' on the shoulder because only sissies get tattoos. He wasn't serious. Jonathan has a tattoo; he was just trying to talk Shannon out of having one at fif…" Her voice faded. "It was the summer Jonathan came home, when Martin…Shannon was just fifteen."

"Had to have been the summer the fort was being built. He saw Harrison's tattoo and wanted one too."

"I guess."

"June, think back. Do you remember that story about taking water outside to wash the pigs?"

She shook her head. "No. But the summer after Martin passed, I don't remember a lot of things. It was a rough time for me." She looked down briefly and then back at Nichols. "You really think Harrison Avery is real and was in our woods that summer? You know this could all still be in his head. All lies and stories. Just a part of his memory before the doctor cured him of imaginary friends."

Nichols slid his notepad toward her, which showed a brief timeline he was working on. "Shannon is fifteen. His dad dies in May; Jonathan comes home and stays several weeks into June. Shannon wants a tattoo; Harrison Avery becomes a friend. Next year, Cherry Bowser's body is found by hunters in early January. What do you think?"

"You don't want to know what I think. But what I want is for all this to be in his head. I wanna get back in my truck and drive back to the farm and live out our lives peacefully. That, Agent Nichols, is what I want."

CHAPTER 26

A list of dark SUVs in Norfolk County had been narrowed down to two sheets of paper. Jemma and Nichols were slowly analyzing each registered address along with homeowner's information when Sheriff Kennedy walked in the room.

"We got two teenage girls waiting in conference room one. They claim they have information about Friday night."

Jemma couldn't hide her excitement as she rushed over to him. "Have you talked to them yet? Are they credible?"

"Not personally, just got the call from Officer Brown. But he thinks they might have something. Come on; they're waiting on us downstairs."

Ashmore and Jemma followed him down the hall and took the stairs down one flight. They immediately saw Officer Brown standing outside conference room one. He opened the door to reveal two normal-looking teenage girls standing huddled together and playing on their phones. At the sound of the door, they looked their way, and Officer Brown quickly made introductions. "Sheriff Kennedy, Agent Rhodes, Detective Ashmore, I'd like to introduce you to Stacie Holt and Leigh Paine. These two girls have some information about Friday night they'd like to share."

Jemma shook each of their hands, thanking them for coming in. "Let's have a seat here. Do either of you want a soft drink or chips?"

Stacie answered, "No thank you, he already asked." She smiled at Officer Brown, who was standing by the doorway. Officer Brown returned her smile and left the room.

They all took a seat, with Jemma and Ashmore across from the young women. Kennedy pulled up a chair on the end of the table. "Ladies, I know you've already told your story to Officer Brown, but I'd like for you to retell the story again, please," requested Kennedy.

"Sure," Leigh replied.

Jemma nodded. "OK. Let's start with your ages. How old are you girls?"

In unison they said, "Sixteen."

Jemma gave them a warm smile. "So why are you here today?"

Stacie looked at Leigh. "You should probably tell them. You saw more than me."

"Yeah, OK, um, well, we came in because we thought we saw what you were talking about in the news conference today."

Ashmore replied, "You two were at the game Friday night?"

They both nodded in acknowledgment. "Except I wasn't feeling well, and Leigh has her license so I asked her to bring me home."

"Do you remember what time you left?" asked Jemma.

The girls looked at each other, and then they both pulled out their phones and started scrolling. "I texted my mom at eight twenty and told her we were leaving," Stacie answered. "She was going to pick me up, but I think my sister had what I had, and she didn't want to leave her alone. Some stomach bug that's been going around."

"I texted my mom at eight thirty-four when we got in the car." She smiled. "It's a rule we have. I text when I'm leaving and then I put my phone away."

"Smart rule. Wish all drivers did the same," Ashmore said as he made some notes.

"Where was your car parked?"

"The parking lot behind the track field."

Jemma looked at Ashmore. He quickly tore off a sheet of paper and drew a square representing the stadium. Then he drew a smaller box and labeled it "shed." Jemma didn't have to ask why he drew that because that's where the body of Melissa Jarman was found. Information they had not yet given the public, just for cases like this one with the girls. Small lines were drawn to mark the fence that Jemma had to follow that eventually opened up to a parking lot. On the other side of the parking lot, farther from the stadium and the shed, he drew another oval to mark the track and field house. There he marked the parking lot the girls were referring to. "This where you parked?"

Leigh nodded after watching the diagram come to life. "I have track practice every morning at seven so I always park there in the mornings. I left my car there because Mom had to check me out for an orthodontist appointment so she just dropped me off later for the game."

"OK, we're following you. So what did you see?" asked Jemma.

"A man ran by my window and scared the crap out of me."

"Did he turn around and see you?" Jemma asked.

"No, I don't think so."

Jemma rolled the pen between her fingers and then stopped as she pushed the map toward Leigh again. "Mark exactly where you parked your car if you can remember."

Leigh drew a line by the field office. "I was in the second row, here."

"And what direction were you parked?"

She drew an arrow pointing away from the field house.

"Was a car parked in front of you?" asked Ashmore.

"Yeah, the parking lot was full."

Ashmore drew her car and marked an "X." "So you are sitting here. Show me where the man ran by."

Leigh pointed between the driver-side door and the car parked beside her. "There." Then she moved her finger forward. "He just kept running between the other cars in the third row."

"Leigh, from the time you girls shut the door, how long passed before you started your car?" Jemma asked.

A moment went by, and Stacie answered. "We climbed in, and we both took out our phones. You texted your mom, and I was making a post on Facebook. Right?" She looked at her friend for confirmation.

"Yeah, that's right. Then you showed me Belinda's post, and then we both responded. But I don't remember if I had cranked up the car yet."

"Are your headlights set to auto?" Ashmore asked.

"Yeah, they automatically come on when it's dark. Oh, they were off. When he ran by, I jumped and looked, but he was just a blur because the parking lot was semi lit."

Kennedy spoke for the first time. "That's good, Leigh. Do you remember anything about him?"

"He was wearing a ball cap and a jacket."

"Anything, Stacie?" asked Jemma.

"No. I was looking at my phone when she jumped and blurted out something like, 'Oh my God, he scared the crap out of me,' but when I asked who and looked forward, I couldn't see anything."

Jemma felt the anticipation begin to deflate around her. They needed more, lots more.

"Tell them what happened next," Kennedy prodded.

Jemma perked up as she realized there was indeed more.

"Well, we backed out, and we had to drive to the end to get out of the parking lot and—"

"Show me on the map," Jemma instructed anxiously.

"Um, well, this parking lot takes you back toward the stadium, and then you turn back to the right onto the main road." Leigh looked at Jemma for confirmation. Jemma nodded so she continued, "When we pulled out, this dark vehicle goes flying around us out of nowhere. I slammed on my brakes as he weaved in front of us."

"You get any of the license?" Ashmore asked.

Leigh bit her lip as she hesitated. "I thought it was Travis. It looked like his car so I sped up. When we got to the intersection ahead, he had to slow, and when he turned, I saw that it wasn't Travis and his Land Rover but a Ford Explorer, black."

"How sure are you that it was an Explorer?"

"Well, with the lights of downtown, I could see it better, and my mom drives one."

Jemma sat back and nodded. "Good. That's real good, Leigh, excellent."

"There's something else." Stacie spoke as she lifted her phone off her lap. "I took a picture. I don't like Travis, and I was going to get him in trouble. But it's blurry."

Time seemed to slow as Jemma reached out her hand to take the phone. She pulled it to her as Ashmore leaned in. "It's not that blurry, and it's part of his tag." Jemma looked up at Ashmore.

Ashmore nodded. "Stacie, we're gonna need to keep your phone for a while."

She gave them a slight frown. "I had figured as much."

"Who knows you're here?" Kennedy asked.

The girls looked at each other. "Well, that's complicated."

Jemma raised an eyebrow.

"We were supposed to be at the library studying, but, um, we weren't. We were hanging out at our friend Doug's house. We saw the news conference and came right over," Leigh said.

Stacie quietly asked, "Can we leave that part out?"

Jemma looked at them. "Girls, thank you for coming in. We greatly appreciate it." Jemma stood and held up the phone. "And Stacie, you'll get your phone back soon." Ashmore stood as well and Jemma looked at Kennedy. "We'll be in the lab."

Kennedy nodded. "Come on, girls, let's go call your parents."

CHAPTER 27

Three hours had passed since June and Shannon Krammer walked through the front doors of the FBI building. Shannon looked mentally drained, and June looked distraught with her dress wrinkled and her hair falling from her bobby pins. Self-consciously, she had run a hand through her shoulder-length hair numerous times as she paced the room, waiting on Shannon. Finally, Shannon was released from Agent Phillips. Agent Cashmere rewarded him with a double cheeseburger and large fries that lifted his spirits. Nichols had personally walked them both out to their truck, and he promised to get in contact if, in fact, Harrison Avery turned out to be real.

A call had been placed to Norfolk with a description. Suspect around six foot or taller, blue eyes with short brown hair. Now Nichols sat with Stepp, Cashmere, and Phillips, staring at a sketch of a man's face as well as his shoulder that had a single baseball with crossed bats below. Nichols finally smiled. "You did it, Cashmere, amazing."

She leaned back with a smile and unclipped her dark hair. She stretched her arms in the air and then stood. "I got a plane to catch. Sorry, but you'll have to buy me that dinner next time, Agent Nichols."

"Count on it. Even better, next time you're in Richmond, my wife will make you a real home-cooked meal, something I know you don't get enough of."

"Got that right, mainly from being called away on a perfectly good Saturday, like today." She gave him a warm smile. "You know wild horses couldn't have kept me away today."

"I'm a man of my word."

"You are. Call me anytime, day or night, whenever you get another one like him."

Nichols opened the door for her as she breezed by. Next, he turned his attention to Agent Phillips, who was still uploading his drawings into the FBI database. "How long will it take?"

"Almost done. We'll search face first and then the tattoo. I'll know something in about ten minutes, just long enough for you to go down and get me a coffee at the café on the corner. Black, no sugar or cream."

Nichols grinned. "No problem. It'll give me time to call Rhodes." Nichols walked over and took a snapshot of the final two drawings. He sent them to Rhodes. "I'll be back in ten."

Once outside, Nichols called Rhodes. "You get the photos to match his description?"

"Yes, perfect timing. We have two teenage girls as witnesses to Friday night at the football stadium. They got a picture on their phone with a partial plate."

"Are you kidding me?"

"No, we got lucky. She thought it was someone else, but anyway, we got four hits on this dark Ford Explorer. Then we cross-referenced the photos you just sent with photos from the DMV. We've narrowed it down to two. We're pulling as much data as we can now, and then we're gonna put a team together and head out."

"Sounds good. Agent Phillips is checking the FBI database now. If he's in the system, we'll know in under ten."

"Call me as soon as you have something. Our targets are about fifteen to twenty minutes out from the station."

"I will. Be careful, Jemma."

"Thanks."

Nichols quickly placed his order and moved to the side to wait. The coffeehouse was crowded with families who had ventured into the city for a day of shopping and strolling. He studied the parents of the young kids. Most looked stressed and worn out. A toddler began to squeal, and a young dad reached into the stroller and unbuckled his son to comfort him. It had little effect so the child was passed to the mother. Nichols thought back to the things Shannon had said about Harrison Avery. Obviously, Harrison wasn't his real name. Nichols heard his name called, and he grabbed the paper box with both coffees and headed back to headquarters.

As Nichols waited on the elevator, he checked his watch. Eight minutes had past. The elevator door opened, and Nichols thought of Jemma Rhodes as he stepped on. He should be in Norfolk with her. When the door opened, he tried to rest assured knowing three other FBI agents from Richmond had been sent to assist yesterday. Two of the agents, Agents Niki Walker and Slater Taylor, had worked closely with him in the past, and both were contentious and hard working.

The door of the office Agent Phillips was using was open. He looked up when he heard Nichols. He shook his head. "It's a common tattoo."

"What?"

"Apparently, if you played high-school baseball or college level in the state of Virginia, you got one."

"Damn. How many are we talking about?"

"Oh, probably hundreds. I did get a couple of hits in the system, all former baseball players. It'll take me a while to sort through them and narrow down the list based on the timeframe we're looking at."

"Get someone else to help." Nichols walked over and placed the coffees on the table. "You know where Stepp is?"

"Not sure."

"I'm heading back out to Virginia. I'm needed there. They got a partial on the license plate from the SUV that tried to run down Agent Rhodes last night."

"Well, that's something. Maybe it'll match the man in our description, and he'll have a baseball tattoo."

Nichols picked up the colored photo. "Could it really be him, our Harrison Avery?" He looked at Phillips. "Sounds like a longshot, doesn't it?"

"It does. But hey, someone was in those woods and built that fort, and someone took and buried Cherry Bowser."

"Yes, they did. Let's just hope it's our River Strangler. If not, then there's another killer out there taking lives under the radar." Nichols shook the picture. "Can I take this with me?"

"Yeah, I printed a couple."

"Great. Thanks for your help today. I really appreciate you coming in on a Saturday."

"Sure, Nichols, be careful out there. This man sounds twisted."

He nodded. "That he does."

***

Back in Norfolk, one block away from the neighborhood of Wood Point, Detective Ashmore pulled to the curb with Agent Rhodes sitting beside him. Behind them, Agents Walker and Taylor came to a stop as well. Jemma spoke the planned route into her headset again. Ashmore and Jemma were to enter the neighborhood at the first entrance, the entrance closest to Luke Carlton's address at 18 Wood Pine Drive. Agents Walker and Taylor were to enter the second entrance, both completing routine drive-bys of 18. Kennedy had four officers who were to be stationed at both entrances in order to keep anyone from entering or exiting the neighborhood as soon as the word was given— something that was sure to cause some headaches for the department on a nice Saturday evening.

"Let's roll." Ashmore checked his mirror and pulled back onto the highway. He flipped his signal and then turned left into the neighborhood. At six o'clock, the only light in the dark night came from the streetlights and within the houses. The moderately sized homes with neatly kept yards were quite peaceful as they circled around a big loop that contained all twenty-eight residences. When they passed the brown-brick home of 18, the two-car garage door was closed, and a few lights were on upstairs and downstairs. They drove by.

At the second entrance, they pulled to the side and waited for Taylor and Walker. Another minute passed, and Jemma saw their headlights. "Anything?" Jemma asked.

"Negative," a voice said over the radio.

Jemma looked at Ashmore. "Let's move in."

Moving at a faster pace than before, Ashmore's red truck and a black Lincoln Navigator blocked the driveway of 18 Wood Pine Drive. All four people quickly got out of the vehicles. Agent Rhodes and Detective Ashmore walked to the front door as Agents Taylor and Walker moved to the corner sides of the house. When everyone was set, Jemma rang the doorbell. A minute passed before a little blond boy around seven or eight came running to the front door. Jemma's breath caught. Soon a woman in her mid-thirties rounded the corner and said something to the young boy that made him halt in his steps. "We got a mother and young boy coming to the door."

The woman opened the door and looked at each of them with suspicion. They immediately produced their badges. Jemma asked, "Are you two alone in the house?"

The mother quickly pulled her son close to her. "Wh…why do you ask?"

"Ma'am, are you two alone?" Jemma asked again in an urgent tone.

"No."

Just then, a man came down the hallway. He had short brown hair and was a little over six foot one. Jemma placed a hand on her sidearm, which was hidden by her jacket. "Mr. Carlton, I'd like you to stop and slowly move up against the wall."

"Ma'am, please take your son to another room," Ashmore commanded as he stepped forward and began patting Luke Carlton down."

"What the hell do you think you're doing?" yelled Luke Carlton.

His wife began to protest as Jemma instructed her once again to take her son to another room.

Luke saw tears forming in his son's eyes. "Shelly, do as she says. This is some big mistake. I'll get this cleared up." She hesitated until Luke spoke her name once again. "Shelly, please, it's OK."

Jemma looked into his eyes and saw not a killer but true raw fear. She relaxed her stance. "Mr. Carlton, are you the owner of a Ford Explorer?"

His eyebrows knotted as he nodded. "What does that matter?"

"Your license plate matches a partial plate of the man who tried to run down a federal agent last night."

He stiffened. "No. Impossible." He shook his head madly. "I heard about the news conference today, but that wasn't me."

"You have an alibi?"

"Yes. Shelly and the boys were with me visiting my parents in Virginia Beach last night. We didn't come home until this afternoon."

"Did you take the Explorer or the Buick?" asked Ashmore.

"The van. How did you know—"

Ashmore interrupted him. "Motor-vehicle registration. Show us the Explorer, please."

Luke motioned down the hall toward what they assumed was the garage. Jemma and Ashmore followed closely. Luke opened the door and stepped forward. "Still parked here since I got home from work at five thirty on Friday."

Jemma studied the front of the vehicle and then walked around to the back to the license plate. She frowned when she read the numbers. Someone had switched tags. The numbers didn't match his original tag number given by the state, the one with the partial license plate in the photo from their two eyewitnesses. Their killer had taken this man's tag that matched his vehicle and replaced it with a new one where Mr. Carlton would never be the wiser.

Ten minutes later, after talking to the wife who verified the story, Jemma and Ashmore left, leaving behind two officers to wait on the crime scene techs to remove the license plate that had been switched sometime prior to Friday night. Jemma fumed in her seat as Ashmore drove. "I knew he was smart, but this? He's borderline genius. He's planned out every detail. That's why he called me Friday night. He wanted us to see the vehicle." Jemma pounded her fist on her thigh. "Bastard!" She shook her head. Ashmore reached over and placed a hand on her balled-up fist. She looked down at his hand, and then their eyes met briefly before he looked back toward the highway. He removed his hand. Jemma looked away and out the window, taking a deep breath. "He's making us look like idiots."

CHAPTER 28

The house was dark at nine thirty when Agent Simon Nichols pulled into his driveway at his home just outside of Richmond, Virginia. The plan was to hug his wife Sandra and his two daughters, Rose and Beth, and then pack a bag and head south to Norfolk. However, all that had changed just a few hours ago. Nichols opened the garage door to an empty garage. He controlled his anger as he glanced in his rearview mirror and watched as the door lowered on his forty-five-hundred-square-foot home.

For the last seven months, Simon and Sandra Nichols had called this old Victorian place home. Sandra had chosen the house last summer while off one day of her seven-day rotation at the hospital. He'd returned from out of town to a home-cooked meal with the girls away for the night at their grandma's house. Immediately, he knew his wife was up to something. The next morning, she took him to their nine o'clock appointment, and an offer was made on this 1920s house the next day.

Simon didn't fight his wife. They'd worked hard and saved over the last ten years of their marriage while living in their first home, the one she liked to refer to as their "starter home." Since moving in, Sandra had worked diligently during her seven days off work on redecorating and restoring their home to its glory days. He'd seen just about everything during her mission to have the house finished by Thanksgiving: his wife covered head to toe in paint, slinging a sledgehammer to bust up tile, and atop of a ladder peeling away wallpaper.

The garage entrance opened up to the kitchen. He stepped in and immediately noticed that the lamp in the adjacent family room was off, something out of character for his wife to do when she left the house. He reached inside his jacket and removed his Glock, and then he flipped the kitchen light and looked around his quiet home. As he worked his way down the hall that led toward the living and dining rooms, he saw a few scattered toys. He flipped the light on in the dining room and found her latest and last project. The same metal twelve-foot ladder dotted with over five different paint colors stood in the middle of the room. He looked at the ceiling and saw where the old paint met the new, where she had stopped.

Nichols continued on, checking the main level. Their bedroom was empty, bed made. The laundry room had a load of wet towels in the wash. He checked behind the door and then moved left down the foyer to the spiral staircase near the front door. Flipping another light, he climbed the stairs. Softly, he stepped across the hardwood floor into a large game room that had been recently converted from two smaller bedrooms. All was as it should be except for Agent Kicker, who was sitting on the floor waiting on him to come home as planned. "Anything?"

"No."

Nichols continued down the hall to the girls' rooms, each painted with a princess theme but with different colors. Beth, the oldest at six, liked yellow. Rose, age four, liked purple. He closed their bedroom doors and walked back into the game room that overlooked the fenced-in backyard where this evening's sequence of events had started.

Sometime around seven o'clock this evening, Beth had seen a flashing light out the window. She promptly left her sister and ran halfway down the staircase to tell their mother, who was up on the ladder painting. Sandra had placed her roller brush down, looked at Beth's face, and then stepped down one step on the ladder where she could see under the thick beam that separated the living room from the dining room. She looked at the four windows along the back wall of their living room. Nothing. It was dark outside as it should be. Sandra was just about to step back up when she saw the light. She froze.

Sandra calmly looked at Beth. "Honey, it's the neighbors. They've been looking for rabbits."

"Rabbits? We have rabbits in the backyard?"

Sandra forced a smile. "Well, no one has actually seen them yet, but their dog has been barking lately. So they're probably looking for rabbits." Sandra slowly climbed down the ladder. "Do you know what time it is?"

Beth screamed, "Movie time? I've already got one picked out."

"Yes. Go get your sister and come on down."

Sandra looked at the front door and found the lock twisted to the lock position. She turned back around and saw the girls bouncing with excitement down the stairs. She took each of their hands and led them toward the kitchen. Sandra saw her purse on the kitchen counter. She hastily grabbed it and then opened the door leading to the garage. She shut the door as the girls started asking questions. "I'm in the mood for ice cream."

"But we have no shoes, Momma, and we're in our PJs," said Beth.

"Drive-thru. Now come on, do you want ice cream or not?"

The girls quickly climbed in the backseat and buckled up. Sandra started the engine, put the van in reverse, and pressed the garage door remote. Finally, the door opened enough, and she backed out of the driveway and sped away. Two miles away, Sandra pulled over in a well-lit parking lot at a shopping mall.

"Where's the ice cream store, Momma?" Rose said as she looked out the window.

Sandra picked up her phone and pressed a number. "I have to call Daddy first. Hang on, sweetie." She heard the FBI operator on the line. "This is Sandra Nichols, wife of Agent Simon Nichols. Someone was in my backyard with a flashlight."

"Ma'am, where are you now?"

"At a grocery store parking lot with my girls, um, in our van."

"Good. Ms. Nichols, can you provide me with the security code?"

"Cinderella," Sandra said as she glanced behind her and gave her girls another forced smile.

"Thank you, Ms. Nichols. I'm sending help."

Agent Nichols closed his eyes. When he opened them back up, he scanned his empty backyard. How frightened his wife must have been. However, she had done exactly as he had trained her. Never investigate anything suspicious, just leave as fast as you can. Relief washed over him as he closed the blind and turned around. Agent Kicker stood. "No movement in the neighborhood, sir."

"Any prints on the backpack?"

"No, sir."

Nichols pulled his phone out of his pocket and called Sandra. She answered on the first ring. "What took you so long?"

"I'm sorry, baby, just had to walk the house first, just in case someone was still watching."

She sighed. "Tell me what they found."

Nichols frowned. He had only told her a backpack was found in the backyard, nothing else. He hung his head, remembering the promise he had made to her years ago when she agreed to marry him. "Two Barbie dolls."

"What? Barbie dolls?" A moment went by. "Was there a note?"

"No, no note."

"Well, that doesn't make—"

He interrupted her. "Their heads were missing and their clothes removed." He heard her breath catch. "They're Beth's dolls."

"What? They can't be. How can they know that?"

His neck tightened with tension. He rolled his shoulders. "The heads and clothing were in the bottom of the backpack. They sent me a picture." His heart sank as he heard her begin to cry. He continued, "When is the last time you saw Beth playing with Lizzy and the one, um, God, I can't remember her name, the one in the blue long dress?"

"Misty. The doll with dark hair is Misty." She let out a deep sigh. "Oh God, Simon! Their hair color matches our girls." Her voice became hysterical. "Are they supposed to be our girls? Is someone threatening our girls?"

He cringed inside and squinted his eyes shut in disbelief that this was happening. He had known this possibility existed, but it was so hard to imagine this was actually happening to his family. "I'm so sorry, Sandra. I'm so sorry."

***

Jemma hung up the phone and walked from the guestroom to Ashmore's living room. She found him sitting in his recliner, looking at the photo sent by the sketch artist from Concord. He looked up at her. "Something else happen?"

She walked across the room and took a seat on the leather couch beside him. "No. Nichols's wife and kids are safe."

Jason picked up a small radio. "Officer Quin, how's the perimeter?"

"All clear, sir."

"Good. Lights out soon. Keep me posted if needed."

"Yes, sir. Good-night, sir."

Since the threat against Nichols's family had been made, FBI Director Bobby Miller had decided to place a post around Jemma tonight as a precaution since both her and Nichols had appeared in news conferences concerning their serial killer. Jemma looked around Ashmore's home, remembering the two phone calls she had received earlier. Her father, Vance Rhodes, had called immediately after her godfather, Agent Mark Mitten, had called. They were concerned for her well-being. She understood, but it just took time to explain everything going on, time she felt could have been used elsewhere. She was on edge but tired, and her brain was trying to shut down for the day. Quickly, she stood again, her anger and nerves getting the best of her.

"Hey now." Jason got up, walked over to Jemma, and took her hand. He squeezed it. "We're gonna find who's doing this. He might be smart, but we're smarter, and we have more resources. He'll screw up; they always do."

Jemma heard the tenderness in his voice as he spoke. She closed her eyes and felt his other hand on her face. She leaned into it. A raw moment of vulnerability briefly passed. Suddenly, she opened her eyes and stepped back. "We should get some sleep."

Jason smiled. "We should. Tomorrow will be a new day; you'll see."

Jemma grinned. "Thanks. You're a good person, Jason, and a good friend to have."

CHAPTER 29

Sunday morning

The bright sun woke Simon Nichols from a deep sleep. He cracked open his eyes, looked around until his vision adjusted, and then sat up. He could hear his wife Sandra down the hallway with Rose. The memory of last night came flooding back. It had taken hours finally to get to sleep after tossing and turning, not able to get comfortable in his in-laws' guest room. It wasn't the bed's fault; it was the thought that his wife and girls had been threatened and possibly could have been taken from him.

Easing out of bed, Nichols grabbed a pair of jeans and a T-shirt out of his suitcase and pulled them on. He splashed water over his face quickly and headed toward the voice of his wife. He found her along with Rose and Beth making pancakes. The girls were taking turns dropping the blueberries into the batter. Nichols swooped up Beth off the counter and gave her a kiss. Next was Rose, and then he wrapped his arms around Sandra from behind as she flipped the pancakes. He kissed her cheek. "Where's your mom?"

"She left a while ago. Her day to open the store."

Sandra's mom and her friend owned a small boutique in downtown Richmond. It was more of a hobby than a job. "And your dad?"

"Ran to the grocery store to get more milk."

As if on cue, they heard the garage door open. "Looks like he's back." Nichols unwrapped his arms from around his wife, walked over to the back door, and cautiously opened it, peering into the garage. Cooper Mound was holding his keys in one hand and the bag of milk in the other. Nichols reached out and grabbed the milk. "Morning, Cooper."

Cooper gave him a weak smile and then a handshake. Nichols had always had a good relationship with his in-laws, but he didn't have to ask why Cooper didn't seem thrilled to see him. His daughter and precious grandchildren had been in danger, and it was all because of him and his job.

"Morning, Simon." He patted Nichols on the shoulder and walked on into the kitchen. With a huge grin on his face, he looked at the girls. "Look at these pancakes, mmm, mmm, these sure look good. Boy, Nana gonna be awfully jealous she missed all of this."

The girls giggled and laughed. Nichols watched the scene unfold. He only wished this was a normal Sunday morning gathering in Grandma's kitchen, but it wasn't. His wife caught his eye. "Hey, Dad, take over, would you? We'll be right back."

Without a word, Cooper dove right in, wrapping Nana's hot-pink apron around his waist, which caused more giggles from the girls. Sandra took Nichols's arm and led him back down the hallway toward the bedroom. She closed the bedroom door and then stepped into him, hugging him tightly, her lips pressed against his. Moments passed as they held each other tenderly, and then finally Sandra pulled away. "Hear anything this morning?"

"No. No one's gonna call me this morning unless they have something." He pulled her back into his arms and touched her face. "They are respectfully giving us space."

"Nice of them."

"We're a family. You go after one of us, you go after all of us. You know that."

She nodded. "I do. I just never thought it would be our family in the middle of a crisis." She pulled away, walked over to the bed, and sat down. "What now?"

Nichols pushed off the door and walked her way. "Stay here, lay low for a while."

"It's not that simple. My shift starts on Tuesday, and Beth has school tomorrow."

"It's first grade. Keep her out tomorrow, and we'll reassess tomorrow night." He sat beside her and placed a hand on hers. "It's for the best. I don't want to take a chance."

She slowly nodded. "I know. Me neither."

"An agent will be posted outside; you'll never be alone."

She leaned into him and placed her head on his shoulder. "Catch him, Simon, and when you do, kill him."

***

Dr. Marlee Hoyt met Ashmore and Jemma at the front entrance of the medical examiner's office. She twisted the key in the front door, locking them all in, and motioned for them to follow her on back. "That was fast." She spoke in a tired voice that matched her appearance.

"You said it was urgent," Ashmore replied anxiously as he followed Hoyt down a hallway.

Dr. Hoyt swiped her badge over a security panel and opened the door. "It is."

Ashmore held the door for Jemma, and they all entered a silent room. "Must be. No music."

Hoyt gave them a half smile and continued walking toward one of the bodies that was lying on a metal table. "I wasn't finished with Melissa Jarman when the call came in about Joy Sutton. Then I get the call from Agent Nichols in New Hampshire wanting me to compare the medical records of Cherry Bowser to our River Strangler's first three victims. I've worked all through the night. Music stopped at two a.m. Believe it or not, I just needed the silence."

"Thank you, Dr. Hoyt. Your hard work could very well be saving a life," said Jemma.

"I hope so. As soon as we're done here, I'm going home for a long sleep. So don't be waking me with another victim. Catch him!" She motioned toward the metal table that was the closest. "Let's start with Mrs. Jarman."

The body of Melissa Jarman was covered by a white sheet to just above her chest, exposing a dark-blue strangulation line around her neck. Immediately, Jemma noticed the slides up on the screen. One was marked Hazel Rice and the other Jacklyn Riggs. "The marks look similar."

"Yes, they do. Can't believe he left the scarf. It's the same silk fibers found on Riggs and Rice, but we'll have to wait and see if there's a DNA match to know if it was indeed the same scarf used on all of them. I got a rush on it."

Ashmore looked at Jemma. "Why did he leave the scarf?"

"To play with us. Send us on a wild-goose chase trying to locate the store that sold him the scarf." Jemma looked at Hoyt. "Was she raped?"

"Yes, repeatedly, with more tears and bruising than the others. A lower dose of chloroform was in her system compared to the others." She frowned. "I think she was very awake when he raped her."

Jemma shook her head in disgust. "What else matches Riggs and Rice?"

She pulled the sheet down to reveal her wrist. "Found traces of the same polyester rope used on Riggs embedded here. I think he's using the same rope to tie them up. Again, it'll take time to get the results of the DNA." She pointed to the other arm. "Her right arm is broken. She must have put up one hell of a fight and scratched him because he cut her nails and dipped her fingers in rubbing alcohol."

"That's what I was thinking. I noticed it earlier when we found her."

"Melissa Jarman must have seen him walking toward her at the cemetery," Ashmore replied.

"Yes. If he's like most serial killers, he doesn't act or dress like one. He must have gotten really close to her before she realized something was wrong and tried to get away."

Hoyt explained, "That would match why there was less of the drug in her system. He probably didn't have the chance to completely smoother her face with a rag that held the chloroform. It would have knocked her out for a little while only."

"So she would be waking up when he got her back to a safe place to rape her." Jemma spoke with contempt.

"That's my theory." Dr. Hoyt turned off the light switch and grabbed the slides of Rice and Riggs from the X-ray panel. "Let's take a look at Joy Sutton. This is where it gets interesting."

Jemma and Ashmore followed the doctor over to the next table. The lawyer's body was covered by the same type of sheet, which was folded below her neck to show a line of bruising. They watched as she placed both slides up on a similar screen and then a third one of Joy Sutton. Jemma looked at the three screens. They were different. The bruising line was thinner compared to the others. Jemma stepped closer to the lighted board. "What did he use?"

"A sharp metal wire. See the cutting on her trachea?"

"Yes, but that's—" Ashmore looked at Jemma. "Our River Strangler used a metal wire five years ago."

"Yes." Dr. Hoyt removed Riggs's X-ray and replaced it with Daisy Gwen's taken five years ago. It was a match. "Her killer used the same type metal wire used on our victims of five years ago."

"What the heck?" Ashmore asked in confusion.

"That's not all." Dr. Hoyt revealed her wrist. "I found nylon-rope fibers embedded in her skin. Nylon rope was used on Gwen, Newberry, and Long."

"Different rope than our newest victims. Whoever killed Joy Sutton is using the same exact methods as our River Strangler from five years ago." Ashmore looked at Jemma. He asked, "Why?"

Jemma didn't answer right away. She was deep in thought, trying to make the connections. She looked at Dr. Hoyt. "Joy Sutton wasn't raped, was she?"

Dr. Hoyt smiled. "Smart lady. No, she wasn't."

Jemma looked at Ashmore. "Very few people know about the scarf, the type of rope used, and the rape. Whoever killed Joy Sutton is trying to blend in with our serial killer." Jemma smirked. "Just like he did five years ago with Laura Stone."

"You lost me," Dr. Hoyt said. "And I'm too tired to try to follow. I didn't find any traces of chloroform but a full toxicology report should come later today. Found some bruising on her skull here." Dr. Hoyt pointed to the place on the back of Joy's head. "Also, tape residue around her mouth." Next, she flipped over her wrists. "Bruising on both hands. She was a fighter."

"Yeah, she was."

"Take a look at this." Joy Sutton's right foot was uncovered. "She kicked something hard and sharp, causing a fracture and a deep gash. She left blood somewhere."

"Good to know. Now we just have to figure out where," Ashmore replied.

Jemma studied Joy Sutton and tried putting all the pieces together. "I don't think she saw him. He struck her from behind and then tied her up." Jemma looked closer at her hands and feet. "She was fighting to get out of something, most likely a trunk." Jemma stood back up and looked closer at her face. "He carried her somewhere safe and then killed her." She looked back at Hoyt. "What about Cherry Bowser?"

Dr. Hoyt removed all the films and walked over to a table. She opened up the file of Cherry Bowser. "Her body was badly decomposed when she was found. She'd been dead and buried underground for at least seven months. The tissue that remained showed very little. But with what I'm able to compare, I would say a sharp, thin object was used to strangler her." She placed two films on the screen and flipped the light. "The markings here on her trachea and her thyroid cartilage match the small, thin lines found on Newberry.

"So possibly the same metal wire as our River Strangler?" Jemma asked.

Dr. Hoyt looked hopeful. "Very likely the same type of thin wire, yes."

"And her hands and wrists?"

"Both tied up, but her body was too decomposed to get a good match on the rope used. Sorry."

Jemma smiled. "Thank you, Dr. Hoyt. Go get you some sleep now. And I pray to God, you won't be needed again."

Once outside in the parking lot, Jemma leaned up against Ashmore's truck, lost in thought. "Joy Sutton's murder has to be related to Laura Stone's. But why?" She pushed off the truck and began to pace as Ashmore looked on. She stopped. "Deluca must have told something to Joy Sutton that got her killed." She looked at Ashmore. "Joy Sutton was a threat. She was killed because she knew something about the death of Laura Stone. We have to go back and look at Laura Stone. We're dealing with two killers, and we need to separate the cases."

"I'm following you, but I worked the Laura Stone case. We dug and dug and didn't find anything."

Jemma neared him. "I know, but you were led to Deluca by her husband. Then you found all the evidence against Deluca in his home."

"What are you saying?"

"Deluca was set up. He didn't kill anyone."

Ashmore couldn't hide the worry lines that appeared. "Agent Rhodes, if what you're saying is correct, the state just killed an innocent man."

"Yes, I know. But think about this. Look at the hair dye. How strange is that? Who dyes someone's hair after death? Someone was purposely trying to make Laura Stone look like the River Strangler's former victims."

"Because they all had dark hair."

"Yes."

"So if all of what you're saying is true, then Laura Stone's death was premeditated."

"Yes, but that's not the worst part of it."

Ashmore raised his eyebrows. "What?"

"Someone close to the investigation killed Laura Stone."

Ashmore shook his head and pushed off the truck. "What?"

Jemma nodded. "How else did all that evidence get inside Deluca's home? The rope or metal wire details were not published in the paper before the trial. All the items found in his garage."

Ashmore covered his face. "Shit."

"I want to see Daniel Stone. Take me to his house."

Ashmore said nothing as he unlocked the truck and they climbed in. Jemma pulled out her phone and called Nichols with an update. Ashmore drove, listening to the one-sided conversation. When Jemma ended the call, he asked, "Are you sure this is a good idea, to just show up?"

Jemma looked at the stack of files in her lap. She pulled out the one on Laura Stone and placed it on top. She opened it. "To drop by on the Stone family without calling? Yeah, I do. I want to know how he handles surprises."

"Well, I can tell you right now, not very well. Especially on a Sunday morning, if they're even home."

Jemma smirked. "Well now, we can't help it's a Sunday, now can we?"

Ashmore slowed and then turned into a neighborhood filled with large homes and circular driveways. "He built this house a year after

Laura's death. No one could fault him. He claimed he couldn't live in his old house anymore and be reminded daily of Laura's helpless body lying on the living room floor."

"And the old house? Was he able to sell it to help pay for this one?"

"No. He tried. Even replaced the flooring and painted the walls. He ended up donating it to a women's shelter. It was a smaller house, and it was already on the market when Laura was killed."

"Wait, I don't remember that in the report. Was there a lock box on the front door?" Jemma started shuffling papers in the file.

"No. It was only on the market three days before the murder and hadn't had a showing yet. So there wasn't anything to put in the report."

"Not even pictures on the Internet?"

He shook his head. "The papers were signed, and pictures were scheduled for the next day. But of course, that never happened."

"So Daniel and Laura Stone had a plan."

"A plan?"

"Yeah, build a bigger home and start a family or split their assets and move on, apart."

Andrew shook his head. "From what I remember, Daniel was pretty shook up by Laura's death. He gave no impression they had marital problems."

"No, he wouldn't if he'd killed her." Jemma looked out the window, studying the sizes of the large homes. "He must do very well."

Ashmore slowed again and pulled into Daniel Stone's driveway. "Yes, he does." The two-story brick house sat on about a half-acre of land. A wrought-iron fence separated his estate from the homes on each side. Ashmore put the truck in park and cut the engine. "Minimum home price is seven hundred in this neighborhood. His probably closer to the one million mark."

"He married so quickly. He would've struggled to afford this with an ex-wife and alimony."

Ashmore looked at Jemma. "What do you plan on saying in there?"

"Enough to rattle him."

Ashmore frowned. They stepped out of the truck, and together they climbed the five stairs that led to the front door. Jemma pressed the doorbell and peered through the bubbled-glass window. Soon a child's voice was heard calling for her mommy. Jemma smiled as the little girl she had seen Friday night stood dead still in the foyer, pointing at them. Daniel Stone appeared and picked her up. He walked over and unlocked the door.

"Detective. This is a surprise."

Ashmore nodded. "Mr. Stone, this is Special Agent Rhodes with the FBI. We'd like to discuss…" Ashmore paused and then smiled at the little girl. "Hello, Ashley. How are you?"

Shyness suddenly consumed her, and she buried her face into Daniel's chest.

Jemma extended her hand. "Nice to meet you, Mr. Stone."

Daniel shifted Ashley in his arms and timidly shook her hand.

"Danny, who's at the door?" A voice rang out from behind him.

"Just a minute, Liza; I'll be right there!" he said loudly over his shoulder. Then he sighed. "Come on into my study; we'll talk there." Jemma and Ashmore stepped inside and followed him down a hallway. He stopped and motioned them inside. "I'll be right back."

Jemma smiled. "Thank you for seeing us."

He quickly turned without a warm reply. Ashley peeked at them over his shoulder, and Ashmore waved. They caught her smile as Daniel rounded the corner with her in his arms. "Cute kid. You seem to know all the kids' names in this town."

"Preschool. It can be a small world," Ashmore replied.

They didn't have to wait long before Daniel Stone appeared again, closing the study doors behind him. "Let's keep this short. After all, it's a Sunday, and Liza has her hands full at the moment."

"Of course," Jemma said as she took a seat that Daniel motioned to. "We've just come from the morgue." She studied his reaction.

Daniel relaxed his haughty expression. "I heard about Melissa Jarman. Our kids play together. Liza is really shaken up. She knew Melissa well. Which is another reason to keep this short." Daniel looked at Ashmore. "What can I do for you?"

Jemma answered. "I have a few questions about Laura that I'd like to ask."

Daniel didn't hide his displeasure. "What about Laura?"

"Why were you selling your home?"

He looked confused for a moment. "That was a long time ago."

"Just five years." Jemma smiled.

"I don't see why this matters. The case against Alec Deluca is closed. He killed my wife, and now he's dead."

"Were you two having problems in your marriage? Were you planning to divorce? Is that why you put your house on the market?"

Rage consumed Daniel. He looked at Ashmore and pointed a finger. "I'm not going down this road again. The police turned my entire life upside down. I had to prove my innocence when there was no evidence, and I repeat, no evidence I had anything to do with my wife's murder!"

The study door opened, and Liza walked in. She looked at Ashmore and Jemma. "What's going on in here? I hear you all the way in the kitchen."

Daniel lowered his hand. "That's the same question I want to know. Why are ya'll here?"

"Deluca's attorney, Joy Sutton, was found murdered yesterday morning. I'm sure you've heard by now. Did you know her?" asked Jemma. She watched Daniel's eyes.

A moment passed. "I knew of her, never personally met her." He looked at his wife. "Everything's fine, dear, go on back in the kitchen. I'll join you very soon." Daniel took his seat again.

Liza, with her hair unbrushed and twisted up on her head, was still wearing a housecoat at 10:00 a.m. Jemma remembered Daniel's comment about her knowing Melissa Jarman well. "I'm sorry about the loss of your friend, Mrs. Stone. We won't be much longer."

She gave Jemma a curt nod and then briefly touched Daniel's arm before leaving them once again. However, this time the study door remained open.

Jemma asked, "Mr. Stone, don't you find it odd that Joy Sutton, Deluca's lawyer, was found murdered like the other women?"

He looked flustered again. "I have no idea who murdered her or the other women, and if that's why you're here, you're wasting your time."

Jemma asked, "Where were you last night?"

Daniel rose in anger. "I was home, with my family." He looked at Ashmore. "It's time for you to leave now. If you have more questions, set up a time with my secretary." Then he looked at Jemma. "We're done."

Jemma stood. "We'll be in touch, Mr. Stone. We'll see ourselves out."

Jemma and Ashmore climbed back into the truck. As Ashmore started the engine, Ashley looked out the blinds by the front door. When Jemma spotted her, she quickly stepped away, and Liza appeared, holding a baby. Ashmore pulled forward on the circular drive. "Did you get what you came for?"

"I don't know. He's hard to read."

Ashmore laughed. "There's a reason why he's our top defense attorney."

They rode in silence to the police station. When Ashmore pulled into a parking slot, Jemma looked at him. "We've got to keep the information about Joy Sutton quiet. The real killer doesn't need to know he made a mistake."

"Because he didn't use a scarf and rape her?"

"Exactly. He thinks he's getting away with murder once again. He just killed the last link to Deluca and his connection with Laura Stone. He's blended in once again with our serial killer."

"If that's true…" Ashmore smirked as he cut the engine. "This is hard to wrap my brain around."

"Yeah, it is. Come on, we have more work to do now."

CHAPTER 30

The conference room on the third floor of the police station was buzzing with activity when Jemma and Ashmore walked in. Nichols rose from behind a computer and walked over. Ashmore greeted him. "How's Sandra?"

"Still a little shaken but pissed as hell!"

Ashmore nodded. "I bet."

Once again, Jemma was reminded that Ashmore and Nichols had been through this once already, five years ago. She had yet to meet Nichols's family, and the chances were good she never would. If history repeated itself, she would be on a plane the day after this case officially closed, heading to a new assignment. She watched Jason Ashmore closely and found herself wanting to meet his daughter and getting to know him better. She quickly shook the thought off when they both looked her way. "Anything from your other cases to make you think this isn't our serial killer?" asked Jemma.

"I've looked and the bureau is on it. But no. I think it's our River Strangler."

"Me too," Ashmore agreed. "The fact that they had their heads missing and clothing removed, it sounds like he was trying to recreate the same image with the Barbies."

"The dolls matched the same hair color as our girls," Nichols said angrily. "He's screwing with my damn family."

"That he is." Jemma placed her hand on Nichols's and squeezed it gently. "We'll catch him." Then she removed it when Kennedy walked in the room. "Kennedy's here. We need to clear the room except for our core group."

"I agree. I'll let him know." Nichols walked over and conversed with Kennedy briefly as Jemma looked down at the files she was holding and sorted them. Within a minute or so, the room had been cleared except for Officers Montgomery, Meriam, Brown, and Lewis along with the three FBI agents from Richmond, Agent Walker, Taylor, and Kicker. Add Nichols, Jemma, Kennedy, and Ashmore and the room occupants totaled eleven.

Jemma moved to the front of the room with Nichols and moved a large, blank white board to the center. Nichols handed Jemma the computer-generated picture of Harrison Avery. Jemma posted it and picked up a black marker as Nichols stepped forward and began to explain.

"Yesterday in Concord, New Hampshire, the FBI interviewed a mentally challenged nineteen-year-old, Shannon Krammer, who claimed to have contact with this man over three years ago. This man, who called himself Harrison Avery, built a fort and camped out in the woods behind Mr. Krammer's house. A few months later after Harrison Avery left, the unmarked grave of Cherry Bowser was found by hunters."

An eerie silence fell across the room. All eyes were on Agent Nichols as he continued. "Harrison is around six foot or taller and has a tattoo of a single baseball with two bats crossed on his shoulder.

Unfortunately, there're hundreds like this in the state of Virginia. Apparently, all the high-school baseball kids want one when turning eighteen, but the tattoo is even more popular among players at the college level." Nichols handed the photo of the tattoo to Jemma, who hung it on the board.

"After the arrest of Alec Deluca, the murders in Norfolk stopped, but during the last five years, the Northeast region has reported over two dozen young women missing."

"Most of the cases can be linked to drugs, prostitution, or simply as young runaways. But there're six cases that stand out differently. All six women were family oriented, strong, driven women who had no reason to up and vanish. Investigations into each case were top notch with absolutely no leads. It's like these women just vanished into thin air, except for one: Cherry Bowser. Ms. Bowser had been tied up, stripped of her clothing, and strangled to death. According to our medical examiner, Dr. Hoyt, she was strangled with the same type of metal wire as our River Strangler's first three victims here in Virginia five years ago."

A few sighs and gasps emerged from the group. Nichols continued, "Many hours have gone into each of the women's cases, with nothing promising and no new leads." Nichols shifted his feet and looked around the room. "They were all cold cases, until now."

"If our information from Shannon Krammer is correct, then we must look at Harrison Avery as a strong suspect for the murders of Dawn Newberry, Daisy Gwen, and Cameron Long from five years ago." Nichols nodded to Jemma and she wrote their names under the picture of Harrison Avery. He continued, "And I believe he's back and responsible for the murders of Hazel Rice, Jacklyn Riggs, and Melissa Jarman." A few murmurs were heard throughout the room, and Nichols paused to let it all sink in. No one interrupted.

Jemma stepped forward and explained their theory. "You might be asking yourself, why is he back in Norfolk? He clearly got away with murder when Alec Deluca was convicted. Well, that answer is looking more and more like I predicted the other day. Our River Strangler wants his credit. He was smart enough to walk away five years ago, but once a serial killer commits murders, it's very rare for one just to stop. The cases that Nichols discovered in the Northeast reaffirm that he never stopped taking lives when he left Norfolk."

"All killers make mistakes. His mistake is returning and taking credit. Not only is he taking credit, but he's enjoying playing with us." Jemma let out a small laugh. "Look at yesterday. We show up at a family residence only to find out that he switched a license plate in advance. Who does this? Someone highly intelligent, borderline genius. Also, he leaves a scarf with the body of Melissa Jarman. These are considered jabs at us, but in reality, the joke will be on him. He doesn't realize it now, but those were considered two big mistakes."

Jemma walked over to another blank board and picked up a marker. She drew an "X" and turned back to the group. "This part does not leave this room." She scanned each face as everyone agreed. "The body of Joy Sutton wasn't strangled by a scarf like our newest victims or raped. In fact, she was tied up and strangled with a metal wire, just like our first victims from five years ago." Confusion quickly spread across the room.

"Whoever killed Joy Sutton didn't know about the scarf, the rape, or how a different type of rope had been used on Jarman, Riggs, and Rice. I believe Joy Sutton was killed because she came into contact with Alec Deluca." Jemma wrote her name under the X.

"Whoever killed Joy Sutton felt threatened that the real truth about the death of Laura Stone would be revealed. Which brings us back to Laura Stone." Jemma added Laura's name under Joy Sutton. "I strongly feel we have a separate killer responsible for the deaths of Stone and Sutton. Alec Deluca didn't kill Laura Stone."

"What about the hair dye found in the sink?" Officer Meriam asked in confusion.

Jemma frowned. "Someone put it there along with all the other evidence found in the garage to make Alec Deluca look guilty of being the River Strangler."

Kennedy raised his hands to quiet his officers. Then he stated, "Agent Rhodes, if you're correct, this changes everything."

She nodded. "I know." Jemma grabbed a sheet of paper from her file. "Laura Stone was murdered. Then her killer tried to associate her death with the River Strangler. Her hair was dyed to match the other three victims and then that dye was placed in the neighbor's sink. Then the killer added rope, metal wire, and soil to the trunk that matched the location of one of the dropped victims."

Jemma picked up a black marker and handed it to Nichols to add information to the board. "Whoever killed Laura Stone knew the following: one, she suspected her neighbor of being the River Strangler, and two…" Jemma looked straight at Kennedy. "And unfortunately, he somehow had access to the confidential information about the River Strangler's case that wasn't made available to the public yet."

Kennedy immediately stood. "This can't be happening," he mumbled as he walked to the back of the room and began pacing.

"We need to separate our cases. We find who killed Laura Stone, and then we'll know who killed Joy Sutton."

Kennedy looked at Jemma and nodded.

"I'd like Agent Kicker and two officers on the Laura Stone case and everyone else still working on the River Strangler." Jemma pointed to the X on the board. "He's done killing. He again thinks he's blended in with our River Strangler. So it's imperative only we in this room know about the rape and scarf. The media cannot find out. If they do, then he knows he's made a mistake."

Officer Norman Lewis raised his hand before speaking. "I know how this is going to sound—"

Nichols interrupted, "Doesn't matter. Every idea and theory is open to discussion."

He glanced at Kennedy briefly. "I know we're separating the cases, but I've seen that tattoo and that person had inside knowledge of the River Strangler case."

"Who?" asked Kennedy.

Lewis exhaled loudly. "Our district attorney, Andrew Lane."

Kennedy shook his head. "Everyone in this town knows Andrew Lane played college ball for Virginia. Besides, why would Andrew Lane want Laura Stone dead?"

"That's a good question. We have to find motive. Who would want to kill Laura Stone? Her entire case needs to be reanalyzed since it wasn't just the lone neighbor with a criminal record," Nichols replied.

"Officers Brown and Lewis, work with Agent Kicker," Kennedy instructed. "Make a list of everyone who had access to the River Strangler case five years ago. And find the damn motive." He looked at Jemma. "God, I hope you're wrong."

Jemma nodded. "I know. Why don't they use another room, and we'll bring everyone else back in and talk about our Harrison Avery."

Kennedy walked out as the board with the X was wiped clean by Jemma. A larger group convened, and the brief continued for another hour as other theories were tossed around and argued among the group. In the end, Harrison Avery's photo was passed out along with his physical description. They were looking for a man in his late thirties to forties who played high school-ball in the Norfolk area as well as college level. A list was made on the board and teams were established.

Ashmore walked over to Jemma. "I can start on new car registrations."

"Or...why don't we take a drive? There's someone else I'd like to visit."

"OK, who?"

"Andrew Lane. I'd like to see this tattoo, and besides, he fits the age of our Strangler. Maybe we can pick his brain on some old players."

"Wouldn't hurt. I know where he lives." Ashmore looked at his watch. "Goes to church—probably home now if he didn't go out for lunch."

Jemma nodded, walked over to Nichols, and filled him in.

"OK. I'll stay behind. I have Agent Walker and Taylor looking into Luke Carlton's whereabouts the last week. Maybe, just maybe we'll get lucky and someone or a video surveillance will pick up the license plate being switched." He frowned. "You think our Strangler might leave town again?"

"No. He's enjoying the spotlight too much, and don't forget the games. Calling me, screwing with your family. No, he's not leaving again."

"Then we catch him, Jemma. This stops today."

Jemma matched his intense stare. "Today." She slowly turned around, found Ashmore, and then left.

***

The Lane family wasn't alone. A white Town Car was parked outside by their open garage, revealing two shiny, matching Mercedes-

Benz E-Classes. Ashmore parked his red truck beside the Town Car. "They got company. He's not going to be happy about an unannounced visit on a Sunday."

Jemma smiled. "At least he's had time for lunch." She got out of the truck.

They walked up the stone sidewalk that matched the stone inlets in their brick home. The dining room French doors revealed seven people sitting around a dinner table. Jemma never broke her stride. She pressed the doorbell, and Andrew Lane quickly came to the front door. "Detective Ashmore?" He looked at Agent Rhodes. "Well, this is a surprise. What's going on?"

Jemma could hear their small children from the dining room. "We'd like a moment of your time. It's important or we wouldn't have bothered your family on a nice Sunday afternoon."

Andrew nodded and stepped aside, opening the door for them. As soon as Jemma stepped into the foyer, Bianca Lane, wearing a wool dress and a string of pearls and without a hair out of place, walked up behind Andrew. "What's going on?"

Ashmore turned to Bianca. "Sorry, Mrs. Lane, to interrupt your dinner, but we need to speak to Andrew."

A scowl filled her face, revealing her onset of wrinkles. "Andrew, my parents are here. It's Sunday for Christ's sake!"

He placed both hands on his wife's shoulders. "Bianca, they wouldn't be here if it wasn't important."

She looked back at Jemma and Ashmore and shook her head. "Fine, I guess we can warm up your food later."

Andrew watched his wife walk away back into the dining room. "Let's go in the study; follow me."

Jemma glanced in the dining room and saw a toddler in a highchair, two young kids, and looks of concern on the in-laws' faces. Jemma said nothing as she followed Andrew Lane through the foyer and left down another hallway. The door to the large study was open. They entered, and Andrew closed the double oak doors behind him. He gestured to a set of leather couches.

"Nice study," Jemma said as she looked around. An oversized oak table that matched the woodwork held a computer, stacks of files, and family photos. The large home, furniture, and décor gave the impression that the Lane family was doing quite well.

"Again, Andrew, sorry about this," Ashmore said as he took a seat by Jemma on the couch.

Andrew sat across from them. "What's happened?"

Jemma opened a file she'd been holding. She pulled out a photo of Harrison Avery and handed it to Andrew Lane. "His name is Harrison Avery, but we don't believe it's his real name. We believe this is our River Strangler, the man responsible for the murders five years ago and the recent ones today."

Andrew took the photo and studied it. He shook his head. "I don't recall ever seeing anyone like this."

"What about this tattoo?" Jemma asked as she produced another photo.

Andrew nodded. "Yeah, I got one myself. It's common." He looked back up. "Our River Strangler has this tattoo?"

"There's a good chance. That's why we're here."

He looked confused.

"We were hoping you could help us out with some old players. We think our River Strangler is local and around your age," Ashmore explained.

"You can't be serious? I mean, it's been a long time, and the thought that someone I knew is a killer?"

"Serial killers look like normal people," Jemma said. "Please try, and also, we believe he left town while Deluca was in prison. Now that's he's been executed, he's moved back, and he's killing again." Jemma noticed a slight change in his demeanor. "Any of this ringing a bell?"

"No. So Deluca wasn't the River Stranger?"

"Correct. He's still out there, and he's returned." Jemma looked around the study and found lots of baseball memorabilia on the wall. A framed picture of Andrew with his son's Little League caught her eyes. He had helped coach. Another shelf contained framed pictures of Andrew in his college years playing ball. Then she saw it, another frame with a group of men all holding gloves. Jemma stood and walked over to the frame. "Are these old players?"

Andrew walked over and picked the frame up off the shelf. "Yeah, every ten years they have a reunion. We all get together and play ball."

"When was this picture taken?"

"That one was the first one I attended. I had just turned thirty. I got another one with the date, just isn't framed." He opened a cabinet and removed a photo album. They were all baseball pictures.

"Someone's organized."

He looked at Jemma with a boyish grin. "Not me, my wife. I give her all the credit for arranging all of this." He found the photo he was looking for. He removed it from the plastic sleeve and flipped it over. "Summer of 2012."

"May I?" Jemma took the photo, flipped it back over, and looked at the many faces. *Is Harrison Avery here? Or did he miss this reunion while he was on his killing spree in the Northeast?* "Do you have more photos of that day?"

"Yeah. On my computer. These two copies are the ones the school sends us in the mail."

"I'd like a copy of those, please, of both reunions."

"Sure."

"And may I keep these for a while?"

"Yeah, not a problem." Andrew took a seat at his desk and pulled up his photo album. Next, he removed a flash drive from his top drawer and made the copies. He handed it to them.

Jemma noticed his hand slightly trembling. She didn't comment. "Thank you. Can you make some time to come down to the station and ID some of these men? It would help speed up our research efforts."

A knock was heard on the door. "Andrew?"

Andrew looked at both of them. "Yeah, but say nothing to my wife; I'll tell her." He spoke quietly. He got up from the desk, walked over, and opened the doors. Bianca had changed into a comfortable velour sweat suit, her pearls missing.

She spoke without an apology. "My parents are leaving."

Andrew turned. "I need to say good-bye. Give me a minute."

"Of course, we'll be right here." Jemma watched Andrew close the door behind him. She looked at Ashmore. "How well do you know Andrew Lane?"

"I was friends with his sister in school. He's older by seven or eight years. I remember when he got that scholarship to play ball at

Virginia. It was a big deal around town and at the school. Now, he sends his kids to a different school, the private school. That usually comes with their own circle of friends. Why?"

Jemma looked around the room. "I don't know, but he seems nervous."

CHAPTER 31

Ashmore took another photo of Andrew Lane's upper arm. Jemma watched him closely. "That's good. Thanks again, Mr. Lane, for your cooperation. Having a real photo instead of a sketch really helps."

Andrew turned and picked up his shirt off the couch. He dropped it. Jemma watched him intently. The short dark hair, the tattoo, blue eyes—Andrew Lane could be a dead ringer for Harrison Avery. Logic intervened; it wasn't possible for Andrew Lane to be their River Strangler. However, what was it that caused their presence to make him so nervous? Officer Meriam's comments rung loud in her head. As the Norfolk DA, Andrew Lane had access to all the evidence during the River Strangler case. Andrew misbuttoned his shirt, and he had to start over. She decided to rattle his cage and find out why he was so obviously nervous around them.

"Bianca hates my tattoo. She thinks the baseball is childish," he commented when he finished.

"Come sit back down."

Jemma walked over to the coffee table and picked up the photo of Harrison Avery. She looked at Andrew as he began to sit. "This could be you."

"What?" He stood back up.

"Yeah, the short dark hair, baseball tattoo, and blue eyes. You're over six foot, aren't you?"

He said nothing as he stood there in shock.

"Sit down. You were working in your office the morning that Jacklyn Riggs was taken. I know you're not the River Strangler." She handed him the photo again. "Look closely; are you sure you don't recognize him?"

"No, I don't know who this is," Andrew said defensively.

"I don't think Alec Deluca killed Laura Stone." Jemma watched his eyes. "But you already know that."

"Excuse me?"

"You've been talking to Kennedy. You know we've been looking closer at the Deluca case."

In a raised voiced, Andrew replied, "Yes, but I thought it was all speculation. Look, the evidence was there, and a jury convicted Deluca of Laura Stone's death." He stood and paced around the room. He stopped and looked at Ashmore and then back to Jemma. "Do you know what this means?"

"Yes. It means people are going to start asking questions."

Andrew slowly closed his eyes and ran a hand down his face. He walked back over and sat on the couch. He looked at Ashmore. "You were here. You saw the evidence. Is this what you believe? We arrested the wrong man?"

Jemma took notice of Andrew's body language. He was getting even more nervous as Ashmore sat there and said nothing.

"This is crazy!"

"You were given a copy of the evidence early on. Did you share that information with anyone?"

Lane looked offended. "No. It was confidential. Why would I risk leaking that information and hindering an ongoing investigation?"

Jemma looked into his eyes. He was clearly hiding something. "I don't know; why would you?"

Andrew didn't hide his anger. "I didn't."

He was struggling within. *Was it guilt?* Jemma wondered. "Andrew." He looked up. "You need to trust us." He quickly looked away. Jemma reached across the table and touched his arm. "What did you do?"

His eyes found her pale hand on his arm. She was slightly applying pressure. He looked up. "I don't know what you're talking about."

Jemma was beginning to lose her patience. "You're nervous as hell and agitated. Hell, you're a casebook example for someone hiding the truth."

He looked at Ashmore for some kind of help. Ashmore continued to say nothing.

"The truth will come out; it always does."

Andrew turned and looked at the study door, and then he lowered his chin and spoke quietly. "I slept with Laura Stone." Andrew let out a deep breath and then buried his face into his hands. He mumbled, "I'm such an idiot. I...I just did it to get back at Daniel." He looked back up with tears in his eyes. "It had nothing to do with my wife. I love her deeply. I..." He shook his head. "I just wanted to screw Daniel Stone for winning that damn case. That's all." He leaned back and wiped his eyes. "Stupid, just so damn stupid, all of it." He grabbed Jemma's hand. "Don't tell my wife. It will destroy her!"

Jemma and Ashmore drilled Andrew Lane with dozens of questions before leaving an hour later. Now they were back at the station, sitting in a small conference room with Nichols and Kennedy. Jemma had recounted the entire story, leaving Kennedy speechless. Nichols, not so much. Not much surprised him anymore after eighteen years of service.

Kennedy laughed as he stood up and walked over to look out his window. "Andrew Lane with Daniel Stone's wife. Unbelievable. Our DA sleeping with the victim. Not only did an innocent man die, but also our DA contaminated the whole damn case! Wait till the press hears this. We're gonna be crucified."

"You will. But we have a bigger problem than the media, Sheriff. We still have two killers out there, and one will continue to strike very soon if we don't find him."

Kennedy looked at Jemma and took a seat.

Ashmore looked at Jemma. "Could we be wrong about Andrew Lane? Did he kill Laura Stone? Was all that remorse back at the house guilt over an affair or murder?"

Jemma stood and began to pace. She rubbed her right shoulder, trying to work the kink out that had formed throughout the day. Suddenly, she stopped. Clarity slowly filled Jemma's mind. "Oh my God!" Everyone looked at Jemma. "When Laura was murdered, Andrew Lane must have known he would be a suspect since he was sleeping with Laura Stone. Sometime during their affair, she must have mentioned her creepy neighbor. Lane panicked. He pulled up Deluca's name and researched him." Jemma noticed their confusion. "Don't you see? After her murder, he planted evidence against Alec Deluca out of fear his affair would become public and ruin him."

Kennedy leaned forward. "That's a big accusation, agent. I've known Andrew Lane since grade school."

"He's an adulterer who panicked." She looked at Nichols. "How many times have we seen this? The lengths a person would go to protect their marriage and family and, also in this case, his job."

"So he takes the information from the River Strangler case and plants evidence in Alec Deluca's home?" asked Ashmore with a look of disbelief upon his face.

Jemma sat. "Yes, that's what I'm saying." She spoke with excitement. "It would put an end to the investigation into Laura Stone."

Ashmore shook his head. "But if he did that, Jemma, then Laura Stone's killer gets away with murder."

"He doesn't care. Not when it comes to saving his family. He said today he never loved Laura Stone, remember? It was just about the sex and nailing Daniel Stone in the process."

Nichols spoke. "If Jemma's right and Andrew Lane used his inside knowledge to plant evidence, then who's to say he wouldn't go a step further to silence Joy Sutton if needed?"

"Joy Sutton," muttered Kennedy. "Andrew met with her a few times as the execution neared. You think she said something to Andrew that spooked him?"

"It's possible," replied Ashmore.

Kennedy shook his head. "I can't see it. I can't see Andrew as a cold-blooded killer."

"Not even if he felt his whole world was threatened and he was on the verge of losing everything?" Jemma prodded him.

Nichols spoke. "Let's back this up. Sheriff, how did Andrew Lane seem after Deluca's conviction?"

"I don't know. Relieved? But hell, we all were. This whole town was ready to pick up the pieces and move on."

"Did he take time off?" asked Jemma.

Kennedy's expression turned serious. He leaned back in his chair. "He did. He took his family to their beach house at Virginia Beach."

"I don't remember this," said Ashmore.

"No, you wouldn't. You had taken a leave of absence." Jemma looked at Ashmore for an explanation, but Kennedy continued so she turned her attention back to him. "He was gone longer than the standard vacation time, maybe three weeks."

Nichols continued, "And no one would question it. We all had put in so many man-hours on this case. I took a week off myself when I returned to Richmond." Nichols stood. "Sheriff, we need to bring in Andrew Lane. There are just too many what ifs and unanswered questions."

Kennedy, with a look of disgust, stood. "OK, but I want your agents and my men still digging into Daniel Stone's cases. Andrew might have cheated on his wife, but that's still a far cry from murder and planting evidence in my book."

"Sheriff's right." Jemma leaned forward and picked up a paper. "Bring him in, but I want his alibi for Joy Sutton and Laura Stone." She picked up a pen and tapped it on a notepad. "Let's get to the conference room. We still have to track down our Harrison Avery."

CHAPTER 32

Music was playing softly in Andrew Lane's study. Bianca had left with the kids to attend a birthday party at the local skating rink. He sat in his nice leather chair, drinking scotch and holding a frame that contained their family portrait taken last summer at their beach house. He placed the photo down and refilled his glass. He looked around the room and saw his many accomplishments; all had been hung on the wall by his wife's loving hand.

Bianca had special ordered matching frames to hold his pitching glove from college and his college jersey. They hung side by side. Another wall held his law degree along with the state of Virginia certificate to practice law. He stared at his certificate. Bianca had wanted to frame his results on the bar exam, but he had told her no. He closed his eyes and thought back to the first day he met Bianca. She was walking down Main Street in Charleston. He'd just had lunch with a colleague from the courthouse where he was interning at the prosecutor's office the summer before graduation. His life drastically changed that day when their eyes locked.

They continued to date the last year of college. They were inseparable, and they took turns making the drive each weekend between Richmond and Charleston to visit. When the baseball season began, their relationship survived and became stronger with his demanding ball schedule. After graduation, he proposed.

They married a year later and moved to Roanoke, Virginia, where he worked as junior prosecutor for the city. There Bianca taught preschool at a local elementary. They were happy and had a five-year plan. However, it took seven years before an opening finally came up in Norfolk, Andrew's hometown. They left Roanoke two years later than planned, a month after Andrew's thirty-first birthday.

For the next four years, Bianca continued teaching, and Andrew slowly worked his way up to district attorney for Norfolk. When Bianca became pregnant with Collin, they began to draw up house plans. Three months after Collin was born, they moved out of their tiny apartment and into this home. Andrew looked at the framed photo of the three of them on the front porch the day they moved in. He tried to remember if it was his mother or Bianca's who had taken the photo. They were both there that day, fussing over the baby while Bianca instructed the movers on where to put each box.

His eyes left the framed photo and found his empty glass. He poured more scotch. Everything he and Bianca had built was unravelling right before his eyes. Laura Stone's face appeared before him. He picked up and drained his glass. He heard Laura's laughter fill the room. He squeezed his eyes shut, trying to block out the memory. She was smiling as he teased her with his hand, sliding from her cheek, down and over her breast, to her naval. They had just made love in Daniel Stone's bed while Daniel was out celebrating a big win against his office. Andrew blocked the memory out of his mind and reached for the bottle of scotch.

The sound of a car pulling into his driveway caused him to turn around and look out the blinds. It was Sheriff Kennedy along with three other officers, climbing out of their patrol cars. He quickly moved away from the window. The doorbell sounded, followed by a loud knock. Andrew sunk into the leather chair and buried his face into his hands. The doorbell sounded again. Slowly, Andrew unlocked the bottom drawer of his desk. He pulled out a gun and sat back in his chair. The pounding on the door sounded again as his eyes found the framed photo of his family sitting on the edge of the desk. He wondered if there was any possible way out. He tried to picture himself explaining it all to Kennedy; how he'd been blackmailed. Would he believe him? Would Ashmore and that agent believe him? He shook his head in despair as he heard another loud knock. He raised the gun to his head.

Outside, Sheriff Kennedy instructed two of his men to check the back of the home. Just as they turned to leave, a single gunshot was heard. "No, no, no, no!" Kennedy pointed at his deputy. "Call an ambulance." He removed his gun and stepped back off the porch. He fired into the glass, shattering it. He reached in, unlocked the door, and entered.

***

Eight miles away, Jemma was presented with a long list of male baseball players in the Norfolk school district from 1983–1998. Another list was made of students who earned scholarships for college-level ball. Then, they narrowed down the list to locals who had come back home and settled down. Anyone who played college baseball and was recruited from a state other than Virginia was eliminated for now. With the help of Agents Walker and Taylor and eight police officers, the final list of twenty-six had come together quickly. The names were added to a board, along with address, job, family status, and any police records. Jemma stood by the board, studying each name and the data. None had been arrested. Eleven had received traffic tickets over the last seven years. All but two were employed. Six of the eight who were divorced had remarried. All had children.

Nichols walked up and stood by Jemma. "What do you see?"

Her eyes lingered over their places of employment. "We have a fireman; he's usually off for two days at a time, but not enough time to make trips to New Hampshire and camp."

"No. What about Louis Walton? Says unemployed."

Jemma shook her head. "I followed up on him. He's working for his father at the dry-cleaning company." Jemma crossed her arms. "I don't think our Harrison Avery's on this board."

"Then we keep digging. Anything on Daniel Stone's cases?"

"Nothing concrete. He had a lot of enemies."

"Agent Rhodes."

Jemma turned and found Ashmore standing by the doorframe. He slowly walked forward. "I just got a call from Kennedy. Andrew Lane just put a bullet through his brains."

Jemma rocked back and forth on her feet. She rubbed her face quickly. "Aw, shit!"

"We should've seen this coming." Nichols asked, "Did he leave a note?"

"Kennedy was at the door when the shot was fired. We think he panicked."

"Was the family home?" asked Jemma, still in disbelief.

"No. Thank God. Bianca was with the kids at a birthday party."

Jemma looked at Nichols. "Lane taking his own life!"

Nichols shook his head. "We got to assume the worst of Andrew Lane, maybe not only did he have an affair with Laura Stone, but he killed her as well."

"And silenced Joy Sutton? Wow." Jemma spoke aloud as she thought. "We need warrants. We check everything: house, his car, and their beach house to see if he indeed killed Joy Sutton."

Nichols agreed. "I'll get the warrants started."

Jemma just shook her head in disbelief. She pushed Andrew Lane out of her head. They had to find Harrison Avery before he struck again. "Thanks, I'll work with Ashmore on our Harrison Avery."

Ashmore noticed the board behind her and walked over. "I know most of these people."

Jemma took a step and joined him. "Yeah? Anyone you think capable of murder?"

Ashmore shook his head. "No. But I didn't think Andrew Lane, a college athlete, successful lawyer, and family man, was capable of murder either."

Jemma looked back over each name. "Wait, the rivalry game." She looked at Ashmore. "Rivalry is big in this town, just look at Friday night. But what about other schools just outside the district that travel in?"

"We need to be looking at the other high schools within a two-hour radius," Ashmore quickly added.

Jemma got everyone's attention in the room. She explained what they were looking for, and everyone got to work as Jemma pulled another clean board to the front of the room.

***

Daniel Stone checked the locks on all four doors on the first floor again. He was getting paranoid, but his mind wasn't able to shake the feeling he was getting in his gut. Looking out from his study window, he saw a peaceful neighborhood on a Sunday afternoon. He released the curtains and jumped at the touch of his wife's hand. He spun around. "I didn't hear you come in."

Worry lines filled her forehead. "Are you OK?"

He looked into her blue eyes. "Yes." Then he grabbed her hand and squeezed it. "No, not really."

"Let's talk." She pulled him over to the leather couch. "Baby's asleep and Ashley's still at the birthday party so tell me all about it. I know it has something to do with our little visitors earlier."

"Yeah."

Liza placed both hands on his shoulders. "You're tense." She began to rub. He sighed as he closed his eyes. Patiently she waited.

"FBI was asking me questions about Laura again."

She arched her brow. "What, that again! How can they dredge this back up all over again? It's ancient history, and Alec Deluca is dead and buried."

"They also wanted to know if I knew Joy Sutton, the lawyer found dead." He grabbed one of her hands that had fallen to his lap. "It's all coming back."

She shook her head. "Oh, Danny, I'm so sorry."

"They made my life a total hell. Not to mention the bad publicity it brought to the practice."

The doorbell sounded, and she looked at her watch. "Too early for Ashley." She stood and walked out of the study with Daniel right behind her. She stopped at the doorway of the study. "Relax, Danny."

Together they walked down the foyer, and they both saw Melody with her daughter and Ashley. Liza opened the door. "That was a quick party." Liza saw Melody's sad look. "What?"

"Maybe the girls should go play," Melody hinted.

Liza slowly nodded and then pulled Ashley in for a hug. "How was the party?"

"It was OK. We didn't get to skate long."

"I'm sorry, honey. Why don't you and Tiffany go play in your room for a while, but quietly, your sister's still napping."

The two girls ran off without a reply. Daniel suggested, "Come on in the living room. We'll talk there."

"Can I get you something?"

"No, I'm fine." They all took a seat. "There's more bad news coming to this town."

Daniel anxious asked, "What happened?"

"The police showed up to get Bianca Lane. It appears her husband Andrew was shot." She looked at both of their shocked faces. "He's dead."

"What? What is the police saying? Does it have something to do with our Strangler?" Daniel asked.

"I don't know. Bianca left, and the party ended. I came straight here."

CHAPTER 33

Sunday evening, Bianca Lane was once again in the company of her parents. Just as they had returned home, they got the call about Andrew. They raced back to Norfolk. One parent sat on each side of Bianca at her kitchen table. Once her children had been picked up at the police station by her sister, Bianca returned home and refused to leave. Now she sat just a few rooms away from a study that had been roped off. Andrew's body had been removed.

Sheriff Kennedy sat across from the grieving family. The house had been searched for any kind of note, but they found nothing. Kennedy couldn't help but think his unplanned visit earlier had pushed Andrew over the edge, therefore, no note or any explanation would ever be given. He couldn't imagine Andrew committing murder, but now he questioned all of it. Kennedy tried to focus on a timeline of Andrew Lane's whereabouts over the last week. If Andrew was capable of ending his own life and framing Alec Deluca for murder, then maybe, just maybe they should consider Andrew Lane the number one suspect in the murder of Joy Sutton.

Times and dates had been recorded in Kennedy's notebook. Bianca had produced her phone calendar as well as Andrew's. Thursday night, Andrew hadn't come home till eight. His calendar had no appointments noted, and Bianca had very little to offer other than

saying he worked late. Jill Eckelberg, his secretary, had confirmed that
Andrew left a few times during the day on Thursday but was confident
that Andrew left shortly after five o'clock. Andrew Lane was off the
radar for three hours Thursday evening.

"Friday night, you and Andrew stayed home, didn't go to the
game. Do you remember what time you went to bed?"

Her perfectly manicured nails hid her eyes. Kennedy's question
caused her to breathe deeply and wipe her red, teary eyes once
more. She dropped her hands to the table and picked up the used
handkerchief. She kneaded the cotton fabric between her fingers. She
looked back up with sad eyes. "I don't see why it matters."

"Sheriff, I think my daughter has been through enough. Can we
take her now?" Mr. Jones asked with one protective arm around
Bianca.

Kennedy treaded carefully. "We're almost done. I just need to
finish Andrew's timeline for the weekend."

Mrs. Jones began to protest, but Bianca interrupted. "We consumed
two bottles of wine that night. Probably around nine thirty."

"Who drank more, do you remember?"

She gave him a disgusted look. "I don't know, me probably."

"So you and Andrew were both asleep in your bed around nine
thirty?"

She sighed. "You want the sex details as well?"

"Bianca!" her mom exclaimed in a mortified voice.

"What? I don't know why any of this has to do with why my
husband put a gun in his mouth!" Bianca pushed away from the table

and stood. She walked over to the cabinet, removed a glass, and filled it from an opened wine bottle sitting on the counter. "We opened this bottle last night. But he was the only one who drank from it." She twirled the glass in her hand and took a long, slow sip.

Kennedy gave an apologetic look to her parents, pushed away from the table, and joined Bianca by the kitchen island. "Mrs. Lane, we've known each other a long time. I need to tell you why I came to your house today. I want you to hear it from me."

She placed the wine glass down and narrowed her eyes. "OK, why?"

"I came by today to question Andrew about his handling of the Alec Deluca case."

She smirked. "Is that it? I already knew about that. Andrew shared it with me Friday night." She took another sip from the wine glass.

"What exactly did he tell you?"

"He was worried about the Deluca case but nothing specific, no. Why?"

"Bianca," he whispered and placed one of his hands on her free hand, which was resting on the granite counter. "Andrew confessed that he was sleeping with Laura Stone at the time of her death. We have reason to believe he planted evidence against Alec Deluca."

Shock registered on her face. Then she broke out in laughter. Her mother and father quickly ran toward her and stood by her side. She pushed them away, shaking her head, still laughing. "This is too much. I want all of you to leave, now!" She rounded the island and came face to face with Kennedy. "I want you out of my house now! Do you understand me? Now!"

He stepped back. "I'm sorry, Bianca, I really am." He pulled out a search warrant from his pocket. "We need to search your home, the beach home in Virginia Beach, as well as Andrew's car." He placed it on the counter and backed away.

Mr. Jones picked it up and scanned the document. "This is about Joy Sutton, the lawyer?"

Kennedy replied, "I'd appreciate if you brought Mrs. Lane back to the station tomorrow morning." He looked at Bianca's wild eyes and apologized again, trying to understand the agony and pain she was suffering. He could offer no more words of sympathy so he turned and left them.

An hour later, he arrived at Virginia Beach. Nichols met Kennedy at the door of the Lane beach house, Drifted Pine. "No sign of any kind of struggle. Forensics is working carefully though."

"We got the car impounded from the house, checking for fibers and DNA as we speak." Kennedy turned around and looked out at the other beach houses. People were staring from their balconies. He frowned. "We got to set up another damn press conference and get ahead of this too. The entire Deluca case has been contaminated by Andrew Lane."

"Yeah, looks like it."

"Oh dear God, if Deluca was truly innocent, we helped the state fry an innocent man."

Nichols shared his pain. He'd been there every step of the way when they arrested Deluca as the River Strangler. Andrew Lane had played them all. "I don't know how he's lived with himself as long as he did. He let a serial killer get away with murder, and now he's at it again."

"If Lane goes down for Joy Sutton, what's to keep the River Strangler from leaving town again, disappearing, letting Andrew Lane take the fall for all the murders?"

"I've been thinking the same thing. But I gotta believe Agent Rhodes is right. Our killer is different now. He's intensified, and from my experience, he won't be able to walk away again."

"But he never did walk away—that is, if he's our Harrison Avery. He's been taking women in the Northeast. He could leave, blend in again, and start over."

Nichols couldn't sweep away Kennedy's logic. "We haven't publicly made the connection with Harrison Avery and the missing Northeast women. You're right, he could just up and leave again, find a new killing field."

"Nichols! We got something."

Nichols and Kennedy both turned toward Agent Taylor, who had been assigned to help with the case. "What?" Nichols asked as they neared.

Agent Taylor held up a clear plastic bag with a small nylon-rope clipping inside. "Found it in the bedroom under the bed. We're also bagging the comforter to take to the lab."

Nichols stepped closer and examined the bag. "Could be the one used to tie up Joy Sutton. Dr. Hoyt should be able to tell us."

"We found some markings on the poster bed. Looks like someone was tied up."

Nichols walked back into one of the smaller bedrooms. The comforter had already been removed, and it was sitting on the floor in an evidence bag. A yellow sticker with the number seven had been placed on the right side of the headboard. Nichols stepped closer and eyed the markings carefully. Something had rubbed the stain off the bedpost. He studied the angle, as if someone was lying in bed. It matched with Taylor's theory. Someone had been tied up for a good length of time. She had struggled. He walked around to the other side but found no markings.

"I think he used the metal frame on the left side. Queen bed, would've been harder to tie someone up on all four corners, and besides, that's not how the River Strangler tied up his first victims. Both feet stayed bound together at all times."

Nichols nodded. "That's right; they were."

"Oh boy! Christmas is coming early boys. Look what we got in here."

Nichols turned and saw Agent Walker crouched down beside an open stove used for heat. He neared. "What?"

Carefully, she used the poker stick to pick up a partially burned object. Agent Taylor opened an evidence bag, and she dropped it in. "I found it on the bottom, under all of the ashes." She stood and moved the object around in the bag. "It looks like part of a heel to a woman's shoe."

"Who burns a pair of shoes?" asked Kennedy.

"No one," replied Nichols. He looked back at the bed. "Get it all to the lab and call Dr. Hoyt. I want her working ASAP."

"I'll make the call." Kennedy pulled out his phone and left the room.

"Let's keep digging." Nichols's phone vibrated. It was a text from Jemma Rhodes. *Working on a new angle. Any luck at the beach house?* Nichols quickly replied, *Maybe, heading back soon.* Nichols pocketed his phone and walked back into the living room to find Kennedy finishing his phone call. "I'm going to head back to Norfolk. Rhodes is working on a new lead."

"Good! Looks like our luck is starting to turn now." Kennedy looked around at the beach house. Many family beach photos of the Lane family were framed. It saddened him. "I'll head back too. I can't stomach to be here anymore."

Nichols touched his shoulder as he walked toward the front door. He knew all too well how personal this case had become to all of them involved.

CHAPTER 34

At the station, Jemma and Ashmore researched a new list of names of players who bordered the Norfolk school district. The list had been shortened to five names of high-school players who had attended the University of Virginia, none of them on baseball scholarships. Three of the five lived out of state and had jobs. A team of officers was verifying their whereabouts for the last five years. Two of the men had returned to Norfolk, Trey Gould and Ken Burns. Ashmore worked on Trey Gould while Jemma researched Ken Burns.

An hour had passed as Jemma completed her file on Ken Burns. Ashmore had left thirty minutes ago to pull an old file on a house fire at Trey Gould's childhood home. Jemma tapped her pen as she read over her notes. Ken Burns was a divorced father of three. His prints were in the system in association with the Boy Scouts; he was a leader of his son's troop four years ago. No priors, not even a speeding ticket. Taxes were paid on an apartment in the Rosewood suburb, where he lived alone. Jemma checked the map that marked their victims' homes and where each body had been dropped. Nothing stood out.

Child support income was listed for Glenda Burns for their three children they shared. Glenda and the kids lived on the other side of Norfolk. Jemma again checked the map. She sat up quickly when she saw it. Glenda Burns lived in the same neighborhood as

Melissa Jarman, the woman found at the football field. *Did they know each other? Is this the neighborhood Ken lived in before the divorce?*

Jemma typed in Ken Burns's employer, Trahm Industries. A company website showed up first on the list. She clicked. Trahm Industries was a trucking company serving the Southeast, East Coast, and Northeast. A lump formed in Jemma's throat. If Ken Burns was a trucker, he traveled. Also, Jacklyn Riggs worked the night shift at a diner frequented by truckers. Jemma picked up her cell phone and pressed Nichols's number. "Hey, where are you?"

"Just pulled into the station."

"Good, come on up to the conference room. I think I got something." Jemma ended the call and continued to read the website for Trahm Industries while waiting on Nichols. It appeared drivers owned their own trucks, and they were commissioned for jobs by Trahm. Jemma made a note of the phone number listed for Richmond, Virginia. Next, she pulled Ken Burns's driver's license. Her heart skipped a beat when she saw his current CDL license.

"What did you find?"

Jemma turned and found Kennedy and Nichols standing there, anxiously waiting. "Ken Burns, an old high-school baseball player. He's divorced with three kids, and his ex lives in the same neighborhood as one of the victims, Melissa Jarman. But that's not all. He works for a trucking company that services the Northeast." Jemma smiled. "He travels."

Nichols got excited. "Sounds like too many coincidences not to mean anything."

"It sure does," Kennedy remarked with a smile on his face.

"I know. This could be him."

"Got a current address?" asked Kennedy.

Jemma looked at the address on file with DMV. "Apartment on sixteen hundred Riley Road, Norfolk. You know the area?"

"Riley Road," Kennedy mumbled. "Oh yeah, about ten miles west of here. It's a nice complex just inside Rosewood."

"You got a plan?" asked Nichols.

"No. Called you immediately when it looked promising. Just compiled everything."

"Where's Ashmore?"

Jemma looked at Kennedy. "He's researching another name, Trey Gould. There was a house fire over fifteen years ago at the home he grew up in."

Kennedy shook his head. "Don't recall it."

"What did you find at the beach house?"

"Some rope clippings behind the bed and the headboard had scratches. Looks like someone had been tied to the bed. Also, we found part of a woman's shoe in a wood-burning stove in the same bedroom."

Jemma looked at Kennedy. "Joy Sutton?"

"Good chance."

Nichols said, "There was a video camera at security checkpoint at the prison. I bet it will show Joy Sutton wearing black heels when she witnessed Deluca's execution."

"If Andrew Lane is connected with Joy Sutton, then I could be wrong, our Strangler just might decide to leave town after all."

Nichols nodded. "Kennedy and I were discussing the same thing earlier. Let's get a team together, go stake out Riley Road, and see if we can locate Ken Burns."

Jemma looked at her watch and frowned. It was now seven fifteen. "I'll go see his ex-wife. Maybe she'll be willing to help us." Jemma rose from her chair.

"Why doesn't Kennedy go with you? It's a Sunday night. Might be surprised by Burns returning the kids from a weekend visit."

"Good point. Definitely a possibility. You ready, Sheriff?"

"Absolutely. Let's go."

***

The Stone house was quiet as Liza was trying to straighten up the kitchen while Daniel worked on a case in his study. Ashley had gone to bed at the same time as her younger sister, Sophia. It had been a long weekend with the late Friday-night game, a sleepover on Saturday, followed by a birthday party earlier today. Liza dried the last pan and put it away. Then she removed two wine glasses from the cabinet and poured wine for her and Daniel. She left the kitchen.

The study door was closed while Daniel worked—something common with two young girls in the house. Liza bent forward and opened the door lever with her elbow. She said quietly, "I've brought wine."

Daniel looked up and dropped a pen. He smiled as he stood. "Perfect timing." He met his wife across the room, and they took a seat together on the leather couch. They sipped from their wine, both enjoying the quiet house and lost in thought.

"You doing OK?"

She looked at Daniel. "Yeah, just hard to get my head wrapped around the idea that Melissa Jarman's gone and she's not coming back. Those poor children."

Daniel took her in his arms. "I know." He held her tenderly. "Don's gonna have a long, tough road ahead of him."

Liza leaned up. "It's just all so crazy. And then Andrew Lane commits suicide."

Daniel took another sip. "I would have never thought in a million years that Lane could take his own life. Why? He had everything going for him."

Liza said nothing. The Andrew Lane she knew was much different from what her husband saw in the courtroom. She listened as he continued rambling. "I mean, I know we've had our differences throughout the years, but he was one hell of a lawyer."

Liza thought back to all the times her and Danny had to be in the same room with Andrew and Bianca at this social function or that. Never once did her husband have the idea that Andrew Lane had once slept with his wife, Laura Stone. She continued to listen to Danny and took another sip of her wine. She knew the lengths Andrew Lane would take to save his marriage and his reputation. His suicide didn't surprise her in the least. She heard Danny speak something that sounded like a question. "Hmm, what, dear?"

"I said let's go to bed. Tomorrow's bound to be a nightmare at work."

"Sure, Danny." Liza placed her empty wineglass down and followed her husband out of the study and up the stairs.

CHAPTER 35

Ashmore walked into the station at eight o'clock. Only four officers were working in the conference room. "Where is everybody?"

Officer Joe Wilson looked up and found Ashmore. "Agent Rhodes and the sheriff went to visit Ken Burns's ex-wife, and Agent Nichols took a team to Ken Burns's apartment. We got confirmation that Burns isn't on a road trip with his rig. What did you find out on Trey Gould?"

Ashmore handed over a printout. "Trey Gould's parents died in a house fire fifteen years ago. Trey inherited a two-million-dollar life-insurance policy. Conveniently, he wasn't home when it happened."

"Whew! Two million." Wilson stood up and called over to Officer Jay Ryan. "Jay, you were here fifteen years ago. Do you remember a house fire where the Gould family died?"

Ryan stopped typing and looked up. "What's the address?"

Ashmore looked at the printout that showed an address under a picture of charred remnants of a house. "Four ten Alexandria Road. Here, this jog your memory?"

Ryan took the printout, studied the picture, and scanned the article. "Yeah, I remember it. I was on call that night. Started in the garage. Owner worked on cars for a living. Killed the husband and the wife."

"You don't remember anything suspicious about the son? Trey Gould inherited two million. He was living with them at the time but out of town the night of the fire."

"Trey Gould…" Ryan mumbled. "No. Can't recall anything other than it being a tragic event."

Officer Wilson asked, "If Trey went to college with Andrew, what was he doing living at home with his parents? What was he, twenty-nine?"

"Twenty-seven. Apparently, Trey didn't finish college." Ashmore shuffled through some papers until he found what he was looking for. "He earned a living with Parkins Chemical Plant from '93 to '98, and then he worked for his dad, Lou Gould's Transmission Company, from '99 to 2000. House fire breaks out in summer of 2000, and Gould has claimed self-employed ever since."

"What's his address?"

Ashmore smirked. "DMV and tax records still have him listed at four ten Alexandria Road."

"He rebuild?" Ryan asked.

"Not according to his property taxes. Who wants to take a ride with me and find out?"

Ryan looked around at the other officers working the phones and studying case files. All were in uniform. "I could use a break. Besides, I've been there before; maybe I can offer some insight. It'll be dark, and you can't see the place from the highway." Ryan slipped on his sidearm and pulled a jacket on. "We'll go in your truck and do a drive-by. If my memory is correct, there're more homes down Alexandria Road."

"Sounds like a plan. Wilson, keep me posted on Ken Burns."

"Yes, sir."

***

It was dark when Jemma pulled into Glenda Burns's modest two-story home. They elected to drive Jemma's unmarked SUV to keep onlookers away. Jemma stepped out and pulled her jacket forward to hide her sidearm. It made no difference though; Kennedy was dressed in full uniform. So much for the element of surprise. Jemma looked around at the surrounding neighbors' homes. Two doors down, two teenage boys were out shooting hoops, and the house across the street had the garage door open and the light on.

The door was soon opened by a young boy wearing flannel pajamas. Immediately, they heard a woman's voice in the background. "Timmy! Get in the bed. I'll get it."

Glenda Burns rounded the corner and stopped dead in her tracks, clearly embarrassed at yelling in front of two strangers at her door. She timidly stepped forward after her eyes registered a man in uniform. Softly she called out, "Timmy, go get back in bed. I'll help the officer."

Timmy looked back at his mom with disappointment but obeyed. They all watched as his little feet ran up the staircase and disappeared. She turned her attention back to them. "It's late. Is something wrong?"

Jemma produced her FBI credentials. "We apologize for our timing. I'm Agent Rhodes, FBI, and this is Sheriff Kennedy with the Norfolk Police Department. May we come in? It's about your ex-husband, Ken Burns."

She tensed and then placed a hand over her chest. "Was he in an accident; was he hurt?" She slowly backed away from the door, nearly in tears.

"No accident, ma'am. We just have some important questions to ask you. May we please come in?" Sheriff Kennedy removed his hat and patiently waited.

Relieved that her ex wasn't hurt, she nodded and pulled the door fully open. "Excuse the mess. It always looks like this after a weekend."

Jemma smiled. "Your home is our least concern, I assure you. Where can we sit and talk without fear of your three children hearing us?"

She opened her mouth to respond but paused. "How…how did you know I have three kids?"

"Tax records." Jemma said flatly.

"Oh. Um, let's go into the kitchen, sit at the table."

They followed her down the foyer and through the living room, which ended at a wooden kitchen table for six. Jemma took notice of the décor and furnishings along the way. Glenda earned a nice income as a stockbroker on top of her monthly child support. The place didn't look too messy to Jemma, just a few toys and books scattered across the room. If this were what someone called messy, she would hate to hear what people said about her two-bedroom apartment. Maybe Ken Burns liked things to be perfect, and she was struggling with what was normal. *Well, something obviously ended their marriage,* thought Jemma.

Quickly, everyone took a seat, and Jemma focused in on Glenda Burns and not the house. "Again, we do apologize for the time, but it's important we speak to you tonight."

"OK."

"Like we said, it concerns your ex-husband, Ken Burns. Do you know where he is this exact moment?"

She shook her head. "No. I haven't spoken to him in over a week at least."

"What about the kids?" asked Kennedy. "Does he call them daily?"

She frowned. "No. The kids only talk to him on his visitation weekends."

"How often and when was the last?" Kennedy prodded.

"It isn't set. Ken travels with his work. But he picks up the kids at least one weekend a month. It's a pain; I have to be flexible, and sometimes it's hard to plan ahead. But I just keep reminding myself it's what's best for the kids, not me."

"I imagine so." Jemma spoke sincerely. "Very selfless of you."

She shrugged her shoulders. "Wait, is Ken is some kind of trouble?"

"That's what we're trying to figure out. When was the last time he picked up the kids?"

She didn't like Kennedy's response, but she answered the question anyway. "Not last weekend but the one before. So two weeks from today."

"Thank you. Do you remember anything unusual about Ken's behavior? Or did the kids mention anything off with their last visit?"

She looked back at Jemma while she searched her memory. "Nothing I can remember. I greeted the kids at the door and waved at him in the car."

"DMV has Ken driving a 2013 red Ford Mustang. Is that correct?"

She smirked. "No. That's his mom's car. He still drives that old Bronco."

"What color?" asked Kennedy.

"Dark green. Why?" Clarity finally washed over her. "You two were on the news. It's that serial killer, right? Why are you here, and why are you asking questions about Ken?"

Jemma ignored her question. "So you didn't get close to Ken; you only saw him from a distance while standing at the front door?"

She crossed her arms. "Won't you answer my question, please?"

"It's an ongoing investigation, ma'am," Kennedy responded calmly. "If you were in some kind of danger, we would have removed you and the kids immediately."

Jemma spoke. "Ms. Burns, please answer our questions, and there'll be a good chance I can tell you more."

Slowly she uncrossed her arms and placed them on the table. "I saw him only from the doorway. We're divorced, OK? We just don't care to walk up to each other and have mindless conversation."

"Understood. Now back to the kids. What did the kids tell you about their weekend?"

She grew uncomfortable. "I didn't ask. I used to, but I really got sick of how he spoiled them, or occasionally he would have a woman friend." She frowned. "Look, they just always came home happy, just like they did this time."

"Does Ken still have his apartment on Riley Road?"

"Yes. The kids would have told me if he'd moved but so would Ken. It's in the court papers."

Jemma turned to a new page in her notebook. "Does Ken have any tattoos?"

"Yes. A few."

"Where?"

"A small scorpion on his foot."

"Any on his arm?"

"Yeah, a baseball on his shoulder that he got in high school."

"OK," Jemma said with a smile. "Does Ken still work for Trahm Industries as a truck driver?"

"Yes."

"How long has Ken been known to stay on the road with work?"

She watched as Jemma wrote. "Oh gosh, maybe three weeks at a time? I'm not quite sure anymore. We've been divorced now for five years."

Jemma continued carefully choosing her words. She needed more info and didn't need her to shut down and get defensive again. "Over the last five years, after the divorce, do you ever remember a time that Ken stayed gone longer than a month, maybe missed a monthly visit with the kids?"

She frowned. "A lot of time has passed since then. Please tell me why this is important. Did he know one of the women murdered?"

Kennedy answered, "Both of you knew Melissa Jarman, correct?"

She nodded. "Yes. But she wouldn't stoop so low as to sleep with Ken."

Jemma knotted her eyebrows, trying to decipher her meaning. *Extramarital affair. The cause of their divorce. She must think it's one of the other women.* "Did he ever miss a visit with the kids?"

She sat back, frustrated. "I can't remember him ever missing a month, but it's not always the same weekend of the month. It could be for six weeks at a stretch."

Jemma nodded and made some notes. Her phone vibrated, and she checked the name: Agent Walker. "Excuse me." Jemma stood and walked to the living room. "Rhodes."

"We got Ken Burns's road logs for the last two years. Also, Trahm Industries called. Not only is Ken Burns not working today, he's been home for the last ten days. Vacation."

"Interesting, he didn't get the kids."

"Gonna take longer to get road logs from the last five years, but his current log has him traveling all over the states the women were reported missing."

"Do you have anything concrete so we can pick him up for questioning?"

"No."

"Damn, you got eyes on him yet?"

"No one's home."

"OK, keep me posted if something changes." Jemma pocketed her phone and walked back to the kitchen. "Sorry." Jemma took a seat and picked right back up where she left off. "Did Ken mention anything about an upcoming vacation?"

"No, why?"

"It's not important." Jemma closed her notepad. "I just have one more question: what caused your marriage to fall apart five years ago?"

She looked away briefly at the living room, as if making sure the kids weren't eavesdropping. "He lost interest in me. I wasn't enough to keep him happy. I don't look it now, but I struggled with my weight after my last son was born." She lowered her voice in shame. "I just wasn't enough...he left me."

An awkward silence formed. In Jemma's mind, there wasn't enough time to convince this woman that her weight gain during and after childbirth was not a good enough reason for a man to leave. She pushed the thoughts away for now and concentrated on finding Ken Burns. "No more questions. But I need one favor."

"What?"

"Please call Ken and tell him you're sick. You need him to come over and watch the kids."

CHAPTER 36

Detective Ashmore and Officer Jay Ryan pulled off Highway 32 onto Alexandria Road, a wooded, tree-lined, two-lane blacktop road. The mailboxes they passed had reflectors, but the numbers were hard to read. The GPS showed address 410 just up ahead around a corner. Ashmore slowed his red truck and checked his rearview mirror; no headlights behind him. His truck lights found a black mailbox on the left without reflectors, and the number read 410. Keeping his truck at a constant speed, he passed by. No house was visible from the road, only woods and a gate.

"That gate's new. Wasn't there when the house caught fire."

"The tax records show eight acres. Wonder what's behind that gate." Ashmore continued to drive, passing a few more mailboxes before the road turned to dirt. "Let's turn around here."

As Ashmore made a three-point turn, Ryan studied the survey printed from the county tax office. "This only shows the house and a large shop. Could have pulled in a house trailer, or maybe he lives in the shop if it's big enough."

The truck was now facing the paved road. Ashmore put the truck in park. "With two million dollars, why just live in a shop—or a trailer for that matter?"

"You think he lives somewhere else?"

"I don't know. I mean, wouldn't you?"

"Yeah. What do you want to do?"

"We could walk up, but then we risk finding dogs or getting shot."

"So we drive up, see if we can open the gate, look around, show our badges if we have to, and leave."

Ashmore looked at the time; it was now eight thirty. "No. We would tip our hand. If he's our guy, he could run."

"Then let's go by foot." Ryan pulled out his weapon and checked it. He slid it back in the side holster and then removed his .22 strapped around his calf muscle under his jeans. "Let's get a little closer though."

A few moments passed before Ashmore agreed. He put the truck in drive and moved ahead slowly.

**

The porch light was on, and lights were on in the living room and the kitchen. When Ken drove up, he would clearly see Glenda still up and waiting on him. Jemma and Kennedy sat in the dark in her SUV, parked down the street facing the house. Two more unmarked cars were placed strategically in the neighborhood, one at each of the entrances.

The radio in Kennedy's hand beeped, and then a voice was heard. "Got movement from a red Mustang. Entering neighborhood now."

Jemma picked up her phone and called Glenda. "Make the call now."

Glenda quickly hung up and phoned Ken's mobile.

"Almost there. In the neighborhood," he answered without a greeting.

"Oh. Wow, that was fast."

"You said you were dying."

Glenda took a deep breath. "I'm much better now. I think I'm just going to go to bed now."

"What? I thought you wanted to go to the ER? Thought it was your kidneys or gallbladder or something?"

"No. I was wrong. I think it was food poisoning. I'm much better now that I've thrown up." Glenda saw his headlights from an upstairs dark bedroom as he turned down her street. "I'm sorry to have bothered you. I just really want to go to bed now." Her breath caught as he pulled into the driveway. *Don't get out, don't get out,* she prayed.

Ken sat behind the wheel of his Mustang, pondering his next move. Finally, he responded, "OK, whatever!" He backed out of the driveway and sped away.

The line went dead, and she lowered her phone. Next, she saw Agent Rhodes's white SUV drive by. She wanted to call the agent back but knew she would get stonewalled again. "Just what the hell did you do, Ken?"

She heard a noise and turned.

"Who you talking to, Momma?"

Glenda forced a smile and walked over to their oldest son, Timmy. "No one. Just a wrong number. It's going on nine; you got school tomorrow." She turned him around and walked him back toward his bedroom with her hand on his shoulder. At his doorway, he turned around and gave her a tight hug. Her heart missed a beat. Timmy was just like his father, charming when he had done something wrong. She watched as he pulled away and leapt back into his bed. She debated on asking questions about his last visit with Ken, but when he turned off his lamp and flipped over toward the wall, she walked away.

Tomorrow, I'll ask tomorrow.

CHAPTER 37

No dog barked as Detective Ashmore and Officer Ryan walked through thick underbrush toward the property of Trey Gould. The moonlight was filtered through the trees above, leading them in the right direction. Old cars and farm equipment dotted the property, and an old metal-framed shop stood about fifty yards ahead with a floodlight casting light over a double-size garage door. Quietly, Ryan pointed to the left, where the house once stood, now completely covered with thick weeds and grass.

Ashmore slowly turned around, scanning his surroundings. "Place looks deserted."

"Let's take a closer look at the cars."

They came to an old, rusted Ford pickup with flat tires submerged in tall weeds. Ryan pulled out his flashlight and opened the door. The sound of the whining metal door caused Ashmore to jump and draw his weapon. He turned around and faced the building. No other lights came on, and no one was running toward them. He turned back around and found an empty cab as Ryan flashed his light. They moved toward the tailgate and read the tag. Old and expired. Ashmore did the math in his head. "Never renewed after the fire."

A '55 Chevy and an '88 Oldsmobile both stood abandoned with thick brush surrounding the tires and bumpers. "Truck and the Oldsmobile belonged to the parents. They weren't in the garage when the house caught fire."

Ashmore turned to where the house once stood and then looked at the shop. "Why would Trey Gould use this address for mail?"

"And why bother blocking the driveway with a gate if this is all that's here?" Ryan flashed his lights at the trees bordering the property. "Doesn't appear to be any roads other than this one."

"Time to take a closer look at the shop." Ashmore led the way, and they found the entrance door on the right side of the shop. Ashmore pulled out a handkerchief and tried the door. Locked. They continued toward the back and found a small panel of windows near the top of the building, about ten feet high. There were no lights on inside. Ashmore looked around, trying to find something to stand on. Nothing.

"There was an old chair by the Chevy."

Ashmore shook his head. "Won't be tall enough. Besides, woven fabric looked rotted. I'd fall right through."

Ryan cussed and removed his jacket. "Climb on up."

Ashmore looked at Ryan in disbelief. "You're close to fifty. I'm not climbing on top of you."

"Aw, shut the hell up. I work out. Come on, you want to see what's in here or not?"

Against his better judgement, Ashmore agreed. "Let me at least get the chair to stand on first. Maybe it will hold long enough to get on your shoulders."

It took five minutes of painstaking moves for Ashmore to stand on Ryan's shoulders. As he handed Ashmore the flashlight, he winced. "Don't tell anyone about this. And sure as hell not my wife. She's on my case enough."

"Don't worry. We have no warrant." Ashmore pressed against the window, and it moved forward. It hadn't been locked. He shined the light inside, quickly scanning the area and looking for signs of life, finding no one dead or alive. Two vehicles were parked in the middle, and tools and old parts filled both sides of the wall. The white Corvette was easy to distinguish, but the other, a taller SUV, was partially hidden by a metal stand. He carefully shined the light, slowly trying to decipher the make and model. No such luck.

"See anything? I'm giving out."

"Got a dark-green SUV. Can't see the make or model." His heart raced as he continued flashing the light. "Nothing definitive, damn!"

"Down!"

Ashmore dropped the light and held onto the window frame as Ryan backed away. His fingers burned with pain before he finally turned them loose and tumbled to the ground.

"You OK?"

Ashmore got up and brushed off. "Yeah, you?"

"I think so. What'd you see, anything?"

"A white Vette with a license plate and a dark-green SUV blocked by a stand of tools. Couldn't tell the make. But both looked to be fairly new."

"That's odd. Why keep cars out here?"

"Yeah. He clearly doesn't live out here, and I didn't see those cars registered in his name, just his F One Fifty Ford."

Lights flashed across the woods beside them. Ashmore and Ryan quickly stepped closer to the building, out of view. A car was heard crunching over gravel, and then it stopped. Ashmore quickly grabbed his boots and pulled them on. "Hurry, move to the woods."

They made it behind a thick oak just as they heard a car door close. Then they heard metal grinding as the large garage door opened, and light filtered out through the windows in the back.

"He's here." Ashmore spoke quietly. "Let's get back to the truck fast. We need to be able to follow him."

"What if he's not alone?"

Ashmore thought about the possibility of a woman stuffed in a trunk. He shook his head. "Didn't look like a place he would bring a victim to. Garage was too full. Come on, I think he's here to change out a vehicle."

Ryan didn't look convinced. "Can we take that chance?"

Ashmore sighed. "If he hasn't left in five minutes, we'll come back. Come on." Quickly, they raced back through the woods toward his truck.

CHAPTER 38

He drove around in circles, confused. Was he losing his touch? Finding his next victim Sunday night had proved to be difficult. He'd had a list from the beginning, a plan, but his desire to speed up and kill again caused him to disregard his previous research. He couldn't wait until Monday morning. He needed the thrill of a kill now. When the sun rose tomorrow, his next victim would be found on Main Street, tied up on a bench at the downtown park, four blocks from the police station. A smile formed on his lips at the thought of driving the law enforcement agencies to the brink of madness.

Soon he lost his smile as he remembered getting the phone call earlier. She'd called again, distracting him from his work. The call caused him to delay his plans. Now that he'd dealt with her, it was time. He saw a place ahead; it was dimly lit. His smile returned as he pulled into the parking lot.

***

They tag teamed Ken Burns for fifteen minutes. Jemma would pass Ken at a light and turn off on another street. Then Agent Niki Walker, driving a green pickup truck, would pull up behind him and follow him another mile or two before turning in the opposite direction. Everyone kept in radio contact as they moved within a half mile of each other.

Finally, Ken Burns pulled into Midnight Rose, a local bar in the front of the Rosewood suburb, about two miles from his apartment. Jemma and Kennedy passed by and made a U-turn. They pulled into the semi lit establishment a row down from Burns's Mustang and waited.

Agent Walker pulled into a convenience store parking lot two blocks away. Agent Slater Taylor and Agent Nichols pulled in beside her in their black SUV. They got out and walked over to Agent Walker. Nichols asked, "You ready for this?"

Agent Walker smiled as she pulled off her blazer, revealing a red tank top with a matching lace bra strap peeking out on her tanned shoulder. "Looks like an easy mark. We'll see if I still got my touch." Walker checked her Glock and strapped it around her ankle, hidden by her boot-cut jeans. She got out and grabbed a black jean jacket from the back of the cab. She pulled it on and then lifted her long, blond curls up and out over her shoulders. She stepped back in the truck, flipped open the lighted mirror, and applied red lipstick. She looked back at Nichols and Taylor. "I'm ready; let's do this."

"I'm coming in about three minutes after you. I'll find a corner booth," Taylor said as he checked his sidearm under his leather jacket.

Nichols forced a smile. "Be safe. I'll be right across the street. Follow your gut on this one. Back out at any time. If this is our man, he's sneaky as hell."

"I will."

"Good, OK, let's move." Nichols got back in his SUV and followed Walker's truck. They watched from the other side of the road as she got out, slung her purse over her shoulder, and walked in. "Agent Walker's inside."

Jemma and Kennedy looked at each other. Their hands were tied. With all the news conferences, they would be recognized if they walked inside. They had no choice but to wait outside with Nichols.

A few minutes passed, and Nichols announced Agent Taylor was inside as well. Jemma replied, "Copy." She looked at Kennedy. "The unknown is the hardest part of this job."

He nodded. "Yeah. Why don't we check in with Ashmore, see what he's got?"

Jemma pulled out her mobile and pressed his name. After one ring, it went to voicemail. She ended the call and gave Kennedy a worried look. "Ringer must be off; went straight to voicemail."

"We'll try again later."

The Midnight Rose was half full that Sunday night when Agent Walker opened the door and stepped in. She quickly scanned the area with her big green eyes until she saw Ken Burns sitting at the bar, drinking a fresh beer. The seat beside him was empty. She walked toward the bar and smiled at the men standing around tall tables and looking her way. She chose an empty seat four down from Ken. A man in his early fifties wearing a black T-shirt with the words "Midnight Rose" written in white with a red rose walked toward her.

"What can I get you?"

Niki twirled a strand of hair with her painted fingernails as her eyes slowly rolled over the choices of beer on tap. "I'll have the Ultra. Thanks."

She heard movement, and she turned in time to see a tall man in his early forties slide in between her and the empty barstool beside her. "May I buy you a drink?"

Niki's eyes raked over his face and build before she returned his greeting with a bright smile. "I'd love that."

The bartender placed a frosted mug with her choice of beer in front of her. "I got this, Harry." The man pulled out a ten and placed it down on the counter. She watched the bartender make change. "I'm George. Haven't seen you in here before."

She laughed. "Now that's a line I've heard before. You got anything else behind those killer blue eyes to offer a girl at the bar?" Her laughter was contagious, and he laughed as well. Harry grinned at her from behind the bar and walked away, knowing she could hold her own with one of his local patrons.

"You're too pretty to be alone. You meeting someone?"

"A girlfriend from work. She's running a little late."

"I got some friends." He gestured behind him to a table with four guys, all looking her way. She gave them a warm smile and waved. "Join us if you like."

Niki turned back around and raised her beer to take a sip, buying some time. She placed her mug back down. "That's a nice offer. We'll see when she gets here." Niki pouted her lips. "She sounded a little down when she called, but I'll let you know."

He slowly backed away. "Good. We've no plans to leave anytime soon." He gave a wink as he turned back and joined his friends. Niki studied his backside in his faded jeans and then slowly turned back toward her drink. She looked toward Harry, who was farther down the bar, helping another patron. She checked her watch to give the impression she was still waiting on someone and then casually turned in the direction of Ken Burns as she glanced at the door behind her in anticipation of her friend. Ken Burns was watching her. She gracefully turned back around and caught his eye. She smiled, and he gave her a quick nod in hello. Niki looked down, picked up her beer, and took another sip.

Niki let a couple of minutes pass, and then she quickly placed her beer down and reached into her purse. She pulled out her phone and brought it to her face. "Hello." No one was on the line as she continued a one-sided conversation. She frowned as she listened to nothing. She turned to the group of men behind her. George was watching her intently. She frowned and shook her head. "No, no don't be," she said as she turned back around to face her drink. "Sure, we'll talk tomorrow." Niki placed the phone back in her purse and drained her beer. When she stood to leave, Ken Burns was standing in front of her.

"What's your hurry?" he asked in a warm, friendly voice.

Niki couldn't help noticing his good looks and subtle charm. "No real hurry really. I just got stood up by my girlfriend."

He shook his head. "Now that's a shame. But definitely my gain." He eased into the barstool beside her. "Let me buy you another round."

Niki heard some laughter behind her but didn't dare turn to see George's friends giving him a hard time. She tilted her head toward the group of guys behind them. "You know a better place?"

Ken Burns eased out of his barstool. "Sure do. Just down the road."

She stood. "Great, I'll follow you."

Together they walked out into the parking lot. Agent Niki Walker looked at him and laughed.

"What?"

She poked him in the chest in a fun, teasing gesture. "You don't even know my name."

He grinned. "You're right. I don't."

She crossed her arms while holding her jacket loosely. "I'm Niki."

"I'm Ken."

A brief moment of awkwardness passed. Niki immediately laughed again, dropping her arms, and swayed side to side as she bowed her head. Then she gingerly looked up at him. "OK, Ken, where to?"

"Just a few blocks. My apartment."

Niki stopped swaying and gave him a serious look. "Your apartment? Um, I don't know about that."

He shrugged. "OK, there's another bar about a mile back toward town."

"I think that's better."

"I'm in the Mustang, just follow me."

She walked away toward her truck. When she placed a hand on the door handle, she turned. "Hey, Ken!" He turned. She slowly walked his way. "I don't feel like going to another bar; your place sounds lovely."

He touched her hand. "All right." He released it. "I'll lead the way."

She nodded and walked over to her truck and climbed in. She shut the door and pulled out her phone with the keys. She placed a call and then hit speaker. "Going to his apartment."

Nichols's voice filled the truck. "Fast work, Walker. Be careful."

Backing out, she saw Jemma's white SUV in the rearview mirror. She relaxed. "I will." Ken Burns's little Mustang turned right, and she followed. True to his word, the apartment was just down the road. She followed him into a well-lit parking lot of a gated apartment complex. He waved out the window at guest parking as he continued through an opening to a parking-garage ramp. Niki turned off the engine. "I'm parked in visitor parking up front. He went into their secure garage. Oh, here he comes. He's letting me in through the front door."

"I don't like this, Niki," Nichols said.

Niki looked at the front door. She didn't see any kind of security. How exactly were they to follow her when she needed them. She had no time to respond. She ended the call and slipped her phone back in her purse. She jumped out of her truck and walked inside the opened door. Ken smiled, and the locked door closed behind them.

CHAPTER 39

Ashmore followed the dark Ford Explorer into a twenty-four-hour shopping center. He came to a stop at the end of the row of cars and cut the lights. The Explorer continued. Earlier, Officer Ryan had called the tag in. The Explorer was registered to Virginia Gould at 27 Park Place Lane, Norfolk. The office was to call back with more information on Virginia Gould as soon as they had it. Ashmore picked up his phone and saw that Jemma had called. He was about to return the call when he saw movement up ahead. He dropped the phone back to his lap.

"What's he doing?"

Ashmore couldn't see from his angle. He moved the truck forward and saw the Explorer pull back out down another aisle coming their way. "Duck!"

A yellow two-door Mazda drove by followed by the Explorer a few seconds behind. Ashmore eased back up in his seat. "Did you see the driver of the car?"

"No."

Ashmore reversed and slowly eased forward. When the car and Explorer turned right at the light, he hit the gas, catching up. The road wasn't as crowded now as the time neared ten.

"You think he's following that car?"

Ashmore safely had fallen back to a good distance. Finally, after another turn, he nodded. "I do."

The little Mazda slowly pulled over on the shoulder, and the Explorer pulled in behind. Ashmore saw the blue light and pounded the steering wheel as he sped past them, changing over to the other lane to give them room. "Son of a bitch, he uses a damn cop light." Around the corner and out of sight, Ashmore was finally able to turn around.

"Call for backup. It's him." Ashmore spun his back tires as they hit a patch of wet grass. He floored the truck back to them. "Portraying an officer of the law is enough to take his ass in now and lock him up." He rounded the corner, and the Explorer was gone. Only the yellow Mazda remained on the shoulder. Ashmore pulled up beside the Mazda; it was empty. He hit the steering wheel again as he looked in every direction. "Where the hell is he?"

"There!" Officer Ryan yelled. "To your right."

Ashmore saw fading taillights. "Where's he going?"

"I don't know. Beaver Drive opens up to the freeway. Hurry."

"What was Virginia Gould's address?"

Ryan looked down at his notes. "Twenty-seven Park Place Lane, Norfolk."

"Where's that?"

Ryan fumbled with his phone as he tried to type in the address.

"Hurry, we're losing them. He's getting on the freeway."

A map appeared on his phone. A route was drawn to Park Place Lane. "It's four miles away, near downtown. I know where this is. The freeway takes you. It's a set of townhomes off Millard Boulevard."

"Call it in. He's got to be taking her there."

Jemma was sitting across from Ken Burns's gated apartment when Kennedy got the call. "What? Are you sure?" Silence filled her vehicle as she anxiously awaited, listening and trying to decipher Kennedy's one-sided conversation. Finally, he ended the call.

"What?"

"We're following the wrong trail." Jemma looked confused. He explained, "That was the precinct operator. Ashmore and Ryan are following a dark-green Explorer. They said he just impersonated a police officer; he's taking someone."

"Where are they?" She started the car.

"On Beech Freeway. The SUV's registered to Virginia Gould at Twenty-seven Park Place Lane. They think the Explorer's heading there now."

***

Ashmore drove harder and turned left, closing the gap between them. The Explorer turned off Millard Boulevard and out of sight. By the time Ashmore was able to make the same turn, a wrought-iron gate was closing, keeping nonresidents out of the small community of about a dozen upscale townhomes. Ryan jumped out of the truck and peered through some shrubs bordering the gate. He saw a garage door closing on one of the homes on the far right. He leaned inside the truck. "He's pulled into a garage and closed the door. Third down from the end. I'll see if I can get a phone number."

Ashmore watched him run around the truck to the small call box and then picked up his phone and called Jemma. "It's Trey Gould. Our Strangler is Trey Gould! But the Explorer is registered to a Virginia Gould. Gotta be a relative."

"I heard. Where are you?"

"Twenty-seven Park Place Lane, parked outside a locked gate to a townhome community."

"I'm on my way and so is help. Did he see you?"

Ashmore replayed the chase in his head. He was never close enough. "No. I really don't think so."

"Is there a number to call on the gate? We need access now."

"Ryan's working on that now."

"I'm six miles away; hang tight. If anyone gets there before me, tell them to stand down until I get there."

Jemma looked over at Kennedy. He'd been on the phone as well. "What else do we know?"

"Virginia Gould was adopted by her grandparents at age four. Her grandparents reside just outside Boston, Massachusetts."

"Boston, that's not too far from Concord."

"There's more." Kennedy stopped talking to hang on as Jemma took a sharp turn on two tires. "Virginia was in an accident that left her mentally challenged. Her parents, Lou and Kate Gould, thought it was in everyone's best interest for their daughter to move in with Kate's parents."

"What accident?"

"Don't know specifics. Happened in the home."

"Is it possible he tried to hurt his sister? Maybe tried to kill her? We'll need to find out and reach out to the grandparents. If he's our serial killer, an incident at an early age could have set him off down this path." Jemma saw Park Place Lane up ahead. She accelerated and then braked and turned. Ashmore's truck was still waiting outside the closed gate.

***

Ken Burns's apartment was nice and surprisingly clean for a bachelor. Niki counted the exits: two. One off the balcony with about a twenty-four-foot drop and the door they entered from the hallway. Two F was a corner apartment so he only had one neighbor. Niki dropped her purse on the kitchen island and walked toward the balcony. She unlocked the door and slid it open. She heard Ken say he was going to grab the beers. She nodded. Stepping out on the balcony, she saw no backup if needed. His apartment was on the opposite side of the entrance and guest parking, overlooking a small pond and a walking trail.

She felt him near, and she turned. Grabbing the beer she said, "It's a nice view."

"Yeah, I pay extra to be on this side—quieter."

She noticed a small bowl of shells in the corner. Remembering he had three boys, she asked, "Who collected these?"

Ken looked to the corner of the balcony. "My nephews."

Niki forced a smile. Right away, she knew his intentions. He was either their killer or she was just a one-night stand he picked up and never planned to see again. The wind picked up, and Niki wasn't wearing her jacket. He pulled her gently back inside and closed the door. She walked through the living room and straight into the kitchen.

Eyeing the knife set by the stove, she casually walked over and ran her hand along the shiny-metal gas stovetop. She turned around, leaned up against it, and drank from her beer.

Ken leaned against the small island in front of her. "You hungry?"

She shook her head. "What you do for a living?"

"I'm a truck driver."

She gave him a look of disbelief. "Really? I thought you would be covered in tattoos and have a beer gut."

He laughed and neared her. "I've got some tattoos I'd like to show you."

Niki placed her beer down on the counter and put both hands on his chest. She looked into his eyes and tried to read him. His eyes showed no evil intentions, only lust. Was he not the killer? Her mind scrolled through a mental list, looking for signs. Nothing. She dropped her hands and reached for her beer once more. He stopped her.

His touch was gentle as he wrapped his hand around her wrist. His other hand touched her cheek and pulled her blond hair away from her face. "You're beautiful. Too beautiful to be hitting bars alone."

Niki didn't break eye contact. "I wasn't supposed to be alone. I was meeting a girlfriend, remember?"

His hand left her wrist and moved up her shapely arm. He leaned within an inch of her face. "Are you sure about that?"

Her phone rang in her purse, and she jumped. "I need to get that, sorry." She moved toward her purse, and he stepped in her way, blocking her.

"Let it go to voicemail." His finger touched her shoulder, and then he looped it under her bra strap.

Niki playfully pushed him back. "No. I need to get it. Could be my friend."

He grabbed both of her arms and pushed her back against the counter. His lips were on hers. Niki relaxed and kissed him back. He let go of her arms, and just as his hands found her waist, she broke free again. She grabbed her phone and turned to him. He was resting back along the island with his arms crossed.

Niki stepped into the living room. "Hello?"

"Get out of the apartment; it's not him," Nichols instructed.

She turned around and looked back at Ken. "Are you sure we have to do this tonight?" Ken pushed off the island and moved her way.

"I'm sure. Move fast and get down here."

"I understand. I'm on my way." Niki frowned as she lowered her phone. "I have to go, sorry."

"I don't think so."

Niki raised her eyebrows. "Look, Ken, something's come up. I'm sorry." He continued her way, clearly not happy. She watched as his green eyes turned hard and his jaw muscles tightened. She took a step back, waiting on his next move.

CHAPTER 40

The security gate to Virginia Gould's townhome community had been opened for law enforcement. The lease was signed by Virginia Gould, but no one recalled ever meeting her. Also, the layout of each home was explained: main level contained 1,450 square feet of living space with a small porch and sliding glass doors. The second floor had only a small loft upstairs, no exit. Officers Norman Lewis and Rick Brown were stationed in the back, watching the sliding glass doors for any movement. So far, none, and the blinds were drawn with the lights on. At the entrance, Officer Joe Wilson and Officer Mark Wayne stood near their cop car on the outside of the closed gate, monitoring closely all vehicles. Any car trying to enter the complex was turned away. People were not happy since the time was nearing 10:30 p.m.

Detective Ashmore and Jemma were huddled with Kennedy near the closed garage door of number twenty-seven, the same garage Officer Ryan had watched the green Explorer pull into fifteen minutes ago. FBI Agents Nichols, Taylor, and Walker had yet to arrive. Time was of the essence, and Jemma decided not to wait. Officer Ryan walked around the corner and headed their way.

"Anything?"

"No, nothing."

Jemma nodded and looked at Kennedy. "We can't wait any longer. She'll be dead."

"I agree. Let's do this."

Jemma walked to the back of her SUV and pulled out a blue long-sleeved T-shirt. She removed her blazer and pulled it on over her silk blouse. Next, she pulled her hair back into a low ponytail and covered her head with a pizza-delivery-logo cap. Lastly, she picked up a cardboard box and closed the trunk.

The sidewalk to each entrance was dimly lit. Only a single light illuminated the small porch. The door was wooden with a peephole. To the right was a narrow window covered with blinds. She stood on the opposite side of the window and rang the doorbell.

A minute passed and no reply. Jemma shifted her feet, trying to calm her nerves. She rang the bell again and knocked on the door. Soon, she heard noise, and she lowered her head so only her hat was visible. The door opened, and a man who fit their Harrison Avery description opened the door.

Jemma barely looked up as she balanced the pizza on one hand and tried reading a number on her receipt with her other hand. "I got one thick-crust supreme pizza for fifteen twelve."

"I didn't order no pizza." He moved to the side and looked toward the gate. "How'd you get in?"

"Sorry, is this not number twenty-six? I just rang." Jemma kept her head low, looking for the house number by the doorbell.

"No, it's not. Next door." Trey took a step toward her and motioned to the home beside him.

Glass broke on the sliding door. Jemma quickly dropped the box and shoved a gun in Trey's gut. Immediately, she saw a scratch along his face and neck. "FBI, don't move."

Trey looked into her eyes and a glimmer of recognition appeared. He knew who she was. "Agent Rhodes, we finally meet." Laughter rang out as his blue eyes turned dark and mean. Swiftly, he raised his arms, trying to strike her, but she was ready. Raising her knee, she struck him hard in the groin. Trey Gould hit the ground, howling. Jemma shoved the gun to his head. "Move again and I'll save the taxpayers a lot of money."

Ashmore and Kennedy ran toward them as voices were heard from within. "Need an ambulance," yelled Officer Norman Lewis.

Kennedy got on the radio and instructed the ambulance that was parked just outside the gate to enter as Ashmore cuffed Trey Gould and hauled him to his feet. Trey tried fighting once again, and Jemma gave a punch to his gut, causing him to double over again. Officers Wilson and Wayne had jumped out of their cop car, which now had on its flashing lights. Jemma looked at them. "Get him to the car."

Kennedy, Ashmore, and Jemma entered the townhome. They saw Officer Rick Brown motioning them down a hallway. Jemma ran forward and then stopped cold at the doorway to a small bedroom. A dark-headed woman was tied up on a single bed. Her clothing had been cut from her body, and a scarf was wrapped around her neck. Officer Norman Lewis was administering CPR and checking for a pulse. Jemma slowly neared. "Are we too late?"

Lewis turned. "I don't think so. I got a pulse, but it's weak."

Jemma instructed Ashmore, "Cut her down." Jemma pulled off her blue T-shirt and covered her body. A paramedic rushed in. They all stepped back.

"She's alive." He touched her neck, pulling away the scarf. Red marks were visible. "We got to move fast."

A stretcher was brought in, and no one said a word as the paramedics loaded her up and took her away. Jemma noticed a video camera in the corner. It was on. She walked over and pressed the stop button. She rewound as Ashmore neared. They watched as Trey Gould entered the room and stripped off his clothing, and then he straddled her, pulling the red scarf around her neck. The woman was unconscious the entire time. The sound of a doorbell could be heard, and Trey Gould released the scarf. They watched as he dressed and left the room. Jemma pressed the stop button and looked at Ashmore with tears in her eyes. "We did it. We might have saved her."

Ashmore pulled her into his arms and held her tight.

Jemma and Ashmore stood outside as a forensic team bagged the evidence. A black SUV and a green pickup truck pulled into the parking lot. Agents Nichols, Taylor, and Walker quickly got out and joined them. Jemma noticed Agent Niki Taylor's ripped shirt. "What happened?"

"Ken Burns got a little frisky when I told him I had to leave. Ended up taking him down."

"We couldn't leave until Agent Walker came out. Looks like we missed everything," Nichols said.

"Not everything. He should be sitting in an interrogation room by now." Jemma smiled. "Come on, let's go bust his balls."

***

Monday

It was 4:00 p.m. when Jemma and Nichols wrapped up the paperwork on the River Strangler. Neither had slept a wink. Kennedy had already given a press conference at noon and another one was scheduled at 6:00 p.m. The night had been long and tedious. The first hour was spent questioning Trey Gould, who eventually lawyered up. There wasn't much he could deny. They had him on video attempting to murder Jessica Finn, the girl taken from the yellow Mazda. In addition, other tapes that were made of the murders of Hazel Rice, Jacklyn Riggs, and Melissa Jarman were found in the living room beside his TV. Trey Gould had not attempted to hide his crimes in his home. In fact, it appeared he enjoyed watching them repeatedly.

Nichols had thrown a punch around 1:00 a.m. when Gould laughed about Nichols's wife and children. Ashmore had to pull him off Trey Gould and threw him out of the room to keep him from killing Gould with his own bare hands. The rest of the night was spent tracing Trey Gould's financial records, trying to connect him with the murders of the missing women in the Northeast. Nothing had materialized yet. It would take more time.

Virginia Gould's guardians, who were her grandparents, had been called at 7:00 a.m. The grandmother had called Trey last night. She wanted to remind him that his sister's birthday was today, and he hadn't called. Other than that phone call, they hadn't talked to him in almost a year. They gave very little information on Virginia's accident as a young child. Her daughter, Kate, and son-in-law, Lou, had only said she slipped in the bath, and Kate had found her unconscious. Apparently, Kate had stepped away only for a minute or two. Trey was six at the time and home that day. Raising Virginia was just too hard for Kate, and her parents were willing to take her.

Since the death of Lou and Kate Gould, Trey had begun using Virginia Gould's identity for purchasing items. The upscale townhome on 27 Park Place, the green Ford Explorer, as well as other vehicles, including a boat, had all been in her name. They were still trying to track down the location of the boat that was titled and licensed during the same timeframe as when the River Strangler had dropped his victims near water five years ago.

Jemma looked at Nichols. "I'm mentally and physically drained."

Officer Meriam walked into the conference room and handed Jemma a manila envelope. "The file on Andrew Lane."

Jemma sat up, rolled her shoulders, and turned her neck, trying to knock out the kinks that had formed. She opened it and read. The nylon rope found at Andrew and Bianca's beach home was consistent with Joy Sutton's injuries to her wrists and ankles. In addition, the safety cord in the trunk of Andrew's Mercedes-Benz E-Class had been cut. A picture of a taillight was on another page. It had been replaced recently. No insurance claim was made, and there was no credit card receipt showing the new purchase. "Joy Sutton's foot was fractured and cut."

"Yeah, we can only assume he paid cash for a new brake light. Still checking with all the body shops; someone will remember something."

"Or not. Money can buy a lot of things." Jemma continued to read. They were still waiting on DNA results for the blanket from the beach house's bed and fibers from the Benz's trunk. The shoes found in the buck stove were still at the lab, also pending results. Jemma turned the page and saw a photo of a key. A note was beside it, explaining it fit Joy Sutton's apartment. She turned another page and found a transcript record of an interview with Jill Eckelberg, Andrew's secretary, who had provided a timeline of Andrew's whereabouts the day Joy Sutton was believed to have been taken. She also had told them that Andrew was planning to hire her, and she had not signed in October 30 when she had visited while Jill took lunch.

She lowered the file. "I wish we could have found Joy Sutton's car."

"That could be anywhere," Meriam said without hope.

"So, looks like Andrew Lane did indeed kill Joy Sutton."

"Looks like it," Meriam stated. "Look at the last page. There's a statement from the prison guard who was on watch leading up to Deluca's execution."

Jemma flipped a few pages until she found it. Officer Knots had explained how Deluca became agitated after a news conference the evening of October 29. A copy of Linda Peet's news report from Channel 12 was included. It was the live broadcast from Lake Maury, where Hazel Rice was found dead. Officer Knots explained how Deluca had demanded to see his attorney, Joy Sutton, and how the real killer was still out there. Jemma looked at Ashmore. "So Deluca, who was innocent, was given hope that night. Something he had previously thought was impossible. Is it possible he saw Andrew Lane with Laura Stone? Is that what he told Joy Sutton to cause her to see Andrew Lane the next day?"

Ashmore shook his head. "We'll never know; they're all dead."

Jemma flipped back through the file. "Paper was burned along with what appeared to be a briefcase at the beach house."

"If Andrew Lane had a key to her apartment and had cheated before, we can only assume him and Sutton were tight as well."

"So Joy Sutton keeps quiet, watches Deluca die, and then what?" asked Jemma.

Ashmore suggested, "Maybe she second guessed herself. Confronted Andrew the next day."

"I remember reading an empty bottle of wine was found beside Joy Sutton's nightstand. Also, the prison reported that this was her first execution," Meriam said in an effort to help fill in the pieces.

Jemma dropped the file and sat back. Officer Wayne walked in, carrying a tray of sandwiches. Jemma eyed the food with suspicion. She had felt sick throughout the night and found trying to eat anything today hopeless. She stood. "I'm heading back to the Rivermont. I need some sleep."

Ashmore gave her a concerned look and then handed her a sandwich. "Here, take it with you."

Jemma took the sandwich. "Thanks. I'll see everyone in the morning before I leave."

"I'll hold you to it." Ashmore got the door.

Jemma walked out and then turned. "Thanks for everything, Jason. We make a good team."

He smiled. "We do. You're welcome in this town anytime. Just hope you don't come back only for a murder."

She gave him a warm smile and then touched his arm. "I'll see you tomorrow. Good-night." Jemma turned and left, feeling his eyes still on her back.

CHAPTER 41

Tuesday morning

Jemma woke up at the Rivermont Hotel at three o'clock. Something she had seen had triggered something in her mind, and she couldn't place a finger on it. Andrew hadn't acted as if he killed Laura Stone; instead, it was a look of guilt. His confession over an affair seemed genuine. She rose from bed after failing to fall back asleep by four. Turning on a light, she walked over to the small table and pulled out her files from the case. She flipped through them. *What is it? Lane had killed Joy Sutton, and Trey Gould was clearly guilty of the recent murders.* She flipped through her files and stopped when she saw the stapled pages given to her by Officer Rick Brown. He along with Officer Norman Lewis had personally been in charge of looking into Daniel Stone's old cases. Jemma picked up the thick stack and began to read. Brown had summarized each of Stone's old clients' cases.

Officer Lewis had arranged each case by date. She looked at the last three cases. All were victories. She looked at the last case that had gotten most of the attention. Stone had gotten his client off due to a technicality. Now, his client walked a free man while a young boy and his parents picked up the pieces. The evidence was there. The boy had been sexually abused. However, an officer had failed to gather proper evidence, and the case had been dismissed.

Jemma looked closely at his parents, Tom and Ruth Biddy. Both worked full-time and attended church on Sunday. The father also coached his Little League, but most importantly, they all had alibis. Yes, they would be mad as hell, but Jemma couldn't see Tom or Ruth paying a hitman. More than likely, they just wanted to move on and help their son pick up the pieces. Jemma glanced over the names that were listed who had helped on the case.

She flipped to the case dated before. Again, she read the summary, this one about a case of domestic abuse. The wife was filing charges, and Stone was defending the husband. During the third day of the trial, the wife had dropped the charges. Andrew Lane had wanted to continue the case, but his hands were tied since his witness recounted her entire claim of abuse. Laura looked at the judge's name on the bench. She flipped back to the other case: different judge.

Jemma looked at the time as she turned to another case. She read the summary: a burglary. No one was beaten or killed. Only electronics were taken from a couple's home while they were out to dinner. Insufficient evidence was found, and Stone's client walked. A different judge presided over the case. Her eyes scanned the other names helping on the case and flipped the page. Suddenly, she flipped back. "Wait, where is Liza Stone? Wasn't she his assistant?" It took Jemma a moment to recall her maiden name: Garrett.

Jemma looked through the cases, and finally she found her name after going back two more. "Where was Liza during these last five cases?" Jemma pulled out the list of people who worked for Daniel Stone. At the time of Laura's death, Liza was not listed. Picking up a pen, she wrote the last date that Liza had worked on a case. Five months had gone by before Laura was killed.

Patiently, Jemma waited as her computer booted up. She sat back down with a fresh, hot coffee and looked through Officer's Brown's file. Everyone in Daniel Stone's office had an address listed along with alibis during the time of Laura's death. Liza Garrett's name was missing from that list. Jemma looked at the time again; it was five-twenty. She hesitated briefly and then picked up her phone, which was charging on the nightstand, and pressed Ashmore's name. He answered on the second ring.

"Sorry to wake you, Ashmore."

"No problem. Besides, I'm up. What's going on?"

"You know that feeling that something isn't just quite finished yet?"

"I do."

She sighed. "Yeah, well, I got that feeling in the middle of the night, and I couldn't go back to sleep. I decided to get up and look back through Daniel Stone's cases."

"Did it help?"

"Yes, I found something off."

"Off? How so?"

"Daniel's new wife, Liza Garrett."

"What about her?"

"She stopped working on Daniel's cases about five months before Laura's death and didn't return until about a year later. Do you know why?"

"No, I don't."

"How fast can we get an address during that time?"

"Shouldn't take too long. I'll make a call, I'll get a shower, and then dress and come over. I should have something by then."

Jemma looked at Stone's case files, still spread out upon the table. "Thanks. I'll keep digging into his cases. See you soon." Jemma ended her call and continued reading. By the time Ashmore knocked on the door, Jemma had created a timeline of Liza Garrett's work history at Stone Attorney of Law.

"Hey, come on in."

Ashmore scanned the room and the unmade bed. His eyes drifted back to her. She turned away from him and walked over to the small sitting area with two chairs and table. Her computer screen displayed her recent search: Liza Garrett Stone's tax records.

"What did you find out?"

Ashmore handed her a printout. "Her mother lives an hour away. She was staying at her home."

"Is the address nineteen Peachtree, Winston, North Carolina?"

"Yes."

Jemma clicked a button, and a new screen appeared on her computer. "Liza paid taxes on nineteen Peachtree last year." She pulled up another screen. "JoAnn Marie Garrett passed away in July last year at Morning Star nursing home."

"Looks like she left because her mom was sick."

"Maybe, or…" Jemma paused, thinking about her theory one more time. "Maybe she was pregnant with Daniel Stone's child."

"Wow, you think?" Ashmore looked confused for a brief moment and then realization filled his face. "Wait a minute. You think Ashley Stone is her daughter and not her sister's child."

Jemma nodded. "It adds up. Why couldn't she be her daughter?" She watched as Ashmore began to pace in the small room, trying to remember the past. "She came back to town after Deluca's conviction. Did she have Ashley with her or was it later?"

"I can't remember."

Jemma shuffled through some papers on the table. "They married in the summer a year after Laura's death. The first time you met Ashley, how old do you think she was?"

"Gosh, I'm not real sure. Young but not too young. Um, Rita will know. Let me call her."

Jemma watched as Ashmore pulled out his phone and called his ex. "Hi, yeah, sorry. I'll be quick. Do you remember when Ashley Stone came to live with Daniel and Liza Stone?" A brief moment of silence went by, and Ashmore added, "Yeah, I know, but what do you remember?" He nodded as she talked and then replied, "Thanks, babe. Go back to sleep. We'll talk later."

The affectionate words and tone didn't escape Jemma. Jason Ashmore still cared very deeply for his ex-wife. She pushed the thoughts away and focused on the work at hand. "Well, does she remember?"

He nodded. "She enrolled in Tracie's preschool at year four, fall semester, but was one year behind. Ashley would have been in the three-year-old class."

Jemma grabbed the pen off the table. "How old is Tracie?" Ashmore quickly looked away. Jemma neared him. "Jason, what is it?"

"We lost Tracie to leukemia."

The floor shifted beneath Jemma's feet. "Oh, God!" she whispered as she held a hand over her mouth. Quickly, she rushed to Jason and wrapped her arms around him. "I had…" she paused as she held him tighter. Time seemed to stand still as Jemma processed it all in her head. She knew there was something, but this completely blindsided her. She pulled back and looked into his brown eyes. "I've very sorry, Jason. I can't imagine your pain."

He touched her shoulders, slightly squeezing, and then let his hands trail down her arms. He released her. "Tracie would have turned six this past March."

"When did she die?"

"Two days after Christmas; she was four."

Jemma took a step back and sat on the unmade bed. The case no longer held her interest as she stared intently at Jason. "Come sit with me." She patted the space beside her.

Slowly, he took the step and lowered himself beside her. She placed her arms around him, and together they fell backward in the bed. Silent tears rolled down her cheeks as she buried her face into his chest. No words were needed as a long silence formed between them. Jemma was just on the verge of sleep when Jason released her and sat back up. She rubbed her eyes and leaned up on her elbows.

Jason stood up and faced her. "Let's take a road trip to Winston. Talk to the neighbors and see what birth records we can find on Ashley Stone."

"OK." Jemma slowly rose to a sitting position as Jason turned, walked toward the small table, and picked up a file. Just as Jemma stood, Jason turned. He dropped the file, papers scattering to the floor. He took two large steps toward her and wrapped her back up into his arms.

His lips found hers as they sank together back on the bed. Tenderly, his hands worked the small of her back under her shirt as he kissed her lips, cheek, and neck. Jemma reached for his knit pullover and began tugging it up and over his head. They stilled briefly as their eyes locked once again. He touched her lips with his finger. "Oh, how I've wanted you since the first day I met you, Jemma Rhodes."

She smiled as she pulled him down on top of her. "Well, that's good to know. I want you too, Jason Ashmore."

CHAPTER 42

The Richmond field office called back with new information. Jemma climbed out of bed and picked up some clothing. Nineteen Peachtree had been sold to Judy Cast, who just happened to be the former nurse who cared for JoAnn Garrett before she entered the nursing home. Jemma made a few notes as she stood, wearing only a tank top. She ended the call and looked at Jason, still lying in bed and making no effort to get up. He patted the bed beside him as he sat up against the headboard with the sheet tangled around his waist. She neared, and he pulled her back down and cradled her in his arms.

She said nothing as he held her tenderly. It felt so good. He was good. She tilted her head back and looked into his brown eyes.

He smiled. "You're even more beautiful in person, if that's even possible."

She sat up. "What?"

"The picture. The picture your dad showed me from his wallet."

Jemma thought back to the first time they'd met. She'd forgotten all about his comment about working with her dad on a case and seeing her picture. She smirked. "Why was my dad showing you my picture?"

"He wanted me to meet you. Said we would have a lot in common."

She laughed. "How long ago was this?"

He shrugged. "I don't know, maybe five years ago. I'd made a trip to Washington, and he was the agent who met me. We spent half a day together, going through some files." He pulled her back into his arms and then kissed her. His hand dove into her thick, red hair. "Can't wait to see your dad again and tell him we finally connected."

She punched him playfully, and he tackled her on the bed. He was on top of her again, slowly pulling her tank top back off. "Um, Jason…um, we need to go." His lips silenced her as he entered her again. Jemma closed her eyes and gave in to her needs. The case was just going to have to wait a little bit longer.

Jemma was behind the wheel when they arrived in Winston, North Carolina. Peachtree was just up ahead in a small neighborhood off Main Street that ran through the historic downtown. Jemma followed her GPS's commands and pulled into the small driveway of a two-story home that looked to have been built in the early 1900s. Beside the home was a colonial-style bed and breakfast.

Jemma cut the engine and eased out of her seat. She looked at the well-manicured yards that bordered the sidewalk; following it would take you back to the town, which was four blocks away. "Nice little area."

Ashmore closed his door and nodded. "Yeah, it is. I've been antique shopping here."

Jemma gave him a look.

"Against my will, of course."

Together they walked up the sidewalk and stopped at the "Welcome" mat. Jemma pressed the doorbell. A curtain moved in the room next to the covered porch. "Good. We're in luck."

Soon the door lock twisted, and the wooden door was pulled open. A brunette in her mid-forties stood behind the locked screen door. "May I help you?"

Jemma gave her a warm smile as she produced her FBI badge. "I'm Special Agent Rhodes with the FBI, and this is Detective Ashmore with Norfolk Police Department. May we come in? We have some questions about your former patient, Ms. JoAnne Garrett."

After a slight hesitation, Judy unlocked the screen door and pushed it forward for them. "Um, sure, but I'll need to get ready for work soon. I'm working the noon shift."

Ashmore noted the time. "We appreciate it. This shouldn't take too long."

They were escorted to the room on the right, the one that was adjacent to the porch. The small sitting room with vintage lace curtains had the original hardwood floors, but the furniture looked new. Jemma and Ashmore took a seat on the floral settee across from the matching oversized chair that Judy claimed. She forced a small smile. "So how can I help you?" She gave a nervous laugh. "It's not every day someone has the FBI at their doorsteps. But thank goodness you're in an unmarked car 'cause then I would've been the talk of the town."

"Yes, I can see how that could happen," Jemma responded with a genuine laugh. "But tell me, there weren't questions when you continued to live here when Ms. Garrett was placed in a nursing home over two years ago?"

Judy's dark-green eyes briefly found the floor before she retuned her eyes to Jemma. "No, not really. I've lived in this home for the last eight years."

"But as a caregiver, correct?" asked Jemma.

"Well, yes. I was hired to take care of Ms. Garrett when she was diagnosed with early stages of Alzheimer's."

Jemma pulled out a small notepad and pen from the inside of her blazer. She made a few rambling notes as a tactic to rattle the witness. She allowed a few more moments of silence to pass before looking back up with a smile. "And what were your day-to-day duties in the home?"

"Oh, well, a little of everything. I cooked, took Ms. Garrett shopping when needed, some light cleaning, but mainly I was paid to be her companion."

"And this lasted until Ms. Garrett entered Morning Star nursing home?" Jemma held her pen by her cheek, waiting for Judy to answer.

"Yes."

Jemma wrote some more notes. Without looking up, she inquired, "And you stayed on in the home?"

"Yes. I went to work at Morning Star. Ms. Garrett's daughter felt it would be calming for Ms. Garrett to know a familiar face at her new home."

Jemma looked up. "So you got to remain in the house and gained new employment with the help of her daughter, Liza Stone. That was very kind of her." She looked at Ashmore. "Wouldn't you think so, Detective Ashmore?"

"Very kind of Mrs. Stone."

Judy began to pick at her nails as they rested in her lap. "Ms. Garrett and Mrs. Stone have always treated me well." Judy spoke quietly as she looked at her chipped nail on her right index finger.

Jemma patiently sat through the awkward silence forming around them.

Finally, Judy looked up and removed her hands from her lap. She ran one hand through her dark hair, pushing it back from her face. "I have work soon. I still need to get ready. Um, I'm not sure why you're here." She looked from Jemma to Ashmore. "Ms. Garrett died peacefully in her bed at Morning Star. I was there by her side."

Jemma tapped her pen on her notepad. "According to the records at Winston Court House, your name is on this property. Did you purchase the home after Ms. Garrett passed away?"

Judy slowly nodded. "I like it here." She looked down again. "It's been my home for many years," she said as she began to pick her nails.

Jemma stood and walked around the small room. "I guess Mrs. Stone would have no need for this home since she's happily married in Norfolk." Jemma opened the lace curtains and looked out at the neighborhood. "Have you seen Mrs. Stone's home? It's quite stunning." Jemma let the curtain fall back in place as she slowly turned and faced Judy.

"I've heard it's very nice."

Jemma smiled and walked forward. "Heard? You never saw it on your many trips to Norfolk?"

Judy looked uneasy. "Trips to Norfolk?"

Jemma took a seat again. "Sure. You and Ashley made that trip several times over the last several years. Especially on your weeks off from Morning Star."

Judy took a deep breath as she sank lower in her chair.

"It's amazing how one's life can be tracked by their use of toll roads," Ashmore said.

She looked at him. "Ashley stayed here after her mother ran off to California. I helped take care of her."

"Funny you didn't mention caring for a child earlier." Jemma picked up her pen and began to scribble in her notepad once more.

"Well, there can be a lot of gossip in a small town when a mother runs off without her daughter."

"Right. And who is Ashley's mother?"

Judy's eyes found the framed photo on the mantle. "Ms. Garrett's youngest daughter, Kimberly."

Ashmore rose from his seat, walked over to the mantle, and picked up the picture of Ms. Garrett with her two daughters, Liza and Kimberly. "When was this taken? Beautiful photo."

"Um, I'm not sure."

He placed the framed photo back on the mantle and turned back around. "When's the last time you saw Kimberly?"

Relief washed over Judy. "Is this what this is about, Kimberly Garrett?" She looked from Ashmore to Jemma. "I've never met her, and Ms. Garrett never talked about her."

"Really, I thought Alzheimer's patients liked to talk about the past, especially the early years."

Judy stood. "Well, yes, of course. She did talk a lot about both her daughters when they were young children. Look, I'm really sorry, but I need to get ready for work. I really don't know anything about Kimberly Garrett."

"No? Ashley Garrett just appeared one day on the porch? Was she in a basket accompanied by a stork?" Jemma asked as she raised her pen to her cheek once again.

Judy frowned. "No. Mrs. Stone brought Ashley here when she was just a baby. Look, I was hired to do a job. I didn't ask questions; it wasn't my place."

"Please sit down, Judy." Jemma spoke sternly. "You delivered Ashley right here in this home. Her mother is Liza Garrett Stone."

She sat as her face turned white.

"Mrs. Stone gave you this home last year in exchange for your silence, correct?"

Judy's green eyes finally looked up and met Jemma's eyes. She slowly nodded.

***

Jemma was riding shotgun in Ashmore's red pickup truck. Sheriff Kennedy followed them, and Officers Rick Brown and Norman Lewis were close behind as they all pulled into the driveway of Daniel and Liza Stone's home at half past six. They were all met at the door by Mr. Stone, who had done little to hide his frown, showing his displeasure of again being disrupted by their unexpected visit.

"Mr. Stone, may we come in?" asked Sheriff Kennedy.

Daniel looked at the police cruiser sitting in his yard for the whole world to see. He looked to his left and right at the few homes in sight. Seeing no one coming and going in the neighborhood, he quickly motioned for them to enter. He looked at Ashmore. "This is twice in one week, detective, that you've dropped by unannounced. My patience is thinning."

Ashmore just smiled, and gave Daniel a pat on the shoulder, as if they were old friends. Then he moved past him into the foyer, infuriating Daniel even further.

"Is your wife home, Mr. Stone?" asked Jemma.

"My wife? Why?"

Liza Stone rounded the corner, rocking their baby in her arms. "Mrs. Stone, glad you're home. We'd like to ask you some questions."

She walked forward with a look that showed her annoyance at their unannounced visit. "I need to change her first." Her perfume lingered as she passed and began climbing the staircase.

Jemma nodded for Brown to follow.

At the sound of his approach, Liza stopped on the staircase and turned. "Oh, I don't think so." She looked at Daniel in disbelief, begging him to do something.

"What's this all about? I heard on the news everything's over."

Running footsteps were heard above, and everyone looked up in time to see Ashley and a friend move past Liza and down the staircase. Ashley paused a moment to look around at everyone. "Daddy, we're going to make hot chocolate."

Daniel gave her a big smile. "Sure, baby, go right ahead. Daddy just has some work to finish up here."

Everyone watched as they moved on, innocently unaware of what was happening in the home, skipping and bouncing along the hardwood floors without a care in the world.

"May we use your study, Mr. Stone? We need to finish up some loose ends," Jemma asked, breaking the silence.

Daniel looked down the hallway toward the girls. "Doesn't look like I have a choice."

"Danny!" Liza shouted sternly, and then the baby began to wiggle and fuss in her arms.

"Liza, dear, just come on back down when you're done. It's fine."

As if she'd just been slapped, she quickly turned and stormed up the stairs. Jemma hid her smile as one officer remained in the foyer, and she continued toward the study with Kennedy and Ashmore following. Daniel took his same seat as before, and Jemma and Kennedy took the sofa across from him. Ashmore stood by the open doorway, waiting on Liza.

Immediately, Daniel began tearing into Kennedy. "This is bordering on harassment, Sheriff. You better have a damn good reason to come back to my home again."

"Now calm down, Daniel. Like Agent Rhodes stated, we've got a few more questions."

Moments passed, and Liza walked by without baby Sophia. They could hear Liza talking in the kitchen to the girls. Finally, she joined them and shut the door behind her. She stood by the closed door and crossed her arms in a defensive stance. "Well?"

"New information has come to our attention." Jemma decided to dive in and put the haughty woman in her place. "I've just learned that you and Daniel are Ashley Stone's birth parents."

Daniel immediately started laughing and shaking his head. He looked at Liza and stopped laughing. She had turned as white as the blouse she was wearing. He looked back at the officers. "Ashley is our niece. Her mother ran off as soon as she was born. We adopted Ashley several years ago." He looked back at Liza, who hadn't said a word. His brows creased in concern. "Liza, tell them. We kept Ashley quiet for years to keep down gossip." When she said nothing, he turned and looked at the sheriff. "You know how the ladies can get. We were only trying to protect Ashley."

"So you told the story about Ashley's mother dying in a car accident?" Ashmore asked. "If my memory's correct, that's the story you gave everyone when enrolling her in school."

Daniel nodded. "We did. Liza and I thought it was for the best."

"To protect Ashley, right?" asked Jemma as she looked at Liza.

Daniel looked back at his wife. "Yes." He stood and walked over to her, placing his large arms around her. "Liza? It's not going to make a difference if they know." He turned to Ashmore. "It's not like they have any reason to talk about Kimberly abandoning her daughter, right?"

Jemma stood and walked over to Liza, who still looked to be in some kind of shock. "You never told Daniel you were pregnant, did you?"

Daniel removed his arms and shuffled backward, looking back and forth at both women. "Liza, what the hell is she talking about?"

"There's no need to lie now, Liza. It will only make it worse; I assure you."

Liza dropped her head and closed her eyes tightly. She uncrossed her arms and tried to reach for Daniel as she looked back up. "I'm so sorry, Danny. I always intended to tell you, but I…"

"Did you kill Laura Stone?" Jemma asked Liza.

"Now wait one damn minute," Daniel angrily said to Jemma, and then he grabbed his wife by the arms and pushed her to the other corner of the room.

"You won't be able to hide, Liza. We have your tollbooth records from Winston to Norfolk the day Laura Stone died and the birth certificate. That's motive. The truth will come out," Sheriff Kennedy said as he tried to intervene between Daniel and Liza.

Spit flew from Daniel's lips as he said, "Get out of my house, now. I want all of you to leave immediately."

Kennedy shook his head. "Can't do that, Daniel."

"Are you arresting me?"

"No. We're arresting your wife for the murder of Laura Stone," Kennedy replied.

CHAPTER 43

Two hours had passed before Daniel was able to see Liza again. He had warned her to say nothing as he stayed behind and arranged a sitter for the girls. Now he was pacing back and forth at the police station in a conference room, waiting on Liza to be brought in. He'd already signed paperwork as her lawyer. The door buzzed, and he stopped. Liza walked in, wearing orange, and her hands were cuffed in front of her. "Is this really necessary?" he asked angrily at Officer Montgomery.

"Just following protocol, Mr. Stone. Buzz when you're done with your wife, um, client."

The door closed, and they stood looking at each other. Liza's eyes were red from crying. Her makeup had been wiped clean. Daniel lost his frown. "Sit down, Liza. You have a lot of explaining to do."

Slowly, Liza walked over to the table and two chairs. He pulled out the chair for her and then took the seat across from her. She spoke softly. "I'm so sorry I didn't tell you about Ashley. I always planned to. It just, well, the timing never felt right."

"That's no excuse, Liza."

She looked down. "I know. The more time that passed, the harder it became." She looked back up. "I'm truly sorry, Danny. Please forgive me."

"Me forgiving you is the least of your worries now. Liza, do you fully understand what they have charged you with?" She said nothing. "They're charging you with murder!"

Slowly she nodded. "I know."

He studied her face. Who was this woman he'd been sharing a bed with for over seven years now? He thought back to when their affair started. They'd worked late, and since Laura was away on business, he'd ordered in dinner for him and Liza. The memory of Liza lying naked atop the board table with files scattered on the floor flashed in his mind. Liza was very in tune with her body and her sexuality, always willing to lock the door any time of day or place. At first, it was purely lust. Liza's curvy body in her low-cut blouses and fitted skirts was always available to him. Add the two-inch heels, blue eyes, and blond hair, and she was every man's dream to work with on a daily basis. However, over time, he fell in love. They were so much alike: strong, driven individuals. He sighed and buried his head in his hands.

Liza reached out to him. "Danny?"

Finally, he looked up. "Liza, you're the mother of my children. My wife. No way in hell I'm gonna let you go to prison no matter what."

A tear rolled down her cheek, and he removed his hand. "Forget I'm your husband because, for now, you're not my wife; you're my client. And if you want me to save your ass, you tell me everything. Leave nothing out. Do you understand?" She nodded. "Good, leave nothing out, Liza. I have to know everything."

"OK, I…I don't know where to start."

"The beginning."

"I fell in love with you the first day I met you. We were working on that Larson case for over twelve hours that day. Do you remember that?"

He nodded.

A brief moment passed. "I know it was just about the sex for you at first, but I remember well the first time you told me you loved me. We were lying in your bed while Laura was away for the weekend. We spent the entire weekend in your bed at your house. It was one of the best weekends of my life. It was also the weekend I got pregnant."

"I wish you would have told me then."

She looked away. "I wanted to, but we had that fight, remember?" She looked back at him. "You said you were going to try and work things out with Laura."

"If I'd known you were pregnant, it would've changed everything."

She closed her eyes and nodded. "Looking back, I should have." She opened her eyes and they locked with his. "You said some pretty ugly things to me that day. I was really mad. When I left the office that day, I decided never to come back and to have the baby on my own."

"And I didn't see you again until after Laura's death, and your body sure as hell didn't look like you'd had a baby."

"No, it didn't. I've always worked hard on my body, you know that, Danny." She gave him a weak smile. "We picked right back up where we left off, like we'd never had a fight at all."

The memory of that day flashed in Daniel's mind. Liza had walked back into his office after Deluca was placed on trial. She had ripped all the tension away from his body. They'd made love like never before, going at it for hours, multiple times behind closed, locked doors. He pushed the thought away. "Liza, it's time you tell me what happened."

She stood and turned away from him. "I made the trip from Winston to Norfolk to see Laura." She turned. "When I got there, she wasn't alone. Andrew Lane was with her."

"What?"

"Your wife was having an affair with Andrew Lane."

He shook his head. "No way, you're lying."

Liza looked hurt as she sat down. "No, Danny, I'm not. Your marriage was broken." She grabbed his hands.

He pulled away and sat back in his chair. "What happened next?" She frowned and looked at the door, making sure it was still closed. Daniel followed her eyes. "We're safe to talk in here. Tell me."

"The pregnancy made me feel sad and needy. When I saw them together, I knew we still had a chance."

He leaned forward and whispered, "Did you do it?"

She knew what he was asking. Slowly, she nodded.

Daniel laid his face in his hands again briefly. Then he stood and walked around the room, trying to process it all. Finally, he sat. "What did you do next?"

"I blackmailed Andrew Lane. I told him to fix what I'd done or I would tell the world about his affair and claim he was the one who killed her in a jealous rage."

Daniel shook his head. "Oh dear God!"

For three minutes no one spoke. Finally, Liza broke the silence. She whispered, "I helped Andrew kill Joy Sutton."

"What? Why?"

"Because Deluca told Sutton that he saw Andrew Lane have an affair with Laura. Joy Sutton became a threat, and we had to silence her."

Daniel stood again and walked away, his back facing her.

"Danny, what do we do now? Andrew Lane is dead, and all the evidence points to him killing Joy Sutton."

He turned and took his seat again. "Will there be any evidence that links you to Joy Sutton? Think, think really hard."

She shook her head. "I was careful. More careful than Andrew, that's for sure."

Daniel removed a notepad from his briefcase and placed it on the table. "Start again from the day you went to see Laura. I need dates, times, places—"

She reached out and touched his hands. "I know what you need. Thank you for doing this."

He squeezed her hand back. "Like I said earlier, you're the mother of my children and my wife. You're not going to prison."

Liza smiled.

EPILOGUE

One week later

The conference room felt stuffy as Daniel Stone walked in carrying his briefcase. He shook the hand of Norfolk's newest district attorney, Wilt Kingston. In attendance were Sheriff Kennedy and Detective Arthur Lamb, who'd worked the first case against Alec Deluca. Lamb had been on the sidelines since his daughter, Jenny, had found the body of Jacklyn Riggs. Now, Lamb was chomping at the bit to get back in the game.

Wilt Kingston opened a file. He slid over the pretrial list that was mandatory after the grand jury decided there was sufficient evidence to charge Liza Stone with the murder of Laura Stone. Daniel took the list and studied it. "This all of it?"

Wilt Kingston nodded. "All there. Nothing's left out."

Daniel shook his head, laughing. "No way you can convict my wife just on this. All circumstantial evidence, nothing more."

Kingston shifted in his seat. "We'll see."

Kennedy placed a hand down over the list. "There won't be a plea bargain, Daniel. Your wife will go to jail for Laura Stone's murder."

Daniel jerked the paper away and stood. "I look forward to seeing you men in court. And in the meantime, a hair better not be touched on my wife's head under your watch."

Kennedy removed his hand from the table as they all watched Daniel Stone leave the room, and then he said, "Defiant to the end."

Kingston looked at both men, adding, "He has every reason to be. He rarely loses."

"And let's not forget Andrew Lane isn't around to tell us what really happened," Lamb added.

Kennedy stood. "I'm not worried. This time we're getting it right. Justice will finally be served for Laura Stone."

Kingston shook his head. "I hope you're right, Sheriff. I hope you're right."

***

The air was crisp as Jemma stood on her balcony overlooking the Potomac River. She had the week off after leaving Norfolk. It wasn't a request; it was an order by Director Miller. He'd felt bad that she didn't mention her vacation time when he sent her to Richmond. Jemma sipped at her coffee as the time neared ten. She hadn't dressed, only showered, and she stood in her bathrobe, watching the river come to life with bike riders and runners along the paved riverbank trail. Her phone rang, and excitement grew in the pit of her stomach. There was another case.

She picked up her phone off the kitchen counter. "Agent Rhodes speaking." There was a short pause, and then she heard his voice. Instantly, Jemma smiled.

"I hope you don't mind, but I'm about thirty minutes outside of Washington."

"Here? As in Washington, DC?"

He laughed. "God, I was hoping you would say that. It would suck to drive all the way up here and you not be home."

"It would."

He laughed again. "I've never truly visited DC as a tourist, only been there for work. I was hoping you would show me around. I got some time off."

Jemma's heart skipped a beat. "I think I'd like that very much, Jason."

"Great, text me your address. I'll be there soon."

"Can't wait." Jemma ended the call and quickly texted her address to the number that called her. Then she pressed the number and entered his name, Detective Jason Ashmore. She shook her head at her stupidity. "I should've never deleted his contact information. What we had was real." She placed her phone back down and skipped to her bedroom to change.

Printed in Great Britain
by Amazon